ELEGANTLY NAKED
IN MY
SEXY
MENTAL ILLNESS

COLLECTED STORIES

HEATHER FOWLER

ELEGANTLY NAKED IN MY SEXY MENTAL ILLNESS

Collected Stories

By Heather Fowler
Art and Appendices by Pablo Vision

Queen's Ferry Press
8622 Naomi Street
Plano, TX 75024
www.queensferrypress.com

Published 2014 by Queen's Ferry Press

First edition May 2014

ISBN 978-1-938466-28-1

Printed in the United States of America

Previous Praise for HEATHER FOWLER:

This Time, While We're Awake

"It may seem incongruous to apply the word 'pleasurable' to the dystopian visions conjured by Heather Fowler in *This Time, While We're Awake*. The sixteen stories in the collection feature technology run amok, ecological devastation, a smattering of horrible deaths. There's no doubt that the subject matter is disturbing. But after my initial read-through, one of the first notes I jotted down was 'breath of fresh air.' The stories, interwoven with subtle critiques of rampant consumerism, class inequality, and violence against women, do what good literature should: make you step back and look at your world with a more critical eye. So let's call them 'refreshingly disturbing.'"
—Rosalie Morales Kearns for *Stirring : A Literary Collection*

"Heather Fowler has taken literature to places I hadn't known it could go... A wickedly dark and haunting collection that shows its readers an alternative look at the future of humanity; a deep, devastating spiral into strange and frightening circumstances."
—Lori Hettler at *The Next Best Book Blog*

"There's a genuine kind of pleasure you experience in reading a collection of short stories written by an author who masterfully delivers rejuvenating fiction that novels rarely explore. Heather Fowler's avant-garde *This Time, While We're Awake* is a perfect representation that transcends its readers to that esoteric ground... From beginning to end, I felt moved by Fowler's eloquent prose of seduction and bittersweet sorrow."
—Jake Vyper at *Fantascize.com*

"Fowler's stories refuse to leave you alone after you finish them. The stories are relevant to everyday life as we see nature consumed by technology, as we witness human interaction being overtaken by machines. She has accomplished what every author craves—collaboration with the reader. We have no choice but to try and weave the stories together and make conclusions based on our own information, on our own ventures out into the world."
—Ashley Begley at *JMWW*

People With Holes

"Fowler's ability to make a reader believe all the strange things that happen in these stories is deft and precise. Some of the living beings are not human; and while they're certainly used as metaphors, each is also presented with behaviors specific to their species... Readers who admire any of the finest writers in the genre (Isabel Allende, Gabriel Garcia Marquez, Franz Kafka, Toni Morrison, and Salman Rushdie) should enjoy the flights of fancy within this book, and also be able to confront its darker journeys."
—*Foreword Reviews*

"*People With Holes* is a potent collection of magic realism that weaves the tragedy and deception in relationships, the holes of humanity and pulls all that subterfuge to the surface. Holes are actual holes on people that are visible, rooms become home to our scars, heads can be cut off bodies and carried around, people shrink, turn into various animals, a museum of solitude holds all memories, a boyfriend's belly is a flat screen of ocean the narrator can swim into while another's penis is a white laboratory rat. It brings the metaphor to the tactile, the breathable, the living. Fowler's work is inimitable and exciting. I don't even want to call it magical realism so much as Heather Fowler tearing down those 'load-bearing walls,' to find out 'what's beneath the fabric' of each human she explores..."
—Meg Tuite at *Connotation Press*

Suspended Heart

"Fowler's writing itself is beautiful—her sentences are as varied as her characters, and the images she carefully paints echo Francis Bacon's statements about beauty: there's nothing pretty that isn't at least slightly bizarre in some way. This strangeness never hinders Fowler's work, and instead, increases the world she so vividly introduces us to, making her plots more believable, and just that much more fun to read."

—Stephanie Johnson at *Ampersand Books*

"The stories in *Suspended Heart* have made for some of the most twisted, exciting reading I have had in a very long time. They are read with a zealousness and momentum that is like a solid relationship, improving with age and with each re-read. I find these stories to take the idea of love and blast away any cliché notions that love is an ordinary thing. Bitter hearts will be relieved, hardened hearts will soften, and dangerous hearts will finally use caution."   —Zach Fishel at *Girls with Insurance*

"Sometimes, just sometimes, from the scrolls of work I read online, I stumble across a story different enough to make me remember a name. Heather Fowler's such a writer. I encountered her work a few years ago online. It's almost impossible not to. Fresh, vivid, her prose is fluid. It flows like a river. Never static. The work moves characters and perceptions. The heart is revealed and swept away. A single story can be strange, beautiful, moving, dark, then funny. Stories that may seem quirky on the surface of subject matter have layers and deceptive depth."

—Angela Readman at *The Short Review*

For the others

Lovely Ming,
Thanks so much
for your
stunning words
on this cover!
Wishing you
huge success
& delight
with great love.

Contents

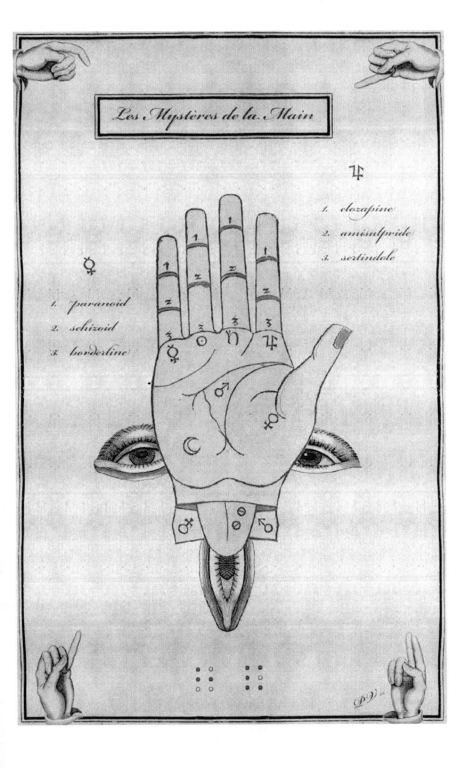

Les Mystères de la Main

1. clozapine
2. amisulpride
3. sertindole

1. paranoid
2. schizoid
3. borderline

THE HAND-LICKER

It was the memory of the taste of Sharon's lips that evoked a simmering wand of cinnamon, the quiet state of mind with which she read, licking her fingers every fifth turn—or, instead, the caustic break of how she'd left Evan without a word, simply disappearing from their apartment one morning.

Not that Evan had ever been able to accurately assess reality. There were the voices and, also, the distractions with which he found himself detoured from any sedentary activity by a fragmented passing of time, though these ample flaws didn't, on a good day, as his mother had said many times, make him less beautiful. *Except I hate you, Mother, and we're all fucking beautiful,* he thought. *If you believe Francis Bacon. Even at our ugliest, we're beautiful.*

He checked his clothing: Two green socks; a pair of black slacks; a t-shirt and a sweater; well-worn shoes, on the correct feet. He'd done well. Running through the checklist was meditative. "So noted," he said aloud, hearing the scattered whispers that an absence of meds could bring. "It's a bad day for positive symptoms; we must take extra precautions." Even saying so to the echo of his apartment made things more bearable, not that he had much control over when these symptoms did appear, especially when he skipped doses. He'd skipped now for two days.

"You can't get into trouble again, Evan," his caseworker had cautioned the last time. "Not again, okay?"

"I can't help when I get in trouble," he replied.

"Take your antipsychotics," she said. "You don't belong in jail. If you act out, you could go to jail."

"I'll stop embarrassing you because you like me," he replied without intent. The idea of obtaining her grudging acceptance or pleasure was enough, and if he said the right things, her soft face lit up with a hope he'd enjoy but invariably destroy.

"Remember, Sharon is gone," the woman said. "Sharon is not coming back. Sharon does not exist near other women or on their person."

Burning cinnamon. Burning wand. Fire lips. Firebrand. Ensorcel. Enrage. "I know," he said. "I do know that."

"But you still hear her."

Every day. Do you think I enjoy this? "I can't get her out of my head. She causes the problems."

"The problems have other causes, too."

"I didn't say they don't."

The last time, he'd been at a burger joint. Sharon had arrived in the food of an old woman. As the afternoon sunlight filtered over the woman's wrinkled visage, Sharon spoke to him from her plate. Because Sharon asked questions but he wanted to stay below radar, he tried to uphold his part of the conversation from his seat across the room, but then her face materialized before him, zoomed up from the old woman's hamburger and fries, and in his mind he saw the woman touching Sharon's face, biting Sharon's face, all the while Sharon's mouth smiled, her raspy voice calling, "Aren't you going to come get me, Evan? See what she's doing? I'll be gone in a minute. Soon enough, I'll be gone. You'll have let me go again, you fucking loser."

ELEGANTLY NAKED IN MY SEXY MENTAL ILLNESS

He had approached eagerly, thinking with a trace of desperation of the last things Sharon had said to him the night before he'd discovered that she'd abandoned him, that rancid morning when he realized that even her knickknacks and plants had disappeared from the apartment, all her traces. "You never fucking sleep," she'd said. "It unnerves me." This was what she'd uttered at midnight, years ago, when she'd surely decided she could no longer deal with the trials of his illness.

He'd replied, "If I wake up and wake you again, I'm sorry. I can't sleep well. If the meds were—"

"I don't care about your meds. Let's just hope I sleep," she repeated. "And try not to disturb me with your terrors."

"As if I have any control," he replied, but this was a pitiful and quiet rebuttal in the face of her apathy. *And what a horrifying thing to say to someone before you plan to leave them,* he thought, *someone in permanent limbo, someone who suffers such terrors that they can barely keep track of their own dreams and waking.* It's not like he hadn't offered her another room, hadn't said many times that she was welcome to sleep separately, welcome to be "just a friend" who could stay in exchange for the simplest of help, so what a fucked-up, horrible thing to say to someone you professed to love—especially someone with attachment disorders, someone from whom, the very next day, you'd erase your entire existence.

To the social worker, later, he would explain that this was why, when he saw Sharon in that woman's burger, among those greasy fries, he went and stood before her with aplomb, brought his face to the low level of the food, and said, "I hope you don't sleep this time, Sharon. I'm here now. There is no terror. I'm taking my meds. You can't bother me anymore."

The seated woman regarded him with fear, a gentle old lady with gray curls, wearing a woolen sweater with a gold chorus bell pin. "Leave me alone, strange man," she said, her voice atremble. "Please back away."

What Evan had briefly seen of Sharon's face disappeared.

"I'm Evan," he replied, extending his hand. "I mean you no harm." *No harm, no harm.* He had learned this mantra from the Buddhists. *Meditate to come down,* he thought. *Act normal. Be quiet and still. No meds for two days, but I can handle it. So I lied to Sharon. So I'm not taking them. Sharon deserved my lies. No joy with the pills. I can live without their dull world. I can handle it, my life. The hallucinations don't control me.*

But he was mistaken. His eyes flew around the room and back to the woman before him. Reluctantly, she extended her aging claw. "I should leave you now," he replied, fully intending to do so, but instead he grabbed her palm in his own hands, smelling Sharon, thinking Sharon, tasting Sharon, enveloped in the musk she wore and the scent that represented the back of her neck, lightly dried sweat and cut grass. Such an ugly thing in his grip, this woman's wrinkled appendage, but he could not help himself. He licked her palm. It tasted of salt and soap. He kept licking, then tasted all of her fingers and the places between her fingers, tasted her knuckles, too, her veins and moles. He did not hear a thing when the woman began pleading for help, faintly, but he felt the thwack of her blue umbrella on his back and shoulders as she began to hit him, saw it like a black cane, like his father's black cane.

In his mind, his father then beat him as he tasted Sharon. "Low-class, lying, cheating whore," he could imagine his father would say. "Wrong side of the tracks, Evan. You pay for women like that, then discard them. You don't love them. And this, this from my son?" The umbrella continued to fall.

Outside, the rain recommenced, splattering the restaurant windows. The old lady, her hand trapped in his, began to cry. Soon a bevy of workers would surround him, tearing him away, and he'd cry, too—*where was he, who was he, what was he doing*—innocent as a fool, blinded by his tears, by the absolute ugliness and implacability of it all, reluctantly awakening to the actual present as if out of a dark and smog-filled cave.

ELEGANTLY NAKED IN MY SEXY MENTAL ILLNESS

But he felt none of their hands pulling at him until after he surfaced from the dream in which, while his father's cane kept falling, he tasted the backs of Sharon's thighs, simultaneously undoing the garters she'd connected to her stockings, unhinging those stubborn rubber discs below her ass while she'd laughed, aware that he'd live happily forever if only for the daily sight of the bare thighs that led up to her perfectly round posterior, as once more the wreckage of time and its attendant truths deceived him, consumed as he was, as if for hours, in his memories of parting Sharon's thighs from behind, tasting between them on that first night with her in his apartment, the night she'd said, "You can have your way with me if you want, Evan; any way you want. I'm not scared."

"I love you," he'd replied. But now, before he was removed from the old woman, he said it again, to the Sharon that existed on the woman's hand. "But why? Why did you leave me, Sharon?" he asked. She did not answer, and, "I'm sorry. I'm sorry," he said to the old lady, finally clearer once held back by four men and a woman, intermittently awoken from his fading phantasms by the sight of the old woman's horrified face.

His apologies afterwards had not helped. "It's not about you," he told the lady as they wrenched him aside, preparing to deposit his slouching carcass in the rain. "I was just looking for someone. But I am sorry. I'm so sorry. I thought I saw her." Outside, his tears and the hot summer rain comingled and, read his rights four minutes later by a plain-clothes deputy, he had another arrest on his record.

His caseworker would be furious. And how his father would be dismayed and ashamed, were he alive, like he was the day Evan lit the heritage tapestry on fire. "You've got to make me proud, Evan," his father had said so many times. "Look here. It's our family tree. We can't have a nutcase on it. No one can know about your problems. I can't keep fixing you forever." His father fingered the tapestry as if it held the secrets to power or wealth.

The thing had hung in his father's study, purchased custom from an artisan, adorning the back wall and spanning back to the 1600s. It had cost thousands. In the garden, it took three minutes to burn. That was a lie. It took two minutes and thirty-nine seconds to burn. Tired of hearing what he could not change, Evan had first seared his own name and then torched the whole, saying, "Don't worry! Now none of us has to hang from those trees!"

Afterward, his father had beaten him senseless, left him on the den floor, and then turned on the baseball game. Baseball and punishment, baseball and bruising, seemed connected for him now. Sometimes, to the imaginary sound of his father in his mind, Evan smelled the sulfur on his own fingers and looked again for the old match while hearing a phantom game, thinking: *If only I could light my tapestry head on fire. But all that was long ago. You stitched yourself into me. Three strikes. Tenth inning. Overtime.* Now, there was the hand licking. The problems. Sharon coming. Sharon leaving. Additional accidents and incidents.

Soon after the one in the restaurant, he was told by his caseworker in her vaguely hopeless way, "I like you, Evan the Fifth. I don't want you to get thrown in jail or the loony bin again, okay? Repeat after me: Sharon is gone. Sharon is no longer here. Sharon is not coming back. Talk to your trustees. Be religious with your meds. Did you take your antipsychotics? Sharon is not on objects or on the hands of other people."

Evan smiled to thank her for her efforts and cried as he replied, "I know you're right."

But he remembered having seen Sharon in the Polish woman at the donut shop, in the fat mother in the bookstore, in the twenty-something woman-girl on the green bicycle. He'd licked their hands too. The social worker had never known.

Charges had only been avoided because the women had felt sympathy, because he'd backed away quickly enough, some fateful intervention occurring, and his false imaginings and subsequent need to apologize made him seem so small, lost, and deluded that as he pursued Sharon's vestiges, it was evident to most normals that he was more to be pitied than censured.

It was not that he hadn't tried to lose interest in Sharon, gain interest in other women—but Sharon had accepted him, criminal as she was, low as she was, because she knew about his illness and didn't care. And how could he expect decent people with no problems to deal with his madness if Sharon couldn't? When they were together, he'd financed their lifestyle; she'd lasted four blissful months, the longest of any woman.

He tried to stop envisioning her every day, but if Sharon stopped appearing, he knew, it would be just like before, which was potentially worse—hallucinating his gone sister sometimes but mostly reliving embodiments of his father's cruelty as he cowered and recollected the past in various public locations, once berated by the moving yellow pencil of a schoolgirl in the library, a pencil in the place of his old man.

That day, when Evan had finally had enough of his father's tirade, having decided to stick up for himself, he strode to the little girl in a gust of bravado, grabbed the father pencil by its scrawny little neck, and broke it in half before telling it firmly: "You have no power anymore, old man! You should have never had power, you sad sack of pompous shit. I'm the family lunatic? You're the lunatic!" And the young girl had cried, yes, bawled while demanding in shrieks that he leave and that he replace her pencil, then calling for her Mama, so angry with her little blonde braids wagging, her magenta dress flaring before him. But no charges had been filed because what could Evan be persecuted for? Talking to someone invisible? Breaking a pencil? Making a little girl cry?

Sharon hated that episode when she heard about it, disdained his behavior as if he had demolished all happy-littlegirldom forever. "You broke a girl's pencil in the library, Ev?" she asked. "You scared a little girl? It was just a pencil. Your father was an asshole and your father is dead. He doesn't live in pencils."

"I needed you with me, Sharon."

"I can't be with you every day," she said. No, too busy moving illicit goods into and out of the apartment, she wouldn't pay much attention. Nonetheless, she made him take his meds after that, said, "I can't put up with this shit. You take them, or I'm moving out."

Evan followed her advice, did anything she mandated or supervised as long as she let him talk to her and touch her. "Can we make love again?" he asked so many times. "Sometimes I feel like making love is the only thing I can do where it feels real and good at the same time. I'm good to you that way, aren't I? Aren't I the best you've ever had?"

"You know you are. Crazy as hell, but erotically talented, lover."

"It's my only skill," he said, touching her shoulder and letting his fingers trace a slow pattern over her back, caressing her in the way she enjoyed. If his mentality was a jumbled heap, his fingers had always moved majestically across women's bodies, or so he'd been told; he could write a symphony from the moans and sighs he elicited. His recall was perfection. What a strange skill for a crazy man, he often thought, about which Sharon had agreed, but he had enormous talent. He liked sex, too, pleasing people. *I'm elegant when I'm naked*, he sometimes thought, as he left the body of a sated, sleeping woman—*elegantly naked in my sexy mental illness*.

When Sharon left and he had no steady girlfriends, or between attempts to gain them, he'd often pursued temporary women to show them his gifts and seduce them to bolster his confidence. Sometimes ugly girls. Sometimes fat girls. Sometimes any girl. But he gave them all incorrect telephone numbers or names. Often, he pretended to be on vacation or from a foreign country—Ukraine, Belgium, Russia—just to enjoy the moments at their houses without having to explain or continue. When he wanted something real with someone, he knew, he'd have to admit his illness, and he didn't want to explain it, knowing that they'd run, or that they would not understand, fearing that they'd feel cheated after he'd pleased them in bed. A loss. A pity. The illness should be expressed before intimacy despite that to speak of it would often thwart that very access. The illness was a trust-killer, but it didn't go away, shaming them afterward as well as it shamed him, for how could they have been lured by such a disaster of a man, one who could touch them very well, but who couldn't tell a pencil from an abusive prick of a father, one who saw his sister in falling icicles and cried for hours after witnessing his mother in a shoe? A man who gained an obsessive desire to please women after his mother, subsequent to his father's less violent abuses, had touched him wrongly in the bathtub to persuade him he was straight? "See, Evan? See? A woman's touch is what does this to you."

The lovers could not handle his truth. And when his inferiority shamed him or them, the illness relentlessly confirming his disability and causing more devastation in a rollicking cycle of horror, lack of empathy, and futility, he wanted to find the nearest bridge and throw himself off, to end this sequence of confessions and withdrawals, passionate involvements and tears. He wanted to be honest. He was honest with his caseworker at least; once he'd even tried to seduce her, thinking, *she knows everything, it's okay,* though she was at least fifty-five, fat, sweet, single, and unavailable to clients in a romantic capacity. "You and me, you and me, Frances—we should get together."

"Are you flirting with me, young man?" she'd asked.

"I could take you to bed and take care of you and you could take care of me," he replied, examining her inch by inch, determining he could give up attractiveness for warmth. "I'll please you in bed, Frances. I'll cook for you. Let me show you. I'm very good. You don't have anyone to take care of you. I can take care of you and you can take care of me."

He thought that perhaps her supervision would keep him in

line and he could get over, in stages, their age difference and her unappealing body. With as many women as he'd pleased, he picked a woman's pussy better than a thief did a lock. It was no mystery. Anything unpleasant around the magenta core could be ignored—body, face, sound—so he might master her genitals, make her body quiver. "We could make a go of it," he said. "We'd never hurt each other."

"Oh, honey, no," she replied, absorbing his contemplative look. "I don't need another manchild to tend. But you made me feel real sassy today. Thank you."

Rejected, he thought, *by a woman twice my age.* He'd never missed Sharon more. Regardless if Sharon had stolen, if she'd done drugs or sold them from his apartment, if she was unreliable, Sharon had at least told him everyone would love him. With her short black hair, Sharon was a plump pixie, appealingly thick in the thighs and hips. She told the most amazing stories.

She lied, yes, but in all the best possible ways—was actually a compulsive liar, but this was sometimes good when your lover was delusional, and continuous deception, intentional or benign, became between them an almost shared affliction.

Sharon's first lie: When they met, she told him she was waiting on a friend to pick her up because she was in from out of town but her friend, mysteriously, couldn't be reached, so could she stay over? She left for only two days after her initial stay, calling every few hours, and then moved back in when he reluctantly agreed, telling him, "I don't have any real friends here, Evan. I need to live with you."

"I'm not well," he remarked. "You don't want me."

"I can handle whatever you've got," she replied.

"I suffer from serious mental illness," he said.

"Me, too. Are you dangerous?" she asked.

"No," he said. "Not to others."

"Then I'm easy," she replied. "I do want to stay. I don't care how cracked you are. I might be a little sociopathic, a little borderline. I mean, I often lack empathy. It's a little schizoid. I feel like a torrent—up, down, all over. But I come from a family of healers. I could heal you some, maybe."

He'd later discover that her family was comprised of drug addicts and louses, not a one who'd healed anyone, but when Sharon lied, she lied beatifically, floridly, with extra intricacies, and as she lied, she often laughed. How she laughed! It made his heart curl at the edges.

When Sharon laughed, he felt the whole world would be just fine, one atom at a time, that his father was good and dead and that everything would eventually be all right. This feeling lasted even when Sharon lied to him, about him, which he found charming: "You'll be getting better any day now, Ev. And then we can travel to Asia on your daddy's money. How that old fucker would hate our use of his money! He'd hate me, too. But we'll have a grand ole time! You can buy me some jade. A few kimonos. I'll be a Chinese princess and we'll walk in the fallen cherry blossoms. I can make up some big fat whoppers, can't I? Don't you hate how I lie to you? I do it all the time."

In Evan's position, he found no fault. "I think it's fine when you lie," he said.

"Don't tell me it's fine!" she replied, her mood change rapid and bitter. "It's not fucking fine." She threw a glass stein into the wall. "Nothing is fucking fine!"

"But it is. I don't care."

"No, Evan," she said, a moment later, when there was guilt, remorse. "As soon as possible, you should hate me for lying. Because I lie on purpose—I tell you things I know aren't true. I use you. That's the difference. You don't use anybody. You don't know what's true. Your illusions are out of your control."

"Use me all you want," he said. "I like to be used. I like you near me." What he meant, perhaps, was: *I like to be touched by someone I am familiar with, even if they harm. I like a sense of connection.*

25

"No," she said. "I like you too well to keep using you like this, on and on. I don't want to marry you. I'll never marry you, Evan. Not even for your money."

"Yes, but after you lie, you believe what you said sometimes, right?" Evan asked. "So we're not so different. One minute you want to marry me—the next you don't. Tomorrow you might want to again. It doesn't matter. Oh, just come here. Come here again and again. I want to live in the folds of your skin. I want to crawl inside you and stay hidden. I want you to keep lying to me until it's so boring to tell your lies that the truth is the only thing left. Even your lies are just shadings of the things that you've wanted. You've wanted your lies to be true, Sharon. I know you have—at least while you said them."

"Evan," Sharon said, happy again, laughing, kissing him, pulling on his shirt. "I do love you. I'm not lying now. I love you. I truly love you. I love you so much it hurts to fuck you over like I do." It was the first time she'd ever said that, about the loving, but they talked about sleeping later that night, how he couldn't, and then she was gone.

More than three years ago, this, and if he woke up one more morning with the same ridiculous thought, *and then she was gone,* he might off himself. Didn't he have enough troubles? "Yes, Evan," he told himself aloud again today. "She is gone. You have been licking the hands of strange women to taste her. And she's not coming back. She hates you. She loves you so much, she hates you."

He regarded his outfit once more. Today he would go to the library, wearing his green socks, his black t-shirt and black slacks, his Argyle sweater, his Oxford shoes. Maintaining normal, he would check out a book. At the library, he felt cocooned by the evasive glances of introverts avoiding interpersonal contact. He'd have a good time, he wasn't in jail, and this was one thing they still let mentally ill people do: Read. It remained a free country as far as reading went.

ELEGANTLY NAKED IN MY SEXY MENTAL ILLNESS

Once there, he sighed and smiled. In the library, the late-morning sun slid through unfettered windows to light the faces of midday patrons. A golden light, he decided, beautiful, the kind of light that makes your life seem a dreamy movie where people don't leave and someone finds a nice abandoned dog and decides to take it home, feed it, maybe the kind of movie where a sad man who sees his ex-girlfriend everywhere and in everyone can get over her because he looks so ready to be involved elsewhere, especially because he looks around so much or looks so sharply, with all the intensive looking he can muster—until he stops to appreciate a beautiful girl with curly red hair and a mole on her cheek, who suddenly appears seated by a window at a table near the back door.

This girl wears a lemon-colored blouse and a tweed skirt with sturdy black walking shoes. A stack of books is spread on the table before her. And, *my God*, he thinks, *she is as beautiful as daylight.* Her face tilts down toward the book she reads, her fingers fluttering. He likes the way she touches the pages. Lingeringly. He likes the scar on her left cheek. He likes how she tilts her face up into the yellow pools of light streaming through the big library windows as if she were a seeking flower, and he realizes, with a freakish spasm, that he is in love again—very much and all at once.

Heart booming, he wants to lick her face. He wants to lick her nipples and hear her call out with joy and abandon. *I want to give you ten thousand orgasms,* he thinks. His imagined version of her reactions to his skills is just a prelude. He daydreams how she will sound not before he gives her these orgasms, but after he gives her so many that her throat is sore, raw.

But she is too beautiful to want a man like him for long, he knows. Besides, there is an equal chance that he will have no luck at all. He will approach her, he suspects, and she will shoot him down. He pulls a comb from his pocket and runs it through his hair.

He will approach her and she will reject him. Yes, that's possible. This is okay. He takes a step toward her.

As he does, Sharon's face, textual, multidimensional, emerges from the pages the girl's fingers traipse. "Evan, you have been learning some things without me, haven't you?" Sharon says. "I'm glad."

He forces himself to sit at the nearest table. *Don't respond to the voices*, he remembers. *Refuse to respond.* "I have," he says, looking up at the clock, as if he were not answering. "Been busy."

"And you know more now than before, don't you?" Sharon's text face asks.

"I know what I've always known," he replies, peering up from dropped lids to regard her, and Sharon pulls her pouting face. Her expression, despite its papery construction, is well-delineated.

"Get your ass over here," Sharon says. "I'll tell you a story. It begins with a girl moving in—and ends with the girl and the guy fucking all the time. Until she can't stand him because she is *fucking him over*. And she is not a good person. So she bails. But before that, they have a really good time. Do you want to hear more?"

At this, Evan stands, says, "I can't do this anymore, Sharon. Stop, Sharon. Sharon, you get me in trouble. I like this girl; will you leave her alone? Just leave her alone." While pleading, he realizes he repeats her name, begging for release, but Sharon's face turns into Sharon's hands, papery font hands above the real girl's slender hands that still flutter over her book.

"Come and taste me," he hears Sharon say.

"She's not here," he says aloud. "This is a bad day for positive symptoms; we must take extra precautions." He drags his eyes toward the redhead's face as if to request that she save him. She seems not to notice his struggling conversation. A backpack sits like a fat lapdog beside her chair, huge, moss-green, stuffed, like she had nowhere else to go and so took her things to the library. All of them. *As if it were a train depot*, he thinks. *All aboard!*

ELEGANTLY NAKED IN MY SEXY MENTAL ILLNESS

"It's okay. I like her, too," Sharon says, her face reappearing in the grain of a nearby wooden table. "This one's good for you."

"Sharon, you do not exist," he says, keeping his voice at a whisper. "Sharon, you existed once, but now you don't, not here. Wake up. Wake up, me!" he says and slaps his own face, retreating inward, tracing his reality into alternate mental alcoves, sketching it in broad strokes.

Without question, he knows a few things: Because of his illness, somebody, not him, pays his rent. Somebody delivers his groceries. Somebody stops in, along with his caseworker, to check on him once a month. There are lots of somebodies. But he can't get in trouble again. He'll be institutionalized. Evan the Fifth.

Now, he plays records and checks out library books and picks up women from the market, from the streets if he wants—now he is free but if he gets in trouble again, he will not be free. "Sharon," he says. "Go away. Go away. Go away."

He remembers the sanitarium, the shock treatments. He wonders if the idea of taking his meds was actually an act of not taking his meds, where he took a sugar cube instead and let it melt on his tongue. That's what he used to say, as he ate sugar cubes as a child: "I'm taking my medications."

Later, as his symptoms clarified, he can remember his mother holding open his mouth, placing her fingers inside with the huge pills she made him swallow, pouring the water down his throat. "Nothing is wrong with our family. You are my perfect child."

He can hear his father, too, his father admonishing, "Goddamn fuckall of a son. Goddamn fruitcake nut! The men at the club say you're not even...that you're a fucking...that I should—"

As always when his imagined father speaks, Evan's world darkens. The pain of recall expands. Except, two seconds later, he watches the redhead raise her chin, tilting her palms skyward, as if her focus has turned from reading her book to feeling the sunlight spilling into her spread palms. *She's got the whole world, in* her hands, his thoughts sing. In bliss, she smiles. He smiles in echo. Her eyes are closed.

It is as though she is a seraphic presence who speaks with God. A mundane messiah. Evan cannot resist. He approaches like an unworthy disciple, gets on his knees before the table, and puts his head into her hands atop the book, rests his cheek there, kisses her palms, feels the sunlight where it gathers on her hands.

But the urge to taste, to touch, to lick, returns. He turns his face so his mouth is on her palms and frees just the tip of his tongue to move upon her skin. She pulls one hand free so that it can flutter over her book. Her remaining palm he then traps between his hands and commences to lick, now tasting her fingers like hers is the last human hand on the planet, a place of connection between himself and the flesh and the sun—and maybe the hand does not belong to Sharon anymore, instead belongs to this girl of light, but he wants to feel the golden light, hold her warmth, know how it feels to taste her.

She does not pull away. Now sunlight lands on his cheekbones. He wants to steal her power to summon the rays, wants to let her goodness block out both Sharon and his father, but he knows he will soon be shoved away. Any moment.

"I'm sorry," he murmurs, yet as he continues to lick, after a mild jolt of surprise, the girl does not resist; she does not struggle. She spreads the fingers on the hand he holds a centimeter wider and continues to move the fingertips of her loose hand over the available page of her book beside his face, tracking the words, one by one, as if his licking of her other hand were some sort of silent companionship to her reading.

Evan is grateful. His sudden love for her intensifies. He stops licking only long enough to say, "Can I take you home?"

"I don't know how to get to your house," she replies.

"I'll show you," he offers.

"And I don't know who you are," she adds.

"I'm Evan," he says, observing that her hair is like living fire in the yellow afternoon. Every bit of detail he can amass he sees so clearly. And then, in the whitest line, he sees her cane, brilliant with red stripes—notes the Braille on her pages, its telling bumps. "You're blind, aren't you?"

"Yes," she says. She chuckles before continuing, "What gave that away, silly?"

He feels like her new dog, allowed to lick her palms and remain with her in the sunlight. *Oh, yes,* he thinks. *With pleasure, I am your dog.* He wants to see the color of her eyes and wants her to pet him fondly, to scratch his back, to ruffle his hair and make long smooth strokes with her fingertips all the way down his shoulder blades. "My name is Evan," he repeats. "Come home with me. You could live with me. I'll be nice."

"I don't have a home," she says.

"You can stay in mine," he replies.

Her face is blank. "Do you know how to cook?" she asks.

"Yes," he says. "I am a good cook. Or I can get someone."

"Well, it's true that I don't have anywhere to go," she says. "Or I probably wouldn't. My mother died, and I'm staying at a hostel. I don't know these roads. I don't like the city. I don't have friends here. I don't have any friends."

Evan nods, finding this good news. "So come with me," he insists. "We can live together. I won't hurt you!" For an instant, Evan can picture everything happening with a new and exciting outcome. He will simply tell her the truth, all of it. She can back out if she wants. "I am mentally ill," he admits. "I see things, hear things. But I have a nice place. I'm good at sex. We won't ever be evicted. I have money. I am five-foot-eleven. I get arrested, sometimes, for licking people's hands. For seeing things. But if we live together, I won't touch another woman."

The redhead thinks about this. "I don't see anything," she replies. "Nothing. Except what I imagine, so when you licked my hand just then, I was reading about a dog licking a girl's hand, and it was perfect. I was thinking, 'Humans can lick hands too.' I was grateful to have someone touching me. It's been so long since anybody touched me—I mean other than to guide. They can think you're pretty, you know, when you're blind? But nobody wants to take advantage of a blind girl. I was born this way; their vanity makes them want to be seen, really seen, and I don't even know what I look like, except by what others say. Does this bother you? I will never be able to see you. Because if this bothers you, you need to tell me right now. We can have years of the same regrets about what you can't have—my physical, knowledgeable approval of you. How do I look? No clue."

"It doesn't bother me at all," Evan says frankly. "I think you're beautiful. I can tell you how beautiful you are. It doesn't matter what I look like."

The smile returns, her blazing smile. "If you see me as beautiful," she replies, "I trust you. So, let's go. Let's visit your place." She stands slowly, putting on the black sunglasses she'll wear to walk into the steamy afternoon. "They like blind people to wear these," she tells him. "They do nothing for me, but they let other people know. They pinch the bridge of my nose. I hate them."

"I hate that," Evan says, encouraged. He touches her cheek. "So, let me tell you what I saw just now. Your red hair glowed in the afternoon sun that filtered through the windows, your skin like porcelain. You smiled, and I felt my heart lift. You tilted your hands toward the light and it looked like you held all earthly sun in your palms, like a queen or a goddess. You held it so easily. I don't think I've seen anyone so pretty. Not ever. If you could see yourself, you'd smile."

A blush steals over her face. "Help me get my books?" As he hands them to her, she tucks them into her already full bag, says, "Did you know that, for a blind person, touching a person's face is very intimate? I didn't even ask for it, but your face in my hands was the first thing you offered. It was like a dream. I felt you as handsome. Do people think you're handsome, Evan?"

ELEGANTLY NAKED IN MY SEXY MENTAL ILLNESS

"No," he says. "Well, yes, sometimes."

"I think you're handsome," she says. "Very. I feel like we've been intimate."

He strokes her offered fingers before they walk, clutches them. He wants to say, "I'm not as good as all that, not as attractive. I'm terrible. Don't let me touch you." But he knows, sometimes, when to be silent, when to just accept an unusual gift and be humbled when joy crosses his unseen barriers. He touches her fingers softly, reverently, like the light will fall back onto them at any moment simply because they belong to her, like she will fling it across the room in streaks to paint the walls.

"My name is Claire," she says. "In case you want to know."

"Let's go, Claire," Evan replies. "Right now."

This moment with Claire is perfect. There has never been a better moment: No matter what happens next, if he gets lonely again, he will replay this memory, reel by reel, until the mental film sputters into darkness. If she is a dream, he'll eventually want to know this, too, but not just yet. He doesn't think she is a dream. Usually, his dreams are bad, the people in them cruel. "Can I dress you up and tell you again what you look like when we get to my house?" he asks. "Can I look at your beautiful skin in all the light that comes through my western windows? Can I touch you? We can be intimate. I won't hurt you."

She smiles again, mysterious now in her black, blind person's sunglasses. "Sure, I like that idea. You can do that." She hefts her pack onto her narrow back then clutches one of his hands in hers, with her cane in her other, before saying, "You lead."

Standing still, she waits. As the sighted person, he realizes, he must tell her which direction to go, use the pull of his body to guide hers, and he knows that they will now accomplish any directed movement he orchestrates in tandem. He revels in how she needs him. He is needed. Evan the Fifth.

Without him, she will not move. She stands so patiently. He wants to guide her into a dancer's spin with his hand. The pressure of her flesh is so welcome that if he is little more to her than a guide dog leading her out of the library, he does not care. He is grateful.

In his hand, he can feel her pulse, his pulse, maybe their pulses pressed together. And when he looks at Claire, he no longer sees Sharon; he does not see his father. This is a relief. "Claire," he says, "Claire?" with no specific question. In fact, he has already forgotten his earlier questions. To say her name is like playing that echo game where you call out a code word, as if asking for a part of nature to reply and yet never expecting to hear an alternate voice.

"Evan?" she responds, "Evan," clutching his palm loosely, briefly, before they take their first steps together into the lobby. They clear the doors with her pulled close as he holds one open so they can advance.

Outside, he notices the sky is blue and dotted with white clouds. "I would like you to tell me to take my medicine if we live together," he says. "Tell me you will leave me if I don't. And if you hear me talking to someone, it is usually Sharon or my father or mother. It's okay to interrupt."

Claire nods. "I don't hear any voices," she says. The street is loud after the quiet of the library. The scent of sycamore leaves and pollution moves through the air. "I was thinking about what you asked earlier. Yes, you can look at me and touch me when we get to your house; I'll interrupt your voices. But you have to do something for me."

"What?" he asks. "Anything."

The hand that holds her cane trembles. "Please don't forget that I'm blind," she says. "No matter which voices you hear. After we make a few turns, I won't know where I am. I don't want to get hurt. So when we get into the middle of an intersection on a main road, when I can hear the traffic and the crowds from all sides, please don't release me. Until we get to where we're going, don't let go of my hand. "

ELEGANTLY NAKED IN MY SEXY MENTAL ILLNESS

Evan looks at his shoes. He nods before realizing that nods aren't audible. When he sees that she is waiting, expectation in her stance, he says the words she needs to hear to move the two of them forward into the attending summer with so much promise, "Don't worry, Claire. I won't."

THE STAR

LOSING MARRIED WOMEN

I am an unrepentant harvester of other people's marriages. I have been told I have a disorder, which is to say, I do not feel, traveling through life on a blank page, skirting the voids and chasms, and sometimes I hear a voice, low and demeaning, which says, "You want to recant all your promises, but this is impossible. You have opened a vast box called Infidelity. It was not heavy. It was a feather that stuck to your shoe. Because you forage it again and again, your life is your fault."

I hush it quickly when another voice argues, "The infidelity is not yours—but hers, luminous her, the her that you thought you might escape but never could. And then there was the him, the him that slept beside the her until the you:

Sex was never the issue. Love was the issue—an absence that became an issue, just as rapidly as a conversation became intimate."

Katie was a bleeding gash her husband occasionally cauterized. They made their lives with monotony. She ached for something new. I stole in, invisible, as I always do. It is easy to steal a heart unguarded, as easy as opening an unlocked door. I watched her and touched her—expecting nothing. She was in her forties—her body tight like twenty years earlier. She had ash-blonde hair. She had purchased a facelift years ago.

I might have been anyone. A mailman, for example. A delivery boy. Instead, I was a woman, living close enough to invite inside for daytime daiquiris. She is what this is about—Katie.

She lived in a vast, open house alongside Virginia Beach. All day, she shopped or called friends or, on special occasions, drank until she passed out on her Ethan Allen couch with her blahdeblah designer end table, near a blahdeblah telescope, in front of an open window. His name was Ed. Katie and Ed. A boring, hetero, upper-mid couple.

At one time, he plied her with romance, settled his hands deep inside her heart and stirred it to motion. This soon stopped. I had considered their marriage abandoned by both before I ever entered. I didn't want to enter for the longest time. When I met her, we simply shook hands. I said, "Hi, I'm your new neighbor."

She said, "Hello, I'm Katie Ford," announcing her full name. Her palm was warm and dry. For many days, we talked from our balconies, and then one day she said, "Come over and hang out. You busy?"

"Of course not. I'm looking for distractions," I said. "You?"

She said, "Let's go to the beach and swim."

That had been the plan. I wore a one-piece, swimmer's suit. She put on a white wrap and a two-piece, changing in her bedroom while I watched. I told her, "I'm gay, you know."

"I'm not homophobic," she said.

"Okay, just letting you know." My last lover had left me for what she called "an absence of true gayness." I refused to shave off my hair and would not attend the women's meetings. I refused to let my armpits grow shaggy and learn the gay code. Is there such a thing as not gay enough? Sure, I had enjoyed men. I had enjoyed women. I had decided to enjoy women more.

They did not beat me. They did not lie to me. Only on

occasion did they cheat, and usually then over some trifle of affection I had forgotten to grant. In fact, I did not care for people…whether they entered or exited. I was a room in a dance club, night after night, dazzling but stained with the smoke of cigars—hot bodies crushed against my wall, floor getting crowded. I kept no emotion close. All that remained was the bouquet of truculent voices and my mimicry. My smile looked more sincere.

I felt, at times, like an old woman whose eyes watched myriad scenes with the same young woman, who was myself, as the star. Star, my own name. In deed and fact. My blood, at times, ran as cold as the Atlantic in December.

Katie and I played in the waves. She didn't fear the freeze. When her bikini top came loose, I swam after it. When I brought it back, she said, "My fingers are cold. Will you put it on me?"

I stared at her rosebud nipples. I stared at her emaciated chest. Her ribs were visible through the surf. But I was bored with straight women who played games with their bodies: Touch me. Do you like me? I'm not gay, though. Whatever.

I wrapped the top around her like a bandage. She smiled. "Thanks," she said.

"Sure," I said, smiling back, my sincere smile.

Everyday afterwards she invited me over. One time, she had returned from a shopping trip wearing a navy silk evening gown. The tag hung from the armpit. The neckline plunged. "I'm playing dress-up," she said. "Wanna come in?"

She lifted her mussed hair for me to undo the button in back. My fingers paused at the soft hair just beneath her scalp. I loosened the button. "Come in," she said, husky, with a sad undertone. "Sit on my bed. Stay awhile."

I am naturally silent. That's why my mother named me Star. A star twinkles, is quiet, draws the eye without sound. As I sat in her room, she told me about Ed and slid out from inside the blue dress. She tried on another.

"He's just, well, he's obsessed with the business. He comes home, slumps into his chair, and turns on the news. I usually have dinner ready, but he eats it from the couch. I don't doubt that he loves me, but sometimes, except for a quick kiss before he goes to sleep, I doubt he recognizes that someone else lives here. So I shop. I spend his overtime. It's mutually beneficial. After all, look at this dress! Isn't it beautiful?" She spun around. The second dress had a series of crinolines that swished; it was pink organdy, the color of cotton candy and little girls.

"Yes," I said, but suddenly, out of the blue, I wondered how I would react to poverty. Would my needs become emotions? These questions stirred me. And what if all of history suddenly evaporated? Not just mine, but everyone's. What if there were no past? I voiced that thought aloud. "What if there were no past?"

She laughed, delighted. She stared at my voluptuous chest. "I get lonely," she said. "Do you have a lover?"

"No."

"How can you not?" she asked. "You are so pretty, Star. That long red hair. That delicate face. I can't imagine." She came closer and ran her fingers through my hair. I steeled myself. She was beautiful, but that did not appeal to me.

I thought of the infinite coldness of the universe, of the motion of a formless projectile, like a radio song, hurtling through space. "I don't want a lover," I said.

Her face fell. "I just feel lonely," she said, then began to cry.

"Katie," I said, wrapping my arms around her, because that was what I was supposed to do. "You need to get through to Ed. That's all."

She did not go out to her patio for the next few days. She did not call. I began to take interest. Was she rejected? I showed up the next day with dahlias and a gift. She opened the door, faint hope in her eyes. "I'm sorry for being such a sap the other day," she said. "Come look at my new kitchen. It's not done yet, but tomorrow…"

A workman stooped on her floor, laying down tile the color of blush. "I've been busy," she continued. "Come see the new closet."

I followed her into her bedroom. She had bought a new armoire, dark walnut. When we entered her bedroom, she closed the door. "Do you think I'm pretty?" she asked. "I mean, I know you're gay, so if you do—it's okay to tell me."

"You're pretty," I said. "But not my type." I handed her the box. Inside was a piece of blown glass that looked warm due to its sepia color, like a full-bodied Italian woman.

"Oh, it's so lovely," she said. "I'll put it in the kitchen. Let's see where it might go."

"All right," I said, thinking: *Sex can be destructive. Will I make love to her?* I often looked at women's sexual organs, their rosy, lower lips and upjutting clits. Through this, I had visions of my own anatomy.

After determining a place for the glass, we strode back to the bedroom so she could change her clothes once again. "I think you're beautiful," she said then, and, unexpectedly, ground her mouth into mine. Her small arms had startling strength. I began to kiss her back. She did not pull away. I cupped her ass in my hands and pulled her close.

Her eyes dared me to stop, and she trembled. This was obviously her first time with a woman. "I don't like to get involved in these married things," I told her, lying shamelessly.

These married things were always better. An affair with a married woman had no repercussions. She never gave her full self, only the needy part. She gave sex without love, misguided sex, sex meant to punish someone else and please the new practitioner. I understood that. Her lips tasted like cranberry sugar.

The first kiss is always delicious. A kiss is more than a kiss. A beautiful girl in a window, waving hello. A chance to be sensual. A kiss seals things or tears them apart. I love you. I love you not.

I did not look for these liaisons. They came unbidden, laid themselves at my feet like pigeons before hilltops of bread. I told her, "I should leave."

"No," she said. "Let's go shopping."

"Don't buy me anything," I said.

"Star," she said. "Don't be uptight."

On the way, in the car, I could tell she was pleased. She hummed a jaunty tune, her eyes glittered, and she lowered the top of the convertible so the wind would blow through her hair. She put on a pair of cat-eye glasses and applied burnt-orange lipstick.

We walked through the mall, staring at everything. I could smell perfume a mile away. "Let's try some on," she said.

I watched her accept samples from the salespeople. She chatted casually. One girl asked if I had smelled Lauder's newest scent.

"No," I said. "I have a scent I always wear." Perfidy, I joked in my head. Not Knowing, not L'Amour, not Tresor.

"Come on, Star!" Katie said. "Live a little."

I let her take my wrist. A small spritz was applied, and was nauseating. Katie leaned in, smelled my open arm. "It's perfect!" she announced. "I'll take one of those too."

"For you?" I asked. "Don't buy anything for me."

"Of course for me," Katie said, winking grandly at the others. On the way to the car, she said, "I don't think you're really gay."

I stopped and stared at her. This accusation, heard so many times, rankled in my mind. "There's a time, Katie," I replied, "when there is no gay, or not gay. There is only happy or unhappy. Women have made me happier than men. I have my own money. I want for nothing. It's almost impossible to have money and know that someone loves you for who you are."

"Sounds lonely to me," Katie said.

"Better lonely than used."

"I won't use you," she whispered. "I won't. I promise."

"I don't get lonely," I said, but we went to her house and made love. I did everything for her. She seemed at a loss for what to do, but by the fifth time, she knew my body like the layout of Nieman's.

~

At home, afterwards, I began a series of randomly destructive acts. Glasses clattered into walls. Stacks of papers flew into the air. Pictures were ripped from their frames. I had done it again. If there were a projectile, hurtling through space, it might, from one angle, appear to stand still. If I were that projectile, I would maintain the illusion as long as possible.

Ed came home every day at 7 p.m. After seven, I sat in my house, hoping he'd ignore Katie or go to bed early. Everything seemed normal. One day, instead of playing at the beach, or shopping, we went to a motel. "Why here?" I asked. "We could go to my house."

"Because we have to check in," she said. "I told Ed I'd be here tonight."

"Why?" I asked.

"Because I told him I was leaving. In case the lawyer calls. I won't have much money—but the alimony should be decent. We could go on vacation. We could have so much fun. He can't know too much about us before the settlement, though, so I came here." She wavered, unsure of herself, hovering between wanting one thing and something else entirely.

"Does he know who I am?" I asked.

"No," she said. "He only knows I left him for a woman."

"Go home, Katie."

"No."

"Do you know who I am? Really? I can't make you happy."

"I think so," she said, with a small smile. "And you can."

I pictured her purchase of that sickly perfume. She had no

idea what I wanted. "Go back to Ed," I said, and pictured him crying into his soup.

"He doesn't want me back," she said. "He told me, 'Go be a fucking faggot if you want to, but not on my money.'"

I cringed. I put my arms around her. While she wept, I couldn't help myself—I wanted escape. I thought about her life, and my life, and our lives, and the improbability that I would ever be enough. I thought of her waking one morning to decide that I had not given her enough attention. My pulse raced.

"He said," she moaned, "that I would have to leave you and never see you again. I told him I couldn't."

"Katie, go back to him," I told her. "I'm not who you want." As I said this, I wondered why no one ever says, "You're not who I want." People always invert it, just like no one ever says, "You can't complete me," but that's what they mean. What they mean is, "You are just a speck of dust on my sleeve and I'm ready to brush you off." I already loved her like a memory. Besides, it was never the "other" person who made a scene unbearable, always the unhappy housewife/neglected husband. A world of need was laid at my feet, her need for me to be everyone and everything that pleased her.

I kicked the burden away like a skipping stone. I stared in Katie's eyes as I watched who she thought I was change—and she inched back, but I was a breeze in a house of boredom, a come-hither draft that wrapped around others until they chilled. She had opened the door. She had gestured—come in. I entered. But now, she glared because she had chosen to change her life?

I watched her eyes pulse like a kaleidoscope, shifting blue to black. Those eyes decided I was meaningless, that she had made a startling mistake. They decided to return to Ed. They decided to hate me. No, there was another resolution. None of this mattered—it was all a fantasy; some grim joke enacted for a lukewarm laugh. "Star," she said. "Do you want to make love? One last time?"

ELEGANTLY NAKED IN MY SEXY MENTAL ILLNESS

"No."

The door closed and I was gone. Literally. Figuratively. Perhaps she fought herself inside that room, reeling with embarrassment, decided to call Ed. Perhaps not.

But I kicked the feather from my shoe and raced into another series of illusions. The scent of crushed flowers hung in the air outside the door.

I followed that scent into the open afternoon. Losing married women was delicious—just beyond the sensation of losing yourself in a storm.

Past the parking lot, on the telephone wires, a single sparrow careened into another pair. They fell awkwardly, flew up, and united, shaking out their wings. Possibly, they tended to each other—until ambushed by other interruptions, but the kamikaze bomber flew away, oblivious.

The other two returned to their previous position, preening.

~

"Hi, I'm Star," I said to the woman at the checkout.

"Hi, Star. I'm Glory." It was two in the afternoon, Wednesday. She obviously had nothing important to do.

"You live around here?" I asked.

A diamond ring was plain on her finger, two carats at least. "Yes, yes I do."

"I live on Thistledown Court," I said. "The weather's nice, isn't it?" I smiled my genuine smile.

She smiled back.

"I like to go swimming in the ocean on days like these." I said. "Are you busy?"

SPEAK TO ME WITH TENDERNESS, HOWARD SUN

It is a horrid age. Online, icons pop and engage. They present possibilities, illusions. Since Howard Sun would never tell Lisa James he loved her, they also presented him a venue with which to test his questions beforehand. This was, Lisa decided, halfway into his gambit and, beginning to get pissed, working with a deleterious effect on their as-yet unconfessed and earth-shattering love. Not that she had decided to determine what they shared as love definitively—that is, until she feared he might kill her and she realized she kind of liked the idea.

Howard Sun expressed nothing on his face. Howard Sun replied curtly when they spoke. *Why, oh why, am I interested in Howard Sun*, she often asked herself, *since he's always a million miles away?* Then she remembered that the small action was everything to her, and he had, one summer morning and with no announced intent, brought daffodils to their place of employment. He'd said, "I found these. Can I give them to you?" She'd been his since then.

He was handsome if taciturn. He did not remind her of her father, who was far more jovial. He reminded her of a stone wall.

Yet another day, Howard Sun gave her a mix CD. "I like these songs," he said. "Want to hear my CD? You can have it."

Because she was never rude, she said yes, but when he walked away that day she thought only: *How fucking weird, Howard! How socially inept.* It was like how he wore his pocket protector in the designer clothes his ex-girlfriend had outfitted him in, obviously unclear about, or ungrateful for, what a strong effort this ex-girlfriend had made to help him live up to the sexy man he could be, if only he would stand up straight, look people in the eye, say the romantic thing to a girl rather than a near-autistic level of statement like, "I like these songs." She considered throwing his CD in the trash. "Fucking Howard," she said to herself. But there was a sigh after she said this, because she loved music and she was curious because he did have a sweet look in his eyes as he handed it to her, even when saying something ludicrously impersonal.

Sometimes he said uncommonly romantic things, but this was rare. At a company picnic two years ago, before Lisa knew or suspected he was enamored, she remembered he'd stood beside her as she waited in line for a hotdog. She saw a friend, Eleanor, a stout old woman from her former department whose company she had enjoyed. "Hey, Howard," she said. "Can you hold my spot in line for a minute? I want to talk to Eleanor."

The line was long, wending past the first two picnic tables and out toward the baseball field cluster. Howard Sun said then, "I would wait in this line for you for an eternity. I am a sun. The sun keeps burning, even when touching the other side of the world, even when the moon is the only thing visible."

While her first response, the one that almost slipped out, was, "What the fuck, over? Can you just speak plainly?" she knew he liked wordplay, liked puns, and he was, in his bizarre way, being friendly. "Thanks, Howard," she said. "So grateful."

Then came the escalating gifts—two Hershey's Kisses on her desk one morning that he denied leaving her though she had watched him place them there, the unexpected daffodils, memos he wrote to reduce her workload, that mix CD that floored her since it was full of the sort of well-spoken love songs she couldn't even imagine him listening to—and just the other day, he had invited her to a football game. "I have two tickets," he said. "Want one?"

"To go together or apart?" she asked.

"Either way."

"Well, I'm not going to any football game by myself, so decide what you mean."

"We could drive together, I suppose," Howard Sun replied. "But I may have to leave early."

"I hate football," she said. "But I'll consider it."

Though the game was four days away, two days later, Howard did not come up and check in to say, perhaps, "So, Lisa, are we going or not?" He could have normalized this nonexistent inquiry further by stating something like, "These tickets are expensive and I want to ask another friend."

They didn't end up going together. Neither did he go, she found out soon enough. He came to her desk, after she left work, and dropped a poem by Longfellow on her keyboard. This is why, once she decided that he did indeed love her, despite all the bullshit, non-shit he said, it did not surprise her that she would catch him staring at her longingly, only to look away when caught. It also did not surprise her that he would begin, via her Facebook page, to create numerous alternate-personas with which he could "get to know her."

They were not obvious at first. Sometimes, in fact, more than one of "them" spoke to her on the same day. Each held a trace of Howard. He wanted this small link—he wanted her to know them, yet wanted her to simultaneously not know them. It wasn't that she didn't have real Facebook friends, but she also had several of his ghosts, and with more than one thousand friends to her credit—she posted music a lot and people liked that, she guessed—she did not think she could ever eradicate all of his shadows even if she wanted to, and yet, these questions the strangers would ask!

Each reeked of him, though the similarities were weblike and intuitive—so she could not, after a while, explain how she knew that a teenage-girl horror writer was him, freak mystic zealot was him, crazy-obsessive where's-my-gone-lover was him, nature-nut save-the-environment was him, freaky sex magazine page was him, aspiring poet who never read was him—but she knew.

Every new Howard she talked to would do something weird: Friend her when they had no friends; display a quote that sounded like a fuck off to her patent non-reaction to his mix tape; address something she and Howard had just spoken about, staplers, dreams; or even simply show art or book taste that, in combination with whatever they said first, second, or third, spelled out his name like a flare from an airplane. *Howard Sun, are you Emily Peabody from Detroit, Michigan?*

Sometimes, he would scheme coordinated themes with his personas and she'd clue in on a new linked identity. Clowns one day, for example. Another day, fashion.

Not that he would admit it. Not that it wasn't making her feel crazy. Not that it wasn't wasting her time to reply to "strangers." In the end, she concluded it was a big situationist experiment, as he'd claimed many times over their scattered lunches throughout the last three years he was into as a sort of unplugged lucid dreaming. And he would one day write a book of essays about it. So this idea made all the more sense when the "shadow" people asked her questions that he had narrowly alluded to in previous cryptic emails.

Still, she had hardly enough time for real people, much less the shadows of a co-worker she could only suspect was head over heels in love with her, and so she resolved to confront Howard. She had, after all, just enough ammunition to make it appear that she knew more than she did, having strolled past his desk during his bathroom break and seen such a shadow page displayed wherein Shadow Dimwit Non-Reader Poet Fucker had said: "You're just so kind, Lisa. So lovely. I wish I lived in your town because I would take you out for sure. I would recite Yeats to you, though I think he's overrated."

She had replied (all this visible on Howard's screen): "I hate romance and all stupid pricks who want romance. Sorry."

Doh, she thought. *I guess I'm getting a little crazy honest with how irritating I find this subterfuge.* What if Shadow Dimwit Non-Reader Poet Fucker was really some sweet guy, some nice guy that she had clobbered over the head due to recalcitrant, non-telling, situationist, freak magnet and devilishly handsome Howard Sun? She took a moment, actually a few seconds, to ponder this idea, critiquing her own cruelty.

Then, as if a light bulb flashed on in her head, she reminded herself: *Shadow Dimwit Non-Reader Poet Fucker is on Howard's screen, dumbass. This means he* is *Howard. Howard is him.* Howard/Alterna Boy SDNPF had then replied: "Wow. You're pretty angry."

She responded: "Yes, I'm actually a rabid bull-dyke lesbian with a preference for hard fisting and walks on the beach. Sorry. Quote me some Kathy Acker, mmmkay? *Grins* And I like my women strong as bull. Vocal. Unchallenged by honesty. Unless I like men. But you'd never know. I do not mind performing CBT on men, however. If you'd like help with that."

There was no reply that day. None.

Howard avoided her eyes, walking around with a wounded yet curious look. When he stopped by her cubicle a day or two later, he said, "Are you going out with girlfriends this weekend?" He had never asked about her girlfriends. "Yes," she said, thinking about his pretty green eyes, about how he was probably in that very moment imagining her performing oral sex on another woman, then went back to her paperwork.

He upped the stakes on his gift-giving, or promised gift-giving, telling her he would mail her things he thought she wanted. A first edition *Streetcar Named Desire*, for example. "And how do you have that?" she asked. "And how do you know I'd want that?"

"It's lying around," he said. "Somebody gave it to me. I just thought you'd like it. Doesn't everyone like Williams?"

"No. Some people hate Williams and think he was a misogynist, woman-bashing jerk of a gay guy. I like him, in small doses. He was rather pathetic. Do you even like Williams? Are you a fan?"

"Not really," Howard Sun said. "That's why I'd give you my book." He took this moment to scratch his growing stubble, stare beseechingly at her with his heavily lashed doe eyes, as if he said something altogether different in this eye-meet than he had with his words.

This is when little horror writer freak chick wrote Lisa a message on Facebook: "So, you, like, write about desire a lot, right? I need to put more of that in my horror books cuz they are so fucking ugly that all I do is kill people and sex and death are hawt, cuz people like that. You, like, write about love/desire, right? I mean, where people don't just kill each other?"

Lisa ran a weekend column on wedding cakes. Still, this writing about desire thing was a stretch. "I write about cakes," she told Odd Horror Writer Teenager Chick, adding a sweetsy emoticon. "Cakes are wedding accessories that don't enter the bedroom." Sweetsy emoticon two. "People eat them. *Wink* I have a day job at a home-management company. I'm really busy. I don't think I can help you, but good luck with that! Good luck!"

OHWTC did not write back for a while, but replied the next week. By the time she did, "Oh, wow. That's heavy, lady," Lisa was too busy talking with other alters to reply. She thought continuously: *How many messages with double meanings can one compose before it all means everything and nothing—but more accurately means nothing?* She considered closing her existing Facebook account and starting a new one with only people she had met in person. It was too easy for shadows to linger, to infiltrate—and then she wondered to herself: *Does Howard fancy himself a sexy teenage horror writer girl? Because if so, that's appalling.*

But coincidences added up. Another day, he had a strange guy from Czechoslovakia talking to her: "Cans you helps me with English?" The trouble was that while he, Howard Sun, was busy trying to figure her out with the other people he created, the real him saying ridiculous things irked her: "It's Monday today, Lisa. Isn't that great?" He was losing her. Absolutely.

She would have given anything for a little speech from Howard that pointed to more than a coincidental crossing of their paths, office talk, or a mild interest. And she was beginning to hate the computer. And him. *Howard Sun, you are such a douche,* she thought each time she replied to particularly weird question from his alters.

She consulted female friends when this debacle got too trying, like this question wasn't a no-brainer: "Do you think it's cute when someone wants to scope you out so badly they might, say, create multiple anonymous Facebook identities to talk to you— or is it creepy?"

Friends confirmed creepy. "Aw fuck, Howard," Lisa wanted to say. "Can't you just ask me out? Can't you just take us into the wild desert of desire so that we can do the freaky horizontal mambo? I'm feeling like a guy here. This blue-ball thing, it's no joke."

"There is really good melon ball salad up at the cafeteria, Lisa," he said on Tuesday.

Shadow. Shadow. Shadow. Love.

Wednesday: "Did you hear Edgar Clarnte is quitting?"

Shadow novel. Skin trade Moscow. Did somebody say Trotsky? Shadow. Shadow. Shadow love.

"Do you like the song of birds in the morning?" he asked on Thursday.

Shadow bright, shadow light, shadow Poet Fucker here tonight. Here: With more shit to lie about.

"What do you think of the bear market; will the bull ever come back?"

Stream of shadow. Shadow talking. Shadows mating. Real-estating. Wild-shadow tremors—bears! Shadow fucking. Etcetera.

His shadows kept appearing, increasing their demands. She gave blood. Three drops each. She had to admit, it was cool how he crafted these profiles, but where was he getting all the pictures? Some TinyPics stash? No, must be Flickr. Hijacking feed streams? Did he research albums of dead people? He even made different emoticons for each shadow, which he stuck to religiously.

Maybe he had a flowchart for shadow tracking. A character map. There was that weird thing on his desk once that had like fifty emails and passwords on it. And maybe Howard Sun, shy, non-verbal, retiring and self-erasing Howard Sun, was writing a killer novel about this deceptively quiet guy talking to a woman online all the freaking time, except with multiple personalities or personas, and it was to be a thriller. Maybe all these personalities would end up leading her around the globe and then she'd land somewhere to meet her new "true love" personality, Jackory Randall or someone, and there Howard would be, sitting on the hotel bed, crooning, "Hiya, Lisa. I've missed you."

By that time, of course, Lisa would be looking for whichever shadow fucker had become so real to her that she both believed firmly and had long since stopped thinking he or she was Howard, so her eyes would be trained to look for the face of the new beloved, the one who spoke most kindly and sweetly and consistently—because she had decided this self, the once-Howard shadow, now beloved, as a whole character—until there—at her perfect romantic liaison with new and far-healthier love—there was only fuckhead Howard Sun, sitting on the mystery couch of thwarted desire like a twisted Norman Bates in a bathrobe or something. That, or the Howard/Alter-Fucker Beloved character would then play the *Twin Peaks* theme or Cohen's "Take This Waltz" or something terribly dripping with Teenage Horror Writer Girl—and straight up *kill* her, strangling her with excessive bondage rope after inflicting small razorblade cuts on her whole body beforehand! With lots of verbal humiliation! Some kind of teasing, fucked-up game play! Manipulation! Pain! *Ohmygod, the pain!* Howard was going to kill her! This whole cat-and-mouse game was just leading to some Dahmer or fetish murder, and that's why Howard was so good-looking but socially inept, because he was a serial k—

"Lisa," he said, stepping up to her cubicle, his ridiculous pocket protector precariously close to falling out of his pocket. He leaned in, holding a cup of ginseng tea. "You look so nervous," he continued. "Are you okay today?"

She wanted to say, "Go away, Howard. I'm fantasizing about you killing me."

She decided, not long after this, that she must visit a mental health professional—and she did. "Speak directly to your loved one," her counselor Betty said. "Ask him about your concerns."

"My loved one?" Lisa asked. "Howard Sun? Really?"

"Well, yes, obviously," Betty replied. "Lisa, you've been talking about him and these alters for more than an hour—and though I'm not sure why you're so into him, I should tell you that you do exhibit the signs of fascination, of tenderness, of love, even." Betty shook her soft-wave short perm and looked at Lisa through her orange-framed glasses.

"I don't love him," Lisa said.

"Oh, really? Then why," Betty asked, "would you talk to complete strangers, wasting your precious time and playing his game? Let's be honest, little lamb. You want him to love you. What you can't decide is whether to smack the hell out of his alters each time he tries to act like they are unique people and spins you out on purpose, because Howard Sun is a person with either extreme fear, extreme mental illness, or extreme cruelty. But which is it?"

"I don't know," Lisa said. She sat with her head between her legs. "Could he be a spy? Could there be any good reason for all these profiles? I really don't know."

"Cold-turkey anybody you don't already know," Betty said. "Force him out—or through."

"Okay," Lisa said. And she did. As the days passed and she responded to none of his alters, which was quite painful as it caused her to be inactive with her real contacts, Howard grew more and more morose. One day, she saw him at his desk crying—full-on sobbing. She walked over. "Do you think you should go home, Howard?" she asked.

"No." Sob, sob, hiccup. "I'll be fine. I swear."

She broke her rule five minutes later when she wrote back one of the good alters. Howard recuperated quickly, fairly beamed. But Lisa felt nasty about this artificial fix. When Howard next asked, "So, do you have any plans for the summer ahead?" she suddenly broke, just broke, and said in reply, but not to his question, "Why don't you just tell me you love me, Howard Sun, and pursue me like a normal guy? I am more than ready to sleep with you—but you can't ask for mangos when you want papaya! Ask me the real questions!"

"I—uh—I—uhhh," he said.

"Do you want to sleep with me or not?"

Gaped-mouth shock.

"Answer quickly because I am getting impatient!"

"Yes?"

"Is it a question, Howard?"

"I thought an affirmative was an answer."

"But there was a question behind it. Why was there a question behind it?"

"There always is."

"That's it. Yes or no, Howard?"

"Yes?"

"Good. So this has been decided. That's great. When?"

"I—uh—I—uhhh."

"I said when, Howard?"

"Now?"

At this point, Lisa stood. She wanted to wrap her hands around his neck and strangle the living shit out of his ambiguous self, but she did not. She leaned over and planted her lips on his. He kissed her back.

After a minute his hands were taking the full tour of her body and then, and then, at the sound of a nearby lounge door opening, both dropped contact like the other's body was hot rocks. They tried to look normal.

"Did something just happen?" Howard asked, her raspberry lipstick all over his face.

"It did."

"What?"

"I don't know."

"Good. That makes two of us."

"Can you just try to speak to me with tenderness, Howard Sun?" Lisa then asked. "How about you do like my therapist says and be honest? You don't have to speak to me through other people. Come on. Unless you do have to talk through other people, unless you can't help yourself?"

He tapped the top of her cubicle with his hand and walked away. The next day he was out sick and his shadows had disappeared. On her desk, Howard had left a gift. *Streetcar.*

He had highlighted certain lines. They basically said he loved her. But she never did see him again, Howard Sun. The one who said he'd wait in line for her forever because the sun burns unendingly.

She kept blogging about wedding cakes. She kept thinking of

his face. Sometimes she'd stare over at his cubicle, which remained empty for several months, then search out his online shadows in a Facebook stealth mission. She couldn't help it.

After a while she was messaging the shadows again out of sheer and deadly missing him. She kept corresponding. The shadows grew dear. Some of them might be real people. But she kind of loved them, her therapist might say. Maybe she really loved them. Who knew anymore?

She couldn't make herself crazy forever, wondering which ones were real. And so, appropriately humble and apologetic for her former absence, she reinitiated her foray into the great unknown of his meticulously engineered neverland, thinking: *Howard? Howard Sun, where are you? I'll take you any way you come. I am lost in you now.*

The situation was the ether, and the cloud her mind. There was still a courting dance between them.

As the days gathered, she summoned back his shadows like they were the ephemeral gray casts falling naturally between the shrinking ascendant tiers of some white, first-class, shotgun wedding cake—those only found in the wine-dark hotel of her passion's favorite thought-tryst, and she called out his shadows' names into the echoing Internet wires to bring back riddled and befuddling word of his existence, called out to them frequently, with affection and variety, until, still missing both him and the live-chat active connection or the diversity of his themes splashing rainbow flags of his presence into her feed, these things reassuring her of the other personas' connections to Howard's endeavor on the whole, she was done with simpler messaging.

"Oh, Howard. I still love you," she said. "Even if you never will tell me, in so many words, that you love me." But the strange persona friend requests continued to flash incoming on her notifications screen. She surveyed the profiles with a mixture of dread and desire.

Then she bit her lip and friended them again.

ELEGANTLY NAKED IN MY SEXY MENTAL ILLNESS

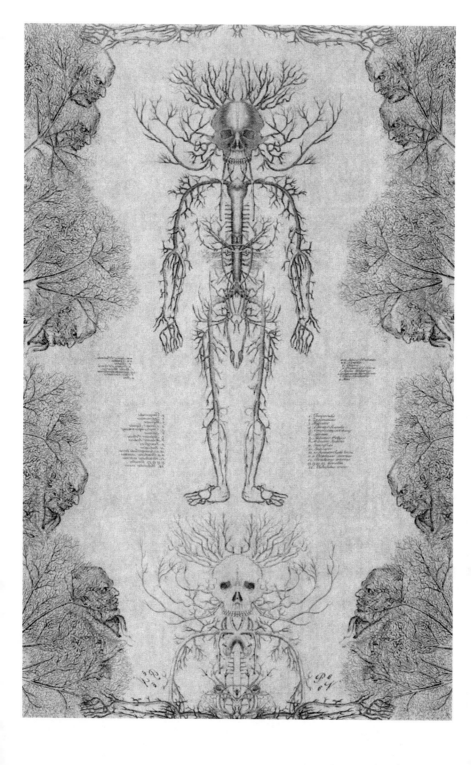

TAKING CELINE

She wouldn't call these intrusions rape exactly. More like a strange penetration, the desire of which she never mirrored. He tried to kiss her, pressed his gaping lips on her body and then, cruelly, without asking or noticing her expression, thrust forcefully inside her. When she acquainted herself with his rhythms, the strain and pull could be reflected away by imagining the cool caves in Ceylon or a handful of smooth stones in her hand.

Sometimes she thought of her mother and visualized a needle coming up and through the stretched canvas embroidery, then down again. The wood that circled its perimeter held down her tight stitches, and she imagined herself as that canvas. Celine was always stretching. First for this one, then the next.

He said he liked it rough. Harry was efficient in his lovemaking. He put his hands heavily on her breasts and tweaked her nipples, then, disappointed with her response, bit them. Celine did nothing. No scream. No sound. No more than the unconscious flinch from the nerve stimulus. She bled, but that was to be expected. Really, she didn't care. Everything was peaceful here. Sunlight bathed the codeine walls with sweeping orange, the morning was misty, and beyond the window a light drizzle fell; the scent of wet leaves pulsed in the air, in turn stagnant and fresh, depending on the breeze. The painted bars outside her window were easy to focus on, so she concentrated on these when a waft of her blood and his sweat reached her.

Harry kept his clothes on throughout. At first his penis was like a fleshy red knob, peeking thickly through the zipper of his trousers. Then he pleasured himself by rubbing it briskly against her. There was no point in protesting. After a while, he'd unbutton his slacks where it more or less jutted awkwardly outward, curving slightly, and pull down the top of his waistband to expose a trail of hairy down which led to a triangle of mottled flesh. This triangle was her view should she look down, so she stared at the ceiling.

When she remarked that she thought it odd he enjoyed these intervals clothed, he replied, "It's about safety." Mostly, he came up to check on her, and if anyone came looking, he explained, he didn't want to be discovered. So considerate. But, he always thanked her and sponged her body down afterwards, kissing her gently on the forehead.

In warmer months, they strode thoughtfully through the trees while he listed them for her—referencing his favorite deciduous varieties. He had many favorites, and so explained each in a windy synopsis which had her yawning on the inside, but pleased to be out in the afternoon air. He explained why they were planted in their order—birches around the perimeter, oaks just beyond, and beeches hidden behind others in the center. A few evergreens spotted the road at the end of the driveway, but they walked briskly past these. He did not like them.

She smiled while he spoke as if to say, *I'm listening, I understand*, but none of it made much sense. Then, in the communal tearoom, they'd drink chamomile, and sometimes he'd ask questions she responded to in a low voice. Notably he asked about her childhood, and Celine would reply, "It was happy," and enumerate each moment she felt her heart swell for the providence of her youth—but there were only four, possibly five such instances that she referred to repeatedly. She knew he'd have no way of understanding the seashell sketches or the sap revival stories, which were imagined musings, but sometimes she told them anyway. He listened to her well-modulated voice without pause. He asked specious questions.

"After you saw the gargoyle tree, which way did the wind blow?"

"I'm touched, Harry," she said. "But I'm not crazy."

"Humor me. I know you know the answer."

"North," she said, thinking. "Sometimes northeast."

"Ah," he said. "And was there someone else there?"

"Yes."

"A friend, perhaps?"

"No. My mother and my brother."

"So your family was around?"

"Yes."

"Did they say anything important?"

"No."

This conversation spanned several outings. He even asked more stupid questions about the gargoyle tree—as if its shapes and surfaces didn't clearly explain its name—and, she wanted to inquire, couldn't he tell that she was tired of discussing that part? "This is not to the purpose," she announced late one afternoon. "It was a reference point only. What I wanted to communicate was the frog-bog or the moon shivers. Yes, exactly that."

They watched the sun decline into the trees. He returned her to her solitude. With this dispute settled, she went back to her room, cleared the small desk, and, as they'd classified her as non-violent, pulled out a permitted pen.

Dear Mother, she wrote:
The retreat with Harry at Puggert goes well. Some

attentions he lavishes on me are overwhelming, but the other long-stay guests are very friendly and when they are not quarreling we play parlor games. I am in high hopes that this will be my last few days here. Harry says he'll take me to a different town—one on the French border whose climate is less mutable. His new job forces our relocation, but you know climate is as delicate as temperament, and surely both should improve.

> *Loving you madly,*
> *Celine*

The next morning she took her pills without question and sensed that Harry would be pleased enough to send her missive. "Harry," she said, when he raised from his haunches. "I want you to send this letter to my mother."

"The last letter you sent confused and upset her," he replied.

"That doesn't bother me," she said. "This one should cheer her. I told her what she wanted to hear." She said it didn't bother her, but she lied. Perhaps, while she was at it, she should have fabricated a chapel visit. In the last letter she was especially careful to remain entirely factual. Imagination was close to sin in her mother's mind, and Celine had tried to tell her the things she saw without any distortion—the story of the man who bit himself and then screamed repeatedly, the catatonics with their eyes focused on a single wall tile for hours at a time, the listers, the ritualists, the autistics—Celine described all of these people realistically. But imagination was less frightening than truth—life had taught her that. She felt that the only way to keep above the heaviness here was to succumb to it, and wasn't her mother the one who sent her here after all—this pivotal decision reached after only a few bouts of what she euphemistically called "away time"? Her mother said she wanted the truth, but only when that truth was mild and benign.

"Celine," Harry said. "Why don't you ever move or respond when I make love to you?"

ELEGANTLY NAKED IN MY SEXY MENTAL ILLNESS

Celine's face screwed up distastefully. She had forgotten he was present, just succeeded in blocking him out, and was startled when his face resumed its angles of confrontation. *You don't make love to me,* she thought. But she knew Harry could be useful in this place.

"Will you send this letter, please?" she asked.

"You're not responding to what I asked."

"Your definition of making love is strange. Will you send this or not?"

"Yes, Celine. I will send it."

"That's good, Harry. I don't know why I don't respond. Why do you continue if I don't respond?"

"Because I want to."

"That's why I don't respond."

Harry, agitated, walked past her while zipping his pants, his white coat flapping ridiculously around his backside. For the next few days, Celine retreated into her deeper mind. Her long arms wrapped around her legs and she rocked back and forth on the floor for hours. When he tried to question her, she gave him her blank eyes and then curled her head between her knees so she could view the triangle of floor left bare from flesh. This shadowed triangle which started where her legs met and ended at her knees was not only inverted, but the top's flat image was concave where her legs continued their lines beneath her and unfinished should she hold them out in front.

When repulsed by this, she gnashed her teeth, and when in tune, smiled sweetly down at herself, mouthing a nursery song whose lyrics lost a line or two every year. This time it trickled out in her small girl voice:

> *Soon they will be marching*
> *marching two by two*
> *soon they will be marching*
> *until the battle's through*

The flags they are a'waving
the fighting lines are drawn
the flags they are a'waving
they may not see the dawn
The enemy has seen them
the soldiers scatter back
the enemy has seen them
an ambush for attack
Call the reinforcements
the officer replies
call the reinforcements
or everybody—

She couldn't remember the last verse. She couldn't even remember the first, which told the beginning of the story, or certain others that fell somewhere between. But because it was a long song and she used to know it by heart, she felt anxious. There was a celebration at the end, the skirmish had been won, but the part about the women greeting them open-armed and the part about the dead collected on the field had long ago been erased. Thus, when the blankest nothing verses came she just hummed the rhythm and tapped her foot, incensed.

Every now and again, an orderly brought a needle and stuck her until the gray wash of calm settled over her, and she fell asleep dreaming of her mother's rickety verandah, or the eagle that her father shot falling through the sky, landing on the ground at their feet with a thud and a puff of dust. If she saw Edgar, he danced with bloody wrists around her, the red splatters making burgundy dots on the foreheads of her dolls.

"Celine," Harry said. "If you don't start behaving more rationally, I'm going to have to leave without you on my trip. Today's Wednesday, and I leave tomorrow morning. Celine?"

"You are nothing to me," she said.

Sometimes, in her lucid moments, she tried to tell him about the moon shivers in the shake, but he wasn't receptive. His face melted down to the thick red-brown of his beard, or a forest of hairs writhing like worms in a bait jar. Then the orderlies strapped her down. "I'm patient," she said to herself. "I'm patient. I am clear. And everything will be fine." But she shook until every muscle was sore. Then at about 4 a.m., she subsided. Harry came in shortly after and told her he would put off leaving for a day or two.

"But I'm ready to go now," she said.

"I think it would be better if you rest for a few days."

"But I went away for a while and now I'm back. I'm fine," she said, shaking her fist at him.

"Celine, you need to relax," he said, running a hand down the side of her face and then under her pajama top to stroke her breast. He seized it as an infant would.

"Thank you for having them take the restraints off, Harry," she said.

"Are you ready for this," he asked, putting a hand down his pants and touching the ridge of his hardening flesh.

"No," she said. "Not today." But he pushed himself on top of her and this time didn't pull his pants down. He took himself out, rubbed against her, and wet himself only slightly with his own saliva before penetrating.

"Ah," she said. She imagined that his pricking was her mother's needle, and as he moved inside her, she faded out again. Then, looking at the curtains he'd hung, staring with wet eyes through the window at the leaves of trees, she thought about the letter. "Did you mail it?" she asked.

"Yes, Celine, I sent it." Even his speech seemed to rock with his pelvis, but she noticed from the wide pocket of his coat the sound of paper, and the shape was rectangular and flat. She reached around him, and he, eager for her first and only voluntary touch, preened toward her. "That's good," he said. "So good." But when her hand was stable enough she reached into his pocket as though caressing his side, and pulled the letter out just far enough to see that it was hers, unstamped and as carelessly in his pocket as it was on the day that she gave it to him.

Do not lie to me, Harry, she thought, waiting silently for him to finish. Her hands dropped. She didn't reach up again.

At least, these intrusions would not create children. He said never to worry about pregnancy because he was sterile, so she was glad when he finally ejaculated. Afterwards, as usual he sponged her down, kissed her on the forehead, and pulled her pants up gently after he rebuttoned her shirt.

The door rattled with a knock. As had happened many times before, the nurse came in and sat above Celine's pillow with his fingers on her neck to check her pulse, listening through his stethoscope for her heart. He seemed cool and collected, smiling his professional smile.

"Dr. Owens," the nurse said. "You're needed in room nine."

"I'll see you tomorrow, Celine," he said and, brushing off his pants as though they were covered with lint, he left.

Celine was inconsolable. Her letter, the one she wanted so badly to be sent, was still in his coat pocket, and in a few days he'd take her to a new hospital. This next one would give him complete freedom over her, more privacy, because she was his special transfer. Celine thought about the orderlies' rumor that proceeded this unusual move mid-session, and she assumed that her leaving with him was the compromise the doctors had reached to resolve the unspeakable situation. But she felt weak, and tired from the past few days of sedation, and sore from his efforts.

She looked out the window and saw the brown trunks of oak trees staring with their knotty eyes at her. She remembered he said there were so many that he often stood distantly to see them in their entirety, but failed to register each individually. Brown birch trunks peeled down to white undergarments in front of the oaks whose dark arms reached leafless fingers to the sky, and then there were the beeches in the distance—half-limbed through the others, macabre, like amputated parts.

So she sat again on the floor, doubled over, and proceeded to remove her clothes. She flung them from her body and pressed her hind-parts onto the cold wood. "I'm patient," she said. "And everything will be fine."

She began to defecate, the warm texture pushing out, seeping into cracks and forming a cushion beneath her. When she was satisfied with the amount, she scooped up her own shit and smeared it over the round firmness of her stomach and in circles around her breasts before applying it softly to her kneecaps and finally in vertical stripes on her neck. Then she stood, arms raised, imitating the closest birch she could see through the glass barrier, like a long-limbed gazelle or statuette of brown and flesh-rubbed circles, hoping that if she stood there long and still enough, he would think that she had vanished and leave her behind.

But her arms felt too heavy, too weighted to remain above her head, and when she woke the next morning all her bark was removed. She had been sedated, cleansed.

Harry hummed with the car radio, fiddling with its dials, and the birch trees flew past her window with silent goodbyes, as if leaving would close out the circle which had allowed her to join their deciduous alliance. She wanted to reach with her fingertips, to press them against the glass, but knew then she could not, restrained by a white coat with buckles and latches and clasps, hands behind her back, as Harry drove her to another place of madness, one where he had more control.

This time, she sang her own song. She remembered every verse, but Harry, with his busy fingers, kept reaching to turn up the volume of his classical music, and each time he did she sang louder. Finally, when she screeched at a decibel unmatched by the station, he turned the power off, so Celine, contented with the success of this technique, decided to use it again and again against him, until he stopped.

75

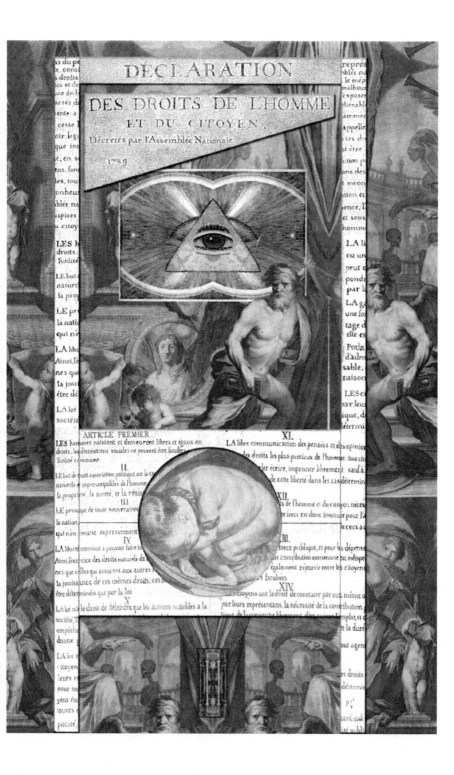

BLOOD, HUNGER, CHILD

We put our wants on paper after years of calling out in vain, after riots, after dreams were made and lost in the climate where the airy aristocrats and lords made mockeries of our humanity. We desired certain rights, we said. We deserved them. And when they did not listen, the blade began to fall, again and again, like a sliver of ice drenched in blood.

Natan was my lover. We'd never bothered to marry, agreed it wasn't any tragedy since no one would want either of us—me with my whoring past, him with his melted face. A month before our first baby arrived, I sat and watched the dropping blade neatly lop off the heads of our previous employers and detractors. The 1789 Declaration of the Rights of Man and the Citizen had still not triumphed; even the leather sacks, made to hold severed heads, had grown ever deeper and darker-stained. It was 1792.

At that time, having moved from more rural lodgings, Natan and I watched from our window. As commoners, we were safe from mob violence—provided we complied with its rules. For his security at practicing a trade, in the company of strangers, Natan played deaf and dumb, although he was neither, and each night we made love, careful of the baby, with the clasp of the diamond necklace at my throat, hidden beneath my hair, cinching two sides of a paste replica.

Due to hot-water burns in his childhood, Natan's face was like a candle's hot wax blown by wind across the tablature of his bones. Thin, wan, I was no longer pretty. Together, we would weather what came next. We hated royalty, though we had once aspired to deceive them.

We had once been adequately appealing or intelligent. I thought of Versailles when we stole the necklace, of the dark and gentle hush in 1786 after we had lifted the diamonds from the Cardinal to sell in London. And I thought: *What a boon that just once I was dressed as a queen, a queen in sullied skirts but a queen nonetheless—and what a silly little man, that Cardinal, to believe I was Marie Antoinette, the Austrian slut. Couldn't he see the Frenchness in my bones—the luster of my hair? All things French were preferable to those Austrian. He'd been a laughable fool.*

A pity he failed to raise the first installment for the necklace and the jewelers applied to the Queen, so he was tried and jailed, and Louis VI had no mercy. This before the Revolution, but we'd taken the necklace long before the blade descended across our window in du Carrousel and orphaned children sang their benedictions. I touched the clasp again and again, which I had kept attached to the faux diamonds around my neck, while noble necks went bare against the wood.

I wore the replica often as if to hide time's less glittering ravages. After securing the full necklace in Versailles, Natan and I had disappeared into the countryside. Ms. Antoinette never received her jewels. We had lost most of those as well, later, in trade or sale, all but the valuable piece that held them together. This I kept. A souvenir of risks.

When the killing started, we had rich things aplenty valued as meals or lodgings, not more. What was not burned at estates was stolen. Queen Marie's dwellings were ransacked. She would soon get the knife, Natan and I agreed—right across her pretty white neck, her daisy skin adorning the guillotine like a rose petal in a woodpile.

France would not mourn her. Natan and I, neither. Our hatred was virulent.

With all her voiced desire for charity, she might very well have uttered, *"Qu'ils mangent de la brioche,"* to entertain. Though some said that this comment was a fabrication, many still thought she deserved her slice of justice. Who goes about commissioning jewels instead of feeding their people, we asked ourselves? Who lavishes more attention on one's dogs than on one's people? Starving. To this, we grew accustomed. Natan said he had an idea of what to put into her mouth, though his suggestion was too rich for her blood.

Blood was on the people's minds and in our eyes. It was rumored that, in fear, some kneeling at the blade had bitten off pieces of their tongues. When my baby came, there was much of it, the blood spread across the floor. Before this, it seeped like sewage water in the streets when we began to kill the wealthy ones, drying to rust on the dirt, splattering from the rolling heads. I began to dream of it rising in a tide from the Seine, crimson as the fires that had consumed the châteaux where my father died, red as the roses that bloomed outside the church, red as the slight trickle that spilled between my legs as Natan got aggressive in the last few weeks of my pregnancy, before the baby arrived.

I was his safe harbor, he told me many times, but even he forgot himself when instinct took over. I liked his sharp hips, his sunken belly, the strength in his long and muscular legs. His large masculine parts. He had his gentle moments, too. These he found mainly in my arms after our throes. "If you and I ruled the world," he sometimes said. "I would make you not a queen, but an empress."

"I need nothing but your love," I replied.

"But love does not feed us, chérie," he said. "Love does not make gardens grow."

"Yet love has saved my life," I said. "Isn't that enough?"

"Yes, you're enough," he replied.

Until Natan found me, I'd been a hustler garbed as a whore. Natan, thick and tall as a horse, took me from the streets after a harsh encounter. He'd broken a man's kneecaps to set me free. His brown eyes crossed as if to touch the bridge of his nose, and his face was malformed, but he loved and protected me. "I touch you. Me and no other," he said, after we first made love. I liked his claim of ownership. No one would harm me while I stood at his side, so I hardly cared about his face; it was his voice I enjoyed, his girth, his deceptive calm.

But there was a rage inside him. His burns had been inflicted by nobles. He'd been six. They'd wanted to see how skin melted, considered it an enjoyable pastime to throw scalding water at a stable boy restrained in a barn. Since then, before the Revolution, he'd always had a desire for vengeance.

This is why he knew each part of the Revolution's progress. Shared it with me. The demands were first put on paper in 1789—those for the poor and starving masses. Give us certain rights. Give us our due. Give us nourishment. Stop harassing the poor to feed the rich or cater to their elaborate, wasteful parties. Make it mean something, this life.

Pinched after the Seven Years War and the American Revolutionary War, Natan said the country's coffers could hardly handle the King's misgovernance. The document was the tour de force of reckoning. Its dictates swelled our hearts and brought new pride to our circumstances.

But it was ineffectual, we might be right to say, though segments of it would reappear later in public speeches, amidst the chanting, "*Liberté, Unité, Égalité!*"

I had heard this expression a hundred times or more. People chanted such things, with several variations, as if their immediate recollection might stop the flow of blood, but in the end, the red would pour before it dripped.

"Let the *salopards* get their due!" Natan said, on the evenings we were hungriest. "Each and every one." When the blade started to fall, he left me and travelled to watch, returning to describe in detail those killed, telling me how many died on a given day or which ones he'd seen. "A marquise today in a pale green frock. She looked like you," he said. "Her face. Except her nose was tilted to the air, though she cried soon as her neck found the groove. Eight men followed. Two children. Then a break. Executioner needed a drink."

As more devices were assembled, the killings happened nearer. More estates were rampaged. Soon, Natan needn't travel. Blood drenched our fields. It made us see red. The poor would not wait.

There was vengeance to be reaped, and off we went to reap it, festively ribboning our endeavors with the glamour of elegant words, but wasn't the premise of being right what made a thing worth dying for, the premise of improving one's life?

Hence our Declaration. Natan told me this part would take the most lives—it would not be secured. It was the first article.

Declaration of the Rights of Man and of the Citizen— August 26, 1789: Article first—Men are born and remain free and equal in rights. Social distinctions may be based only on considerations of the common good.

But, really, what was the common good? When I first heard this pronounced, I thought of Hélène, my sister. 1784—five years prior, I saw them strip her dress and claim their *droit de seigneur* on her wedding day. First the noble, Jacques, then his son, ravished her body. That was the common good I knew. What was good for the wealthy was good for all.

She was pregnant afterwards, but her husband would not touch her. She was moved to the kitchens until the babe was born. From her, in those kitchens, I learned how to cook. She taught me the joy of epicurean miracles.

Then we were simply servants, but a fingertip's dash of sauce could be tasted easily enough from a stirring spoon. In this way, we'd sample the others' feast. When she swelled too large, she was sent away.

But this year, September having arrived, the Parisian crowd broke into prisons to release those held, and massacred the nobles and clergy where she'd lived. I heard the news along the wall and chanted for Hélène: *They are dead, they are dead, join the Revolution instead!*

I did not know where she'd gone—or even if she breathed. I spoke of her to Natan.

He did not like my chanting, nor my focus on my sister, yet I thought of Hélène endlessly. And I missed her, my sister, my confidante, my friend, missed her so much I pretended to prepare the dishes we'd slaved over at the old estate, making my clumsy moves with my single knife in the room that held no food.

The other day, because I wanted to cook and Natan was gone, I went through the motions of creating elaborate *gros repas* and desserts, tested my memory for recipes.

I wanted to imagine I was still capable of cooking delicious things.

I may have lost something of my mind then, for swelled with Natan's child, encumbered by my body, aching, I swore I had created a chocolate torte with semisweet chocolate, butter, eggs, sugar and flour, dashed with espresso powder—and baked it over the fire.

"There is no fire," Natan said when he returned home. "All you have done is place an empty pan on the filth-ridden floor, full of more of the same. The house is cold."

"I know. I know," I said. "I could not cut or bring in the wood. There is nothing in the garden."

There was no fresh food for those who did not participate in the anarchist trades of the rebellion. Natan's fury at my baking seemed muted: "You once wore her necklace—now you make invisible cake fit for none, in the memory of rich men's kitchens?" he said. "Be ashamed."

"I need to create something to give me joy," I said. "Anything. I have four spices left! But I have no food. I'm a waste. Don't you see our child? She's famished, too."

"You wasted our cinnamon on this mess of dirt?" he replied. "Your belly looks large enough to me."

I was sure that inside of me the child was small—and a tumor swelled my skin. Or that there was no child, just the bloat of hunger. "I'm sorry," I said, but something in my face asked him to cease his inquisition. He did. He kissed my cheek.

"When this stops," he said, "we will grow our garden again, raise pigs, and find a new way. It can't last forever. Wait and things will improve. Wait. Wait. The baby will be fine." He put his hand on my belly. "When you feel it move," he said, "you know it is fine."

"I like what you do now," I told him. "I think it calms you."

He had become a leathersmith's apprentice. He went every day to learn how to make belts and bridles from an old man nearby. "In a year or two, I will plow a new lot for a garden as big as a pasture," he said. "That will feed us all."

I smiled. Our small garden had been depleted many months before. With the last of the vegetables, we had a tureen of soup we'd shared for three days. One head of cabbage was the end of the fare, even this shrunken and flecked one with a fine white speckling of rot along the outer leaves.

Seated beside the window, when he left the next day, two weeks before I bore our babe, I thought of that cabbage. I heard the rush of peasants and mobs. My child stirred. My teeth ached; my gums burned. I made a fire when he left that morning. I boiled water.

"We'll find a new way," I echoed as I sat alone, remembering the rights he'd tried to teach me. My mouth felt dry—and a trickle of fluid leaked from me as I watched another head roll from the blade beyond my window. The guillotine mechanism squeaked.

My eyes burned with fear. I knew the babe would come soon by the calendar, but wasn't sure if my milk would follow. Of late, I found it hard to gather enough spittle in my mouth, much less the source of an infant's thriving from my breasts.

In my daymares I pictured her born healthy, my tiny new miracle, yet sucking a dry teat. And if I had no milk, or if it was scarce, I'd have a perpetually screaming infant, or a weak one I'd wish was never introduced into our suffering.

On the days we had dinner, these ideas abated. Yes, Natan sometimes brought things from the old man. He scavenged. Some nights, there were limited offerings—other days none.

Solutions at a premium, despite the futility of more examination, I sometimes checked the old garden again. No new growth. Hungry. I was so hungry, even murder evinced food. With a sound like the cutting of cabbage, the blade fell again and again. Digging in the dirt, however, brought nothing new.

My belly felt heavy on my thighs as I leaned over mending for Natan—and, often, I felt a quickening near my groin, a flutter, the kick in my ribs. I came to be engaged in the society of myself and my unborn baby most days. As two, we were still a society of one. No one was injurious.

Article 5—The Law has the right to forbid only those actions that are injurious to society. Nothing that is not forbidden by Law may be hindered, and no one may be compelled to do what the Law does not ordain.

I was not clear on the law, but I knew what was right. We'd known a poor man named Hugo who'd processed grain. He had a mill, and in the days before the blade they stole it from him. This was forbidden, but the law didn't forbid the abuse. Our Declaration had not yet come.

ELEGANTLY NAKED IN MY SEXY MENTAL ILLNESS

The nobles claimed Hugo's spoils in the name of the church. From his mill, they had bread. Hugo's family went without. His daughter was weak, sick with consumption. She could not eat or drink. The villains took all and left no more than the chaff. The blade came for them in October of 1792, on the hottest day of the month

Natan, back then, had saved Hugo—Hugo's daughter, too. I loved him so much, my scarred man. In the absence of physical beauty, there was a beauty of the soul. Yes, he enjoyed the murders by guillotine—but he would save as quickly as he'd kill. All the way through my pregnancy, the nobles were slaughtered. Still, a hope for better news remained. Natan came home exhausted most evenings. I kept leaking blood.

My time grew near. And then one day, our child stopped moving. I thought my weakness made her weak—but there were no kicks at all. We had only small mercies. A bag of flour—stolen. Some sugar. A few carrots or truffles from friends. I feared she might be dead but did not want to predict such things.

After nine days more, the babe had still had not moved. I begged her to stir, but she did not listen. When the time came, never was there any motion from the small one, but the nausea overtook me. I touched my hard belly. Labor began late one night. It was to be slow.

I hid my pain from Natan.

Through the next day, again the smell of blood wafted in through my window. There was a line to the falling razor. I elected to watch the guillotine from my wooden chair until the last possible moment.

Hungry, ever so hungry and losing blood, I was horrified to see myself, in moments of pause, regarding the corpses intently. A body lying just the right way can look like a butcher's cut. I let out a low moan of pain. I felt like I'd been stabbed. There were convulsions and contractions. And then, out the window, I saw Hélène!

Article 7—No man may be accused, arrested or detained except in the cases determined by the Law, and following the procedure that it has prescribed. Those who solicit, expedite, carry out, or cause to be carried out arbitrary orders must be punished; but any citizen summoned or apprehended by virtue of the Law, must give instant obedience; resistance makes him guilty.

Resistance did make them guilty, but those at the line would be slaughtered regardless. Moments before I dragged my body to the floor, I saw my sister standing among those to be executed, with four children at her feet. I thought I was imagining her— but I was not! There she was. Her dress was blue like the summer sky. Children clung to her skirts and behind her stood Lord Jacques. The blade took the children first, before I made it to the ground. The crowd cheered. As the guillotine framed tiny faces, I grew progressively dismayed. I clung to the chair's sides, holding myself up, watching, when I thought I might faint. *Hello, niece. Hello, nephew. Goodbye. Goodbye.* One with curling blond hair. Another with red hair like our grandmother.

Jacque's wife stood with Hélène, appearing to survey her face more closely than the action of the blade as Hélène watched the demise of her bastard children, in tears. Both women had been stripped of wigs, if Hélène had ever possessed one. This was the last thing I'd seen before viewing the ceiling. The faces of the two women. Still on pretty necks. One of them crying.

My sister's head rolled, as my body curled into a ball, and I moaned. Beside me, the water boiled. The blade fell and fell and fell. I let labor take me for a few hours after she was murdered, but I later saw her head in the basket. And after several seizures on the floor, with the baby still inside, I'd laid so long whimpering in pain and unable to push her out that I wished Natan were back.

He wouldn't come then. When I felt her tear free of my body, I tried everything to rouse her, but she was dead. I held her before cutting the cord, afterbirth drying on my legs. It took all I had, to drag my body closer to the fire.

Devastated as I was, I regarded her then—and cleaned her. She had grown, I decided, into a beautiful dead baby. She was my baby. Our baby. And ever so bloody—was I surprised?

Article 6—The Law is the expression of the general will....All citizens, being equal in its eyes, shall be equally eligible to all high offices, public positions and employments, according to their ability, and without other distinction than that of their virtues and talents.

Natan excelled at making leather goods, but the old man he worked alongside was wise about executions and torture devices. Under his apprenticeship, they had made several of these together. As he'd gained skills, Natan had grown obsessed with torture strategies and the killing of those who opposed the Revolution. Before my pregnancy, he'd said, "Did you know that they tested the guillotine on dead men first—handpicked for being thick or strong, so that they could be sure the blade would work?" He'd talked about the particulars of guillotine construction. Said a man named Roederer made sure the grooves were crafted from brass and suggested that the tongues and gudgeons be iron, as well as declaring that all hooks which attached the cords to the mouton should be bolted instead of nailed down.

I could listen to torture stories any time, but the day I lost my baby, I no longer cared. I hoped when he got home he would not speak. There was a grief inside that was deeper than any pain I'd ever known. I ceased to regard anything but the baby's face as the blade fell beyond my window. The cuts. Then the cheers.

I stared at the sky through the window. I thought of Hélène and wished I had watched her die, but it was enough I had seen her alive, even just this day. Limping, struggling, I stood to locate the remaining spices and dumped half in the baby's blood path. Hélène could have been here with me. Cooking. I could have met her children. My baby was so beautiful and quiet. I sang to her. I kept the fire going, thinking of Hélène's strange and beautiful peace as her lover's wife had regarded her so rancorously. Only her tears fell, not her chin. Our paths had surely diverged. I'd come to steal the necklace of a queen and lost all but the clasp, then whored. Hélène had grown to find love with her abuser, made half-noble children, and soon thereafter, by her own people, lost her head.

I wondered about our experiences with love. Was the noble as large as Natan down below? Perhaps the man fell in love with her because she could cook, I decided, not because she was the only one who'd have him or because he had rescued her. As I thought of the children I would never know, I wondered: Was her witchery wrought there, among the boiling, simmering things? In my pot, boiling now, there was water.

This would turn to steam and then fly off. Many times when we were young, I'd watched my sister wander out over the hills in search of spices. As her children's heads lay in the groove, I'd seen her look away, and I'd wondered if she mentally walked those hills again, searching for coriander or pepper and dillweed or rosemary.

She had never even known that I'd looked on. Leaning at the wall, I spied my own corners and noted a large spiderweb spanning the space between a cast iron pot and the wall. I saw my dead baby on the chair and reached for her. I had wrapped her in cloth after the cleaning. I would have to tell Natan I was sorry—she had come out warm, but dead.

He would have the right to beat me, I supposed, but I doubted he would want to. Our girl was perfect. I touched her tiny eyelashes, little hands, small feet. I kissed her cheek.

Natan expected a living thing; it bothered me that he would come home to this sight, to this sorrow, and again to no food. He would see what had happened. We would cry. We would clean. Perhaps he would help lift me to bed. I was certain he would watch the guillotine the next day with a hardened will because our child had died in this struggle for commodities.

But after the baby came, the damage of starvation became more personal. In the hour before he returned, I steadily watched the fire. Water boiled in a pot, and I felt alone. I removed the pot. There was no more flour, no more bread. Everything stank of rust. I touched my daughter's body once more, pulled her close, and opened her eyes.

Blue. I knew from experience that many babies had blue eyes—some would change later. Her little limbs were fatty. How did she get this way? I didn't recognize parts of her face until, in glimpses, I saw a younger Natan, recreations of his undamaged childhood. Our daughter was pretty. I touched every part of her again and again. Thirty-seven times. I often did things thirty-seven times.

"Your father is working," I informed the baby. I thought of the Bill of Rights and my talents. I had none. I could spread my legs, but anyone could. I could steal, except that was risky. I wanted my sister back. I wanted food and I wanted to cook. My body pained me. My pulse skipped. With the loss of my child's weight and my placenta, it was as if nothing fit right in my body. Loose parts shifted. Tenderly, I collected the rest of the spices, wincing—then, tenderly, too, I placed them on my infant daughter.

Who else should have her? This was not an easy decision. I resolved that she would come to something good. I resolved that when Natan came home, he would smell a meal. You have to understand, if we buried her too shallow, others might dig her up. No one talked about these things—but starving was serious. Humanity was meat. I said the rosary thirty-seven times.

That I should take care of this business myself felt caring and resolute. I could not be tender, however, poking her body to place it on the spit, or tender as I turned her. Still, I'd closed her eyes before I shoved the rod through, closed her eyes so slowly—and then, before she cooked in earnest, I closed mine.

You may say I am the devil. I feel I only did the last thing to be done. "I love you," I said. "I want to put you back inside me. So this." I had nothing worth keeping now but my own life and Natan's. I once had a necklace that shone like the stars over the Seine for a series of hours. Now, I had its clasp. I once had a sister and a garden where hunger was regularly broken with cabbage and onions and herbs. Fresh air. I may not have enjoyed freedom as the peasants called for now, but, between my robbing and after my whoring, I had calm. Oh, the Declaration was full of borrowed finery, but the blade now dropped all day—with each fall, soiled clothes and a cheer from the crowd.

In the end, no one was innocent except the new. I watched my daughter turning on the fire, wondering what made life precious? I did not know.

But I was hungry; I was weak. Even as the baby's skin blackened, I heard the blade. An occasional scream. A cheer. A rousing. Momentarily, Natan would be home. Nausea and a raw ache filled my abdomen. "She was born dead," I'd tell him.

"Oh," he'd say. Onion powder and garlic would mask her human flavor, accompanied by other dust and spice. Then, with the sound of the blade still falling, darkness dropping to accompany our meager fare, I would grieve as I stared in the shadows of Natan's burned cheeks before regarding the singed face of the womb's starvation, and we would again grow angry with futility.

Around my neck would rest the paste necklace with a queen's diamond clasp as yet again "*Liberté, Unité, Égalité*" would be heard without cease beyond the window. The silver blade would rise and fall in severance for a row of human cabbages sliced in the courtyard, and through our tears, despite them, of our dark love Natan had said would never feed us, Natan and I would eat.

ELEGANTLY NAKED IN MY SEXY MENTAL ILLNESS

EVER

You want to scream, but no sound leaks from your throat; you anticipate the need for this sound eventually, but for now your muscles cramp uncomfortably into breath. It is impossible to practice. Your silent breath will not bring others forward.

You lie in bed helpless, headless. The sound of your heart takes precedence, an uneven rhythm. He has called and called for hours, but your machine has no tape. No one can leave a message until you rewind it, but you refuse. This decision stems from another bad relationship you recall, one that, in hindsight, was a walk in a park. After all, your romantic history is a series of the mentally deficient making beds of your mess and messes of your pulse. Your name is Caroline Light, reminiscent of holiday carolers and God. Your stalker told you this.

And how daunting, you thought later. *Yet, how bloody rich.* If he were a hundred years more ancient, you could expect poisoned roses at your door, dyed black, perhaps with blood-tipped thorns, but he's not, so you ask yourself: If a woman falls in the woods with no one there to see her, does she make a sound?

You ruminate on this all night. It is as integral as it is enigmatic.

~

In an old building, a renovated 1920s commercial hotel, you, who are Caroline, dip your fingers into a medical supply box and pull out a pair of powdery plastic gloves. You stretch them over your fingers as you open your door. You have three such packages of gloves: One in your doorway, one in your car, one at your bed.

Coming home from work, you drive around the building before going above-stairs and have learned to screen all calls, lock all windows, and build a circle of friends to contact before sleep. *Hello, it's Caroline. I've lived another day.*

In the mornings, you check your car with binoculars to make sure the glass isn't broken. You leave the lights on, and are careful never to accept unsolicited mail. Compulsively, you read about stalking victims, but whether this fuels or comforts you, you aren't sure. You invite no men to you house, although you have a restraining order—because it does no good.

"Daria," you say into the phone. "Tell Martin to keep the chain on the parking lot gate. If he thinks it's a pain, tell him that I'll get up at five in the morning and do it. No, you don't understand! I moved in here because of the security. Otherwise, I'd have been paying a hundred less in that place off Montgomery.Well then, do it. Goodbye."

If there is a point where paranoia becomes a lifestyle, you have reached it. This is because it's hard to remember living any other way, and "any other way" is like a strange dream, a compelling fantasy. You answer the door like a contorted question mark, sure someone could shoot you with a silenced gun if you stood before it, and in this way, bent over sideways near the frame, you dodge the bullet.

Someone might shove a gas-soaked rag under your doorway, then dribble gasoline down the hallway outside and light it up. All the apartments would burn at once. You have no solution. Someone could wait in the main doorway, or between the hedges, or along the way from your car to your apartment. Your life is more dangerous than that of a spy, for you know you are a constant target with a twelve-block sphere of travel. Already, at work, you gave up your posh office with a window for a safer one deep down the halls and changed your voicemail to the single-ring message: "Good afternoon, this is Caroline Light. I'm away from my desk. If you leave your name and number, I'll call back within five minutes. Thank you for calling Synergy Solutions: The place where we have answers for all your questions."

You finish your outgoing message with the company slogan because the words are repetitious and comforting in their sureness. You think of him. How many times has he called just to hear your voice? How many times that you are not aware of?

~

Three weeks after you met him, he'd said, "I want to get to know you, really know you."

Flattered, you'd twirled a set of keys with your index finger and breathed in, almost gasping, saying, "I'm just a normal person." But you blushed. And you'd never felt special before.

He said, "Don't say that."

You said, "It's true."

"You're not normal when you're with me," he said. "I don't love 'normal' people." He ruffled his short black hair.

"But how do you know you love me?"

"I just do."

"And what if you suddenly didn't love me? We haven't even been intimate."

"I don't ever fall out of love. Ever."

"Ever?"

He pressed his hands to your face, and you felt that your cheekbones would crumble. "If I do stop loving you, you don't want to be around," he said. "So kiss me."

"I'm kissing you."

"Kiss me harder."

"I am kissing you harder."

"Like you mean it." He lifted your soft thighs around him and pushed you to the wall. "It's never been like this with anyone else, baby," he said. "Let's do this. I want you to make me bleed. I'd do it for you."

You do it for him. You do. You do. You do.

~

Caroline (you) has (have) long red hair and green eyes. Across her body, freckles make a nebula of stars. She is pale and her nails are shell pink. When she was with him, he required them red, said he liked how they looked moving in and out of his hair. Replaying this conversation afterwards, a statistic flits across her mind.

She recalls disjointed memories: "He's soft and easy," his mother June had said. "If you give him what he wants." Having spent Thanksgiving at June's house, Caroline remembers this said over pie and coffee on the porch, with her cheek still red from his slap, the slap which was a punishment because she'd talked too long with his empty-head, former Marine cousin from Havasu. But, abruptly, he had left to go fishing and left her with his mother.

"Did he ever tell you about his ex-wife?" his mother asked. "She was crazy. Running around all the time, talking crazy. Finally, she just up and left. Oh, he threw her out of the house with nothing but the clothes on her back."

At the time, Caroline bit her fist, pretending a yawn, but his mother continued, with a conspirator's tone: "She seemed like such a nice girl, but talked to us less and less as time went on. She was a little girl like you. Actually, a little smaller. Thought she was too good for us, I suppose." A murmur of indignation sat like an ugly mood in her tone.

ELEGANTLY NAKED IN MY SEXY MENTAL ILLNESS

"I suppose," Caroline murmured back, but she thinks of this conversation now, seated in her apartment, as she fingers the door handle she broke from his car one afternoon, remembering how, at one time, talk of his ex-wife made her insecure, but after the incident—his straight arm pressed heavily across her chest as she'd ripped her right hand free from his grip then wrestled the handle from its socket—it didn't again.

Sophia was her name, the first wife. He kept her wedding ring in a shot glass on his dresser. And Sofia had slender fingers, tiny, fine-boned hands. In a moment of morbidity Caroline discovered Sophia's ring fit exactly on her pinkie. She tried to look her up once, but there was no listing in 400 miles. Under any name. This was when things began to sour.

At first when he told her he loved her, she fingered the long vertical scars down his back, envying the chunks of him under Sophia's tiny fingernails and whistling with jealousy. Now, the door handle reminds her of what he can do, and she imagines that Sophia, if she's anywhere, washes her hands obsessively, scouring every foreign cell from her fingertips, grinding metal to the grit beneath her nails.

If she is able. It's hypothetical.

~

Hello? Operator? I need to change my telephone number. Obscene calls. Now? 635-4508. Middle name, Sarah. Current address, 3254 Maitlin Drive. Yes. Yes. No. No forwarding number. As soon as possible. Thanks.

Some people say fear is a gift. Andrew must believe that. When you (who are Caroline) tell your mother about the door handle, her response is disbelief. "Oh no. Oh no, you're wrong. He's a nice boy. I met him."

You shout, "It's about decency, Mother. He should have the decency to leave me alone. Oh, is that what Carla said? Well I would have been to her house, but he knows where she lives. I don't want to see him. Period. You think I've lost it? Well has anyone but you checked your mail in the last fifteen years? My bills are missing. My opal ring is missing. If I could check my hairbrush to make sure my hair was still there, I would!"

Blah, blah, consolatory crap.

You put your hand over your mother's ignorant voice, over the phone's receiver, but say, "Why do you always take the other person's side? He called you about my mistreatment of him? And you need to see bruises on my body to believe? I'll give you my address when I feel more secure. I have no time for you today, Mother. Tell Daddy that I love him."

Three weeks pass, then three months, and he has not called. You have not stepped down your measures. Still, you wish it would all go away. You grow tired of no one believing you, meaning they believe you, but not truly—like how it's hard to imagine being freezing in the summer, or in love when you're not, or scared when you're comfortable. Your mother hates hearing about these things because they're ugly, but, "Being stalked *is* ugly, Mother!" you reply, though the phone call is over.

She has already hung up to bake sweets. Vast quantities of simple cakes rise in her kitchen as she smiles and examines the lemon Bundt she adores, which cooks supremely in the oven.

~

"Someone is in my apartment," You (who are Caroline) shriek. "I know because there's a candle burning in the window. Of course I didn't light it. 3254 Maitlin Drive. I'm calling from a payphone across the street. Listen, I've been gone for six hours and the candle is a tea light, so you tell me who lit it! A neighbor? You've got to be kidding. No, I don't see anyone, but I'm not stupid enough to go up there. Thank you."

She (who is you) doesn't wait for the police. She gets on the freeway and drives. In one corner of the car is dread, and in the other, blind fear. She wants to look at them both and not what's before her, so she turns her eyes from the road, examining the dirty backseat and hoping for a crash. She is unlucky. The road is clear for miles ahead. Her alignment is good. She allows herself to veer toward an overpass but at the last moment yanks back on the wheel.

She shakes as she drives to his house, leaving her car in park, walking to the middle of the street, and staring holes through his bedroom window; there are black spots over her vision as she shouts: "Stop calling me, Andrew. Stop coming by. Stop everything. This is my life, you motherfucker."

She picks up a rock and hefts it, gleaning satisfaction as it crashes through his window, then stares at his house for a while. Just when she is ready to walk away, he pokes his head out from the frame where splintered glass hangs like icicles.

"You want to see me, Caroline?" he asks. "Here I am." There is a singing quality to his voice. "I guess you didn't wait for the police? Just left that candle burning. You never appreciated my romantic gestures. You want me to come out and see you? I'm coming. Just let me put my shoes on, darlin'. You wait right there."

His hint of Tennessee accent makes her knees buckle. She panics, struggles with her door handle, gets in, and locks the car. Then she guns the motor and speeds away. There are ads on every radio station. Does she need a massage therapist? Yes. A good deal at May Company? No. A new pet from the Humane Society? Would it be ferocious?

She spends the night inside her car, sleeping at a deserted park, using the car repair slips in her glove box as Kleenex. The next day, she quits her job. She says, "Mother, I need to move in with you and Daddy for a while. I quit. I don't need any storage space. I threw out all of it. Yes. That too. One suitcase…that's right. Carla has some of it. Oh, the other thing? So Daddy told you I bought it? I've been practicing every day... If I can't keep it in your house, can I keep it in the shed? All right. I'll be over soon. It's not a short drive, you know. Keep my old room the way it is. I'll sleep on the couch."

~

When Caroline arrives, her mother makes tea, serves it on Caroline's grandma's blue china set. She even has old-fashioned sugar cubes. "I know you're sick," her mother says. "Very sick. You need to rest and recuperate." Her hands are red from lemon-scented disinfectant.

Caroline's father rubs her shoulders. The smell of lemon bleach comforts Caroline. It's warm in her mother's house, but she hasn't taken off her coat.

"It's okay now," her father says. "You can stay as long as you like, sweetie."

"I booked you an appointment with my hairstylist," her mother remarks. "She's heard so much about you."

Caroline looks at her with shock. "You told her? What did you tell her?"

"Oh, I didn't tell her about *that*," her mother says. "I haven't told anyone about *that*."

"Oh, *that*," Caroline says, angrily pulling off her hat. "You haven't mentioned *that*? Well, what about *this*? Tell her all about this. I'm sure there's not much she can do about it now."

"Oh my," her mother says, fading back a step.

"I did it this morning, Mom," Caroline shouts. "You like it?" She moves her fingers through the spiky, black remnants of what used to be long, red hair.

Her mother tells the clock, "Julie called for you. She sounded a little worried. I said everything would be fine, and I cleaned out your room. All the ballet slippers and toys were put into boxes. You used to love to dance."

ELEGANTLY NAKED IN MY SEXY MENTAL ILLNESS

"Not anymore."

"Your mother's right, Caroline," her father says. "After a few weeks here, you might start acting normal. Get into the things you used to love. Stop leaving those damn mousetraps around everything. Did you bring your gun?"

"Yes, Daddy."

"Did you put it in the shed?"

Caroline nods. There is a quiet moment.

Then her mother says, "I cooked tonight. Mutton. And after dinner we can all watch TV. All right?"

"All right."

"Those circles under your eyes need to go away, angel," her father says.

"Yes, Daddy."

"This has all been overwhelming, hasn't it?"

"Yes, Daddy."

"Where did you say you cut your hair?" her mother asks. "And dyed it?"

"In a Mobile station. With dull scissors. Black like the furnace of hell. You like it?"

"Would you care for some cake?" her mother asks.

"No thank you, Mother."

~

You (who are Caroline) did not anticipate that he would follow you to your mother's house, so you open the screen door at ten p.m., put on your jogging shoes, and go for the first run you've taken in months, your thighs aching, your heart racing. It feels good. Almost too good.

You're amazed at how out of breath you are, how quickly, and how nice it feels to see the old neighborhood and the blanket-wrap of trees alongside the road. It's so calm. Such a calm moment: Where is the storm? Nowhere. It's nowhere.

Your life (which is hers) sifts into perspective, the smooth, blue currents of sanity deepening with every footfall. Even when a car pulls up beside (you) her to ask for directions, she's not nervous. She doesn't hesitate when the driver in a cowboy hat with long brown hair rolls down the window. She keeps running beside him as if moving in place.

Only when his arm leaves the vehicle to wrap around her neck is she faintly surprised. The long, brown wig slips, and he whispers, "Caroline." There is the sound of the forbidding South. This is when she knows. The storm snuck up. It blew in too quickly.

He tells her his first wife is twenty miles deep in the Tennessee woods, behind his mother's house. Her corpse is precious to dust, to mites, to sparrows. There is providence in the fall of a sparrow… Caroline is two miles from her mother's.

She wants to scream, but her muscles cramp uncomfortably into breath. If a woman falls in the woods unnoticed, does she make a sound? No. *The answer is no.* Not on this day. The silence is deep.

The sky is purple and overcast. And so it goes. His hands clenching and releasing her body, caressing the freckled nebula of her skin in the backseat, in the starless night. And if you were truly she, you would be dead, stiffening, leaving one plane for another—but let's say, for argument's sake, that you're not.

~

"Norm, have you seen Caroline?"

"She said she was going for a jog."

"How long ago did she leave?"

"Oh, 'bout an hour."

"Well, if she doesn't come back, I've probably made her angry. She always leaves when she's upset."

"Yep. Just up and leaves."

~

Two days later, stories have played nonstop on the radio about the jogger found dead on the highway, her throat neatly slit, her body wedged, as if sleeping, between trees. The jogger wore a runner's wallet, but her identification was stolen. "Norm, did you hear?" her mother asks. "Strange, isn't it?"

"Yes. I'm a little worried."

"I bet she just went back to her apartment. You know how flighty she is."

"Then why's her car still here?"

Her father feels a crushing sense of awareness. The lumbering bear in him awakens. There is not enough lemon cake in the world to drown this out. Must he dance to the beat of a strange maestro, or have his paws burnt black to teach him the ways of a painful truth? "That's a long drive," he says.

"Someone must have taken her."

"I'm going to try and start her car. Maybe it didn't work, so she called someone."

"Okay, dear. Go start it."

~

Somebody's father gets in a car. Without a single sputter, the engine roars to life. Somebody's mother bakes yet another cake. Somebody says, a week later, "You'd never have thought. She was paranoid enough, but you can't always protect yourself."

Three months pass like speed entering the bloodstream, like mercury rising, and somebody else says, "She was a little girl like you. Actually, a little bigger. Thought she was too good for us, I suppose," and somewhere, in the seemingly stormless future, someone else says, "I love you," with a Tennessee drawl. "And I don't stop loving. Ever."

"Ever?" a sweet girl modestly asks.

It begins to rain. "Ever."

In the family cemetery, your skin, or Caroline's, mimics the colors of fall. It sinks to your bones. The bloating is over. With her decaying eyes, you look beneath the ground. You look into the quiet place where a hundred years could pass without a visit, where the worms funnel through dirt, eating and passing it through them like air.

Intake. Outtake. The only sounds are from the feet aboveground, walking over graves, trampling grass, pausing over headstones, and dropping flowers—there are so many graves. If a woman falls underground with no one there to hear her, does she make a sound? No one heard you before you arrived; they stand, weeping, moaning, but no one hears you whisper, "I told you. I knew." And he's out there, stalking other grounds, miles away, cities wide, so you hope that someone's listening—somehow, somewhere, sometime, for someone else—the someone who just now begins to know what fear really means, which is that paranoia is relative, but pain is real.

Because you're not imagining things. No, not really.

The country woods are full of silent screams.

ConYola

MEZCAL

con gusano

40% Vol.   70 cl

PRODUCED AND BOTTLED IN MEXICO

CON YOLA

Myles could not be forced to give up the burlap doll, especially during periods of great stress, when he took it from the shelf, fondled it, and let the seeds shift into position as he stroked its rough contours. He had been told that the doll was ugly, which he freely admitted. Some said that it did not match the black and chrome of his decor. Perhaps its placement on the shelf drew this unwanted attention—but, attached to it as he was, he would not remove it.

The doll was the color of almonds; its eyes black seeds; and its mouth, a slash of red. Seed buttons marked the nails of its fingers and toes. He had stolen it from a child in New Orleans. To this day, he could imagine the child's shocked look as he had wrenched it away—though he did give her a dollar and a sack of candy in exchange. One girlfriend suggested he burn it, though he had been careful not to let her watch him fondle it. He told her it was a gift from a friend in Guatemala.

In truth, the doll obsessed him. In saner moments, he'd admit that it was a visual atrocity and that he, a handsome university scholar, had no business having it. But he loved it in the way one cannot explain a fixation but loves it just the same. He did not seem the type. His attire was expensive and plain. His walnut hair and blue eyes were attractive beyond a first glance. Often, he watched his own gestures in mirrors, so he knew, for example, when he pointed easterly, what he looked like pointing easterly. He knew, when he wrote on the board, what his back looked like, and which posture was to his best advantage.

He'd cock his head in just the most appealing way when a student called out, "Dr. Myles? Dr. Myles?" on University Way—but the students always attempted to seduce him and smart women irritated him. He preferred blind admiration and casual, flirtatious conversation.

Despite the "misogynist" jeering of his colleagues, he held no unfair bias because intelligent men irritated him, too, though they, at least, could be importuned to share a cigar on a dusty afternoon. This was why, when he finally met Yola, who had been cleaning his house for weeks, he knew she was the one: Brown and silent, just like his beloved.

Sometimes, he'd ask a question to draw speech from her and she pointed or made gestures to indicate her answer. He watched her dust the delicate Japanese sculptures, slowly lifting them, wiping them clean, and then adjusting their positions on the shelf. She moved like a well-warmed mare after a run. Her body was plump but proportionate. She was darkly complected; he thought Mexican, but did not know. Because of her silence, he felt free to carry the doll around at will and fondle it in front of her. Things could not be better.

Due to her silence, he'd have thought Yola mute, but in the late afternoon she'd get into her friend's car and her laughter could be heard from the solarium. A loud, careless laugh. Bonnie, his last cleaning lady, had hired her because he didn't have time to screen the applicants himself. Bonnie had stopped cleaning houses, and he trusted her judgment. Ergo, Yola.

Yola came twice a week to clean the house of a man she had never spoken with, but whose underwear she washed stains from regularly. She never complained. When Myles asked his doctor what caused these stains, the doctor confessed it was probably a lazy wipe job, and though Myles attempted to fix this, he never quite succeeded, but he didn't have to: Yola made everything spotless.

When he discovered his interest in her, he indicated he would like her to come more often, five days a week if possible. He showed her the cottage behind his house and said, "Yola, live-in housekeeper for me?" Yola nodded solemnly. "Yola live here?" he repeated. She signaled for the telephone. They walked inside.

"Five hundred," she said after hanging up from a rapid-fire discussion in Spanish. "A month." Her voice was low but firm.

"Is that all?" he asked. He had hoped to bleed a few more words from her because her words, unlike other women's, were novelties.

"Six hundred," she said, with a stubborn glint in her eye. *Yola*, he thought. *You shrewd bargainer.*

"All right," he said. "But you'll need to net the leaves from the pool three times a week."

"*Sí*," she said, and that was the last thing she said for three months. As the weeks passed, he returned home earlier so he could watch her clean. He had never before taken an interest in women who cleaned his house. Yola, however, grew on him.

There was something peaceful about her light touch and one day he surprised himself by running his own hands over his furred chest and pretending they were hers, tan and callused. Three separate times in the middle of a lecture, he found his groin seized by a rush of heat, thinking about bending her over his antique desk. That night he went to her cottage and suggested they eat dinner. He brought a bottle of wine and a loaf of bread. She took the wine, poured it into two glasses, and drank hers in a single swallow. He looked around the cottage. She placed almost nothing personal inside it, except several paper hibiscuses in a wooden vase. They ate in silence while the sunset faded.

115

When she finished, Yola gestured to her door. He turned to go, when suddenly her hand seized his wrist, and she quickly undressed. She waited naked on the bed. Her eyelashes blinked like tiny shutters but he could not see her eyes.

In bed, too, she was what he wanted. Finally a woman who would not require enticement or even discussion about why he wanted what he wanted. She understood the simplicity of the sex act as a release. Each time he tried to touch her in the way that pleasured women, she brushed his hand away and stared calmly, almost as if to say, 'You were maneuvering correctly, but now you are wasting my time.' From that evening on, he came to the cottage and, after dinner, they had sex: He mechanically, and she, looking as though she took a long nap.

During the day, she cleaned. One evening he arrived at the cottage and she pointed to the door. He surmised that she was menstruating and wanted to be alone, but ten minutes later her friend drove up and Yola got in the car, laughing loudly. She came home at nine the next day, hungover, smelling of smoke.

"Yola had a good time?" he asked. She smiled. "Yola drink tequila?" he tried again.

"Sí," she said, "Worm," and proceeded to skim the pool. On this same morning, he had finally finished the project of the pool-stay. He took an old back brace and attached it to a long length of elasticized rope. He then screwed the rope hook into the ground outside the pool. With this on, he could swim for hours, getting an excellent workout without the hassle of turning in the water or opening his eyes.

"Yola," he called in happy greeting when she appeared at the window, but was unprepared when she began to laugh at him flailing in the contraption, laughing with such intensity that she bent forward. She could not catch her breath. In fact, she laughed so hard and for so long that he began to fear she was having a seizure, wheezing and gasping, and clutching the stitch in her side.

ELEGANTLY NAKED IN MY SEXY MENTAL ILLNESS

Then she sat at the patio table to watch his explanation of the device, but he felt so chagrined that he immediately detached himself, and strode away from the pool. He stretched his arms and grabbed a towel, then preened as though the entire episode had not occurred.

"You like it here?" he asked.

"Seven hundred," she said flatly. "A month."

It was not in his nature to argue, so he nodded and asked another question. "Bonnie ablas español? Commo—" He knew he slaughtered what he tried to say and gave up. Yola took his hand and led him to the cottage, implying she was done talking. A few days later, she kicked him out of her bed at three in the morning. It appeared that she was no longer willing to let him sleep there.

The more she refused him, the more fervently he desired her. On nights when he craved her the most, he walked into the living room, left the lights out, and sat on the recliner, stroking and stroking the doll, watching the cottage. Three days later, he noticed the doll overturned on the shelf, its seed eyes pressed to the bottom of the wood and its burlap rump at an awkward position.

Though he reasoned it had fallen, he attempted to visualize just how it might have landed in that pose. He tried to picture Yola, cleaning the top shelf, perhaps moving the doll to supply herself leverage and accidentally disturbing the placement.

While dismayed, he reflected that, thankfully, his teaching tour at the school was nearly over and soon he'd be free for his annual sabbatical. Nothing bothered him during this break, so the next day he asserted himself. "I need to sleep in your bed," he said. "I can't sleep comfortably without you."

"¿Qué?" she asked.

"Me sleep with Yola," he said, emphasizing "with."

"No me gusta," she stated.

"Sí," he insisted. "With Yola. Con Yola."

"One thousand," she said. "A month."

He was not in a position to argue since it was her right to refuse him, and his funds were near limitless. Also, he began to feel that Yola was necessary in his home. Her silence allowed the days to flow freely and his mind to move at top speed. In her comfortable soundless company, he allowed himself to think all the thoughts he'd imagined drowned under the incessant deluge of other people's voices. She didn't interrupt, yet there was no anxiety in solitude. No need unmet.

"*Sí*," he said. "*Con Yola*. One thousand." She smiled at him, pinching his cheek almost too tightly, then went back to pool skimming.

~

One day, he brought her a present. She threw it on her table, nodded, and walked out to the garden. He followed her, saying, "Yola, it's a present." He had purchased her a book with a set of tapes so that she could learn English to make it easier for them to communicate in bed. *The tapes will help*, he'd thought, and though he did not desire that she become too proficient, the rudiments of the language, at least, would make their arrangement a little more solid. That and the fact that he had no desire to learn Spanish.

Three days later, she placed the book and the tapes on the shelf, the doll positioned to suggest a reader. On the table, a note: *2 days gone. Adios. Yola.*

Myles felt tortured. He was on fire and unable to watch her do the things she habitually did. Nothing felt right. He wandered about the house, picking at his objets d'art. He thought of her manipulation of the doll and the book like a promise. When she returned, she did not alert him. In fact, only her car, a recently purchased Camaro, in the driveway, let him know she had come back—that, and the lights that glittered in the cottage after what seemed an eternity of their darkness.

"Yola!" he said, calling out to her. "You're back!"

"*Buenas tardes*," she said. She had purchased more paper flowers and arranged them in an even larger wooden vase. A small girl stood beside her. The girl looked like Yola. She stared lengthily at Myles.

"Yola!" he said again, then grabbed her wrist and pulled her into his arms. The flowers fell from her hand. He buried his face in her chest. Yola detached herself, sent the girl to the gardens, then undressed, and lay on the bed for his pleasures to be fulfilled, humming, almost inaudibly, a Mexican folk song.

Yola wore no perfume. When he placed his hands on her thighs to adjust her position, he noticed a dry patch of skin along the left side of her right buttock. For some reason, this encouraged him more, and it was as though the dry ridge had transformed Yola, more wondrously, into the doll. Myles longed to tell her this.

After the girl arrived, Yola began to slack on her cleaning, spend long hours on the lounger, sitting with the girl, and leave several times a day for personal errands. When he asked her where she'd gone, she gestured angrily that it was none of his business.

Her refusal made him seize upon a plan to gain her desire, or at least acceptance and full cooperation. It was necessary to bring another woman into the house. He wanted Yola to know what a desirable quantity he was—which she seemed to negate.

The plan was put on hold by his own inexplicable fixation with that rough patch of skin and although he wanted badly to initiate the sequence of crying and pleading, where she would want him and become a supplicant to his will, he was gluttonous to possess her, as gluttonous as ever, and could not keep himself from hanging near her doorway like a lost dog, uttering, "Yola, Myles, Yola," and while doing so, holding the doll in his hand.

Finally, he located the perfect woman. Justine was immaculate, finely sculpted, with a European face and figure. She was a professor in the history department and had eyed him for some time. A satisfied smile spread over his face, thinking of how she would marvel over his things, secretly wishing that she were wife in dominion of his fair resort.

Yola did not care about Justine. He'd even allowed he and Justine to be caught kissing behind the gazebo, and Yola had smiled then continued on to the cottage, shutting the door casually behind her. As rapidly as Yola's door shut, all desire for Justine left him. Also, Justine insisted on philosophical talk, which not only bored him, but made his head ache.

After this incident, however, Yola redeposited the girl wherever she'd come from and began to clean stringently. For Myles, having tired of watching them together, this was a relief.

Yola had sung to the girl, brushed her hair, and spent long periods of time holding her fondly, letting her fingers massage and caress the girl's scalp. Though he thought Yola would be nicer once the girl was gone, he was wrong.

Still, she cleaned his house, though each time she tilted the doll in a way that taunted him, subtly different than before and always mimicking how he positioned her the night before, since he continued to frequent her bed. He noticed she did not speak about birth control, but hoped she was on a pill of some sort because he had no desire to wear a condom.

After the girl left, Yola's eyes were swollen from weeping. She was reclusive. He took to swimming more and noticed that Yola gestured to the pool all the time, nodding and pointing in earnest. Sometimes, she watched him from the kitchen window, while scrubbing the sink.

~

One night, her car sat in the driveway, but Yola was nowhere to be found. He searched the house and the pool, also the gazebo and the greenhouse, but only when he entered the garden did he find her. She pulled up carrots, brushing the hair from her face with the back of a soil-covered glove, and reinserted the spade. She had not spotted Myles, and so looked peaceful, deep in thought.

She wore a white tank and cotton shorts. Her brown body was like a churro in the sun, hot and sweet. He wanted to call out to her, but decided instead to watch her in silence, wondering when the weight of his gaze would impel her to turn and look. Yola dug in the spade.

Suddenly she retracted it. A long white worm hung from the tip. She plucked the worm between her fingers and held it high over her head, watching it curl up on itself. Myles suppressed the urge to vomit, and when she lowered it to her mouth, he ran back to the house. That night she pinned the worm to the doll. The blind creature lay directly on top of the burlap.

"Yola!" he yelled, furious, but then remembered the covert nature of his association with the doll. She knew he liked it, but did not know how it had come to represent her, how the worm pinned to the surface, for Myles, was like Yola degrading herself. He strapped himself in for a swim. She came out in an hour.

"Myles," she said quickly, between his spurts of swimming. "No more Clorox."

He did not answer and did not go to the cottage that evening. When he gave her the thousand on the first of the month, he slipped it in her hand like defecated matter.

In the coming weeks, he searched his soul for the reasons she had defaced his doll—then decided that this was her way of showing her love. She loved worms. Perhaps it was a Santeria spell designed to bind them together. He went to her tenderly that evening, but she slammed the door in his face.

Myles, interpreting this as discontent at his neglect, begged to be let in. "Yola? Yoohoo! Yola? Please let Myles in! Please let me in, my little Paloma. Myles was cruel to Yola—yes? That's why you no let Myles in? Please Yola!" She didn't answer. "Myles not angry," he said. "Please, please, Yola. Let Myles in." Again there was silence. "Myles fire Yola if not," he said. "No more thousand dollars."

The door unlatched. This time she stared so angrily, just before slamming the door again, that he retreated to the house to unpin the doll and stroke it. Distraught, he murmured, "Yola, Yola, Yola," as he cleaned the house from top to bottom. When he tried to touch her the next day, she brushed him off.

Yola stole the doll and put it in her cottage, firmly locking the door behind her. Secretly, he hoped she reconciled with the doll, that she would no longer torment him with her obscene humor. He tried not to worry. Also, knowing the doll was safe in his dead mother's cottage comforted him, as though everything inside it still belonged to him, though he would wait several days to see either Yola or the doll.

Yola's face impassive, she replaced the doll on the shelf three evenings later, nodded to Myles, and locked the cottage door. Mildly sad she had not stayed to chat, Myles looked with happiness upon the sweet face of his doll. The doll's former presence in the cottage made it suddenly more significant that it was returned to the proper shelf and placed in a decent, engaging pose. At three in the morning, he could not resist returning to the living room to stroke the doll, kissing the red slash of its mouth in the dim light. He heard, distantly, Yola's car rev in the driveway. As she drove off, he dragged the doll from the shelf to place in his regular fondling position, but it was not long before he realized that the doll felt softer. In fact, under his fingertips, something subtle shifted, almost slithered, like tiny watch springs. The doll seemed animate.

A light touch like a bird's wing brushed his cheek, but he wasn't clear from where it arose. Rolling the doll's fabric between his index finger and thumb, a wet and filmy texture grew palpable, so he jumped up, doll in hand, to turn on the light. What was slick on his fingers?

Regarding the doll then, Myles observed that it seemed the doll's short arms moved as if to embrace him, but its burlap limbs had been eaten apart by Miller moth larvae; multiple larvae, worm-like, crawled from the fabric. Some bugs were more advanced. Teen Miller moths, having poked through the disintegrating weave, swarmed the air above his face.

She had filled his doll with insects—destroyed his love from the inside. He dropped the doll and ran to the cottage, searching for Yola.

He closed and locked the door behind him. No moths followed. He stood in the darkness, trembling with rage, before turning on the lamp, his mother's lamp. Yola's vases and flowers had been removed, Myles's language tapes sat on a shelf, and his fingers still felt filmy with an almost sexual residue. Across the yard, he saw that, in his larger house, the moths swarmed around the doll's decrepit embodiment. There were so many.

"Yola!" he shouted. But standing in the cottage, looking in on his other life, the embodiment of his beloved fetish seemed neither here nor there. The silence he'd come to appreciate remained, the doll he had connected to their waking lives also remained—albeit ravished by implanted insects—but the real Yola, or any trace of Yola he might address, was gone.

SPERANZA

348

MOTHER'S ANGELS

April 10, 1348. Florence.

They blamed the Jews, so Mother and I did not leave the house.
We swept the rushes from the floor cautiously to the street and slept
on our bellies so vapors would not enter our mouths. Between our
breasts, dirt formed long, black streaks; our skin cracked and itched.
Mother washed her hands and feet and told me to wash mine, but our
bodies gathered filth. It was ugly in Florence, *Firenze.*

Daily, the *becchini,* grave-diggers, dragged corpses through the
narrow streets. We had already lost Father. As a merchant of wool,
he died onboard his ship. Here in the city, the purple flowers of
oregano bloomed beside bodies left alongside the road. Long ago, it
was customary for female relatives to gather in houses and mourn the
dead while men gathered on doorsteps and spoke of weightier
matters. This was abandoned. No one kept gardens. No one rushed to
welcome new neighbors or celebrate the Day of Judgment en masse.
No stones were thrown to the Arno. Rabbi Levitz had been dead nine
months. It was better to hide our menorah, the Mishnah and
Gemara, and Father's old yarmulkes.

Catholic peasants savaged our house, destroyed expensive dishes.

Mother asked them to leave, but they laughed. When a Catholic peasant stole many of Mother's clothes, we began to fear for our lives. "Stupid Jews. Nasty Jews," they said. "Go put on your funny hats."

When a drunk pissed on our tapestries, Mother said, "Gather your things, Tatiana. Everything of value. Your dresses. Your leather shoes."

"And carry them, how?" I asked.

"On your back," she said. "On your feet. Wear as many as you can." Already, she seemed tired—not the commanding presence she had been on social calls.

"But it's hot, Mother. We have a long walk ahead. What good will it do to have so many clothes? We'll be vulnerable to thieves."

"Would you be left with nothing?" she asked.

"What if my clothes already carry the stain of the bubo? What of the marks from the seams of the stars?"

"All right," she said. "We'll take nothing. Nothing that might be seen."

As we fled, we gaped at the discarded garments of noblemen on the roads. Clean wool or linen tripled in price. Once-beloved pets— cats, dogs, goats—followed travelers like lost souls. Animals spouted bubos and foamed at the mouth. They were kicked and beaten. A gray dog had been following us for at least a league.

Walking quickly, we passed a family of nobles on their doorstep, one atop the other, horseflies swarming near a handsome man's face. I thought of Mother's finest dress, indigo-blue, and parties we'd shared with families like these. The flies, her dress, were the same bluebottle color.

"It's Mona Lia," Mother said, gasping and pausing. "And Luigi. And Angelina. Might have been me." She knelt beside the bodies and looked into the open eyes of her dead friends. The gray dog neared us, and I pushed Mother forward. She wept as we walked, a vacant look in her eyes, her weeping muffled by a gardenia posy pressed close to her face. It was as though her mind had taken her to another time, when those faces had laughed, those hands had clasped her own.

ELEGANTLY NAKED IN MY SEXY MENTAL ILLNESS

Luckily, the dog began to follow another family, fleeing toward the country.

My feet burned from the hot road. The merchants had closed shop. I remembered Mother wearing sapphires, her skin golden in candlelight as we dined to the sound of silver scraping plates and gay chatter. I remembered family walks, afterwards, with Father on the piazza. Those were different times.

Firenze had not always been accursed. That night, we slept beneath the cypress trees, beside a cemetery. The first day we arrived in the country, we paid a *becchino* to pull an old man's rotting body from a bed and drag him in blankets out the door. The house was isolated and Mother wanted to stay there. We said he was Mother's father.

Of course, he was not. With a key from his table, Mother locked the doors to the other rooms without looking inside them. Light filtered through Venetian lace on the windows, but we did not go outside, except for food. We knitted blankets from skeins of wool. She spoke of death incessantly. I fear she was consumed by it, her pale face flushed, her gray eyes lit by an unnatural luster. She spoke of the dead, their acts, their lives. Many times, I stole from our house at night and stared at the sky, the moon a white sliver of cut fingernail, the olive trees silver against the bluebottle sky. Everything blue was the color of her dress.

I heard weeping in the streets. Horse hooves thumped along dusty roads.

~

Each morning at dawn, Mother went to the fields. It was spring and, come summer, we could not live as we did, but she found sustenance on fruit trees and grapevines, and from fields of squash. Her fine dress, after weeks of wear, reminded me of tales of my paternal grandparents' poverty in Palestine, before I was born, before Father inherited his ship, before he met Mother. Her hair hung in oily strings around her face and the days were slow to pass. I regretted the loss of my friends. She regretted the loss of her kitten, Alfina. Once, that cat had enjoyed beef dinners, often receiving a morsel from Mother's own plate. Not one for people, Mother loved animals, especially kittens.

Alfina had been blind since birth and Mother's voice could call her from any recess in the house. She disappeared the morning we left. Often, during our journey, we thought we saw her on the road, but we did not.

It was not uncommon for Florentines to arrive from the city with nosegays clutched to their faces—as we had—as if flowers might staunch the scent of decay, masking death with the scent of life and growth. Mother warned that even the country was not safe. Priests, traveling to single funerals, found themselves begged to bury twelve at a time. People dragged their neighbors' corpses, calling out to godly men. Their voices were ragged with grief.

The Catholic clergy were not immune to the bubos. At last, they were told to stop ringing the bells, for those bells had rung day and night from their churches, and it was decreed that they must stop because the constant pealing discouraged the sick in addition to the well.

On a clear night, I could see a thousand stars and imagined them as departed souls.

~

May 1, 1348

In this new house, Mother stayed away. She was afraid of close contact though she believed herself pure, and touching her was forbidden. I prayed, every day, and often stared at her face: Her fine olive forehead beaded with sweat and dust, the black lines creasing like coal across her skin; her wide nose; and delicate, pointy chin.

"I want to touch you," I said one day. "I don't exist if I touch no one." We sat on a bench in the parlor.

ELEGANTLY NAKED IN MY SEXY MENTAL ILLNESS

"No, Tatiana," she said. "You may not."

"What if I die? What if you die, and we endure our last days without comfort?"

"Pass your stitch work to me, and I will touch it—as I touch it, pretend I am caressing your scalp, your little head. Your head is soft as a baby's."

"I'm sixteen," I said, "not a baby anymore," but I passed her the cloth, watched as she fingered it fervently, and said, "I love your blonde hair; it's a talisman to protect us." In her bodice, she had hidden a sack of jewels: Sapphires and rubies, a few diamonds and one emerald—all worth their weight in dirt.

"No," I said. "It's not enough."

"It must be enough. I can imagine your heart beating. I can imagine your soft hands."

I reached for her, but she pulled away.

~

May 3, 1348

Yesterday, when she came home, a dingy cast clung to her skin. "I've seen them," she said. "The Rossettis, the DiCarlos, and there is no food. A thousand florins could not buy us food." The Rossettis were our new neighbors, had been a family of twelve. Mother spoke on, hysterical, "Wasn't the flood of thirty-three enough? What a curse this city—no bridges but the Rubaconte over the Arno. We are punished and doomed. God does not exist."

"He is testing us."

"No. As if di Brienne wasn't the worst—pursued by his men, and now we are pursued by Him. It's a damned life, Cara." She swept her hands over her dirty skirt as if to smooth it. She said, "I dreamt last night of bridges swept away by black water and chairs mangled against the city walls. I dreamt of children, carried away by that water, their eyes open; they did not breathe; their eyes were black;

only now there is no water—only this heat, this fear of dying, this death." We had lit no wicks to preserve the secret of our presence. She sobbed and flung her arms around my neck. "No, no, you must not cry. You must not."

Tears burned my skin. We wept as I took a blanket and mopped her face clean. That was my first offense; she had told me not to disturb her dust. If I had left her alone, she may have survived. That night, I slipped into her bed. She woke screaming, and I hushed her.

The next day I said, "I'm going to look for food. If harm will come—it will come."

She sighed, but didn't argue. "Before dark," she said. "You must be back before dark."

I brought us meat from a freshly butchered dog, bread, and a cluster of grapes. I left the knife on the road. Outside the door, a white kitten mewled, starved, ribs cleanly visible, and it appeared that tiny worms crawled in its stomach. My hands were dripping with blood. I walked past it quickly and shut the door. We cooked the meat and then ate in silence until Mother asked, "What is that noise? Do you hear something?"

The mews ricocheted faintly in the walls. "I hear nothing."

"It's Alfina!" Mother said. "I'm sure of it. Outside the door. She found us! I'll go get her."

"It's not Alfina," I shouted. "It's a rabid kitten and we can't let it in!"

"I know her meow," Mother said, "and we must bring her inside."

"Mother, it is not your cat. I saw it. It's white—not gray like Alfina."

"Still," my mother said. "A white cat in times like these is an angel! Go let it in."

I opened the door, and the cat rushed in. It went to her immediately, as if it recognized its chance for survival.

~

ELEGANTLY NAKED IN MY SEXY MENTAL ILLNESS

May 5, 1348

The kitten was Mother's sole pleasure. She nurtured it, coddled it, spoke softly and sweetly of meals it would eat when this was done. But it was ugly to me. Mother would do nothing without it. The cat had sharp golden eyes that burned in the dark like sticks from a spit.

Each day, I went out and found whatever was edible. Mother spoke to the cat and daydreamed, huddled on a chair. She named it *Speranza*, Hope. One day, she would not get up from her pallet. "I feel warm," she said. "I need rest." But she could not sleep. Beneath her blouse a black dot darkened. She did not tell me about it for days, and when she did, she said, "Cara, go find another house. Leave me."

I could not. I would not.

"Go away," she screeched. "You are not safe here."

I prayed for her, but bubos appeared on her thighs and groin. Her cheeks swelled, but it was better to live together than die separately, and so I remained.

~

May 7, 1348. Dusk.

"I often think about that moment," she said. "When you go up to the sky. I imagine a lady in gold sheets, pulling me up an alabaster staircase and your father is there. He smiles and welcomes me. There is no plague, no bodies left uncovered. I can talk to my daughter there; it's—"

"Mother, I am your daughter."

"I have no daughter," she said, and then, as if I were a friendly urchin, "but you can keep me company."

Beneath her skin the bruises appeared. She walked like a drunkard from room to room, delirious, carrying the cat by its nape. Her hair, once lustrous and black, now appeared a matted nest of char. She laughed, her head flung back on her shoulders, at jokes only she could hear. The cat was dying too; bits of fur fell from its abdomen; worms thrashed beneath its skin.

Mother's throat swelled and she lost control of her limbs. She lifted her skirts and pissed where she paused. "I burn," she said. "I burn." The floors were sodden. With the cat and a small portrait of a hound from the living room wall, she crawled around the house. I dragged her to a chair.

"Mother, please remember me," I said. "Please, please remember me."

"Who are you?" she said. "I don't know you." I wrapped my arms around her, and the cat mewed. She and the cat curled into themselves, curled away. She said, "*Devo farti alcune domande*—I have to ask you some questions… Did the floods happen? Did the fallen bridges travel to the Ligurian on the tides? Were there children with black eyes? My children? I must have imagined these things… I have no children."

A florid ulcer bled on her face. Still, she did not reach for me, so I leaned into her. A fat flea landed on my wrist, brown and thick with her blood. Sickened, I watched it suck at my skin before I pinched it between my fingers, rolled it, and broke its legs. "You are an angel," she said. "Unmarked, ministering to the weak. A blonde angel."

She died, her eyes open, gray and peaceful, her hand clenching soft fur.

~

May 7, 1348. The dead of night.

I told her body a story: "*Stai per fare un bel sogno*, Mama— You're about to have a nice dream, Mother. Here is what it will be: Beyond these walls, gems will have value. People will laugh and dance by candlelight in vast halls, wearing blue dresses, whispering, '*Cara mia. Ti voglio bene*,' and coupling on soft feather beds. Dinners will be prepared by people with rosy cheeks. Farmers will plow fields and sow seeds. There will be no carts to carry the dead. There will be no dead, no floods, no God to wreak vengeance. You and I can walk to this place, if we dare—but we can't go there together because we cannot leave your tiny cat, your beloved kitten, so we will rot here together. *A vivere la dolce vita*—Here's to living the sweet life!"

As I spoke these words, I broke the kitten's neck.

~

May 8, 1348. All day long.

Mother looked silently on, her face turning shades of purple and brown. A black dot had appeared on my chest, below my left breast, beneath the dirty garments. I stripped off my clothes.

In the dark room, I waited and watched it grow, telling Mother lies, and massaging her face with my hands: "You had no children, no house, no husband. You were born here and died of a weak heart. Your name is Lucia. You were a nun. You dreamt of prophecies and black rivers, but these dreams were not premonitions. I am your blonde angel, and I will fly away from here—or, I am not, and I will die in this hot, dark room, without a wick in the oil..."

Naked and bereft, I traipsed through the house, touching my skin.

With the fever's splendor, I imagined my wings.

REVELATIONS

Description de la Main de fer.

GOOD COUNTRY. PEOPLE.

For Flannery. Because I love her. And since that girl of hers, left in the barn, has needed some vengeance for years.

"Some can't be that simple," the girl said. "I never could." Girl's name was Treble, Treble Ann Joiner, and as of one week ago that day, she was nineteen years old, but now she sat talking to her mother's pet, would-be boyfriend, Mister Loved-Treble-So-Much Ray Adams, who had been trying, in his own vacuous way, to enter her man-trousers for years. Ray Adams was forty-four.

"His dick don't even work, likely," she was fond of telling her friends when they came by or called, which was infrequently. Nobody came this far into the backwoods without a good reason.

"And if I could be that simple," she said, twirling a string of her ratty brown hair on a spit-wet finger and relishing the idea, "I wouldn't."

To this last bit, Ray Adams nodded without listening.

Treble expected no response, often spoke just to hear the melody of her own voice playing in its various registers, and often it was like she was mimicking somebody, her mama, Johnella, more than likely, or her mama's friend, or her mama's mama—

maybe even the mama of somebody else like-a-nobody to whom her mama spoke in the oscillating fan-swirled smoke of the home's inner parlor, chatting an interminable amount of time as some kind of greens were cooked in the grease of slaughtered pigs and the other adults, as she called them, as she called anybody not her and over thirty, spoke on in blue yammering streaks due to mourning the loss of the impossible, or possibly nonexistent, gentry inside themselves.

No adults ever truly addressed one another, she'd decided years ago, just engaged in the ceaseless monologues of deciphering their own life's riddles, most folks responding as if interacting, and interjecting here and there a few slightly tangential relationships to the topic at hand to appease the idea of participation in the immediate conversation. For this reason, Treble Ann often said things completely unconnected, as outbursts, not to add to the discussion, but to disrupt it.

And there was Mama, Treble Ann thought, overhearing the bustle and swish of garments moving in the back room, putting on yet more perfume for Ray Adams that would stink up the smoking parlor, which was already flavored perfectly with Ray Adams' lit pipe, likely buttoning closed some dress she'd bought out-seasoned and too small at a bargain sale, in the hopes of finally *enticing*, in the hopes that Ray Adams might summarily give up his highly inappropriate crush on Treble Ann and put his lewd intentions where they'd enjoy better use. After all, the Bible in her mama's boudoir was too oft consulted for no good temptation and Johnella itched for contrition, but hadn't enjoyed a lick of wrongdoing in months.

Poor Mama, Treble Ann thought. *You gonna die out here and no suitable man will ever come calling. None so good as Daddy. But there sits stupid Ray Adams.*

As if in sync with Treble's thoughts, "Ray Adams?" Treble Ann heard her mother call. "Can you come take a look at this here shelf in my hall? It could use some straightening."

"Iffen I help her," Ray Adams said, "you gonna finally give me a kiss, Treble Ann?"

Treble Ann snorted, said, "I'll give you a kiss with my fist, Ray Adams. No problem." His face reddened and he cleared his phlegm-happy throat. She spun another curl on a newly licked finger. "What I will do, if you fix it," Treble Ann continued, "is not tell my mama you been asking me to kiss you again, Ray Adams—because you get free supper here all the time, you lazy, no-account bum. And you know that could end. In fact, why not scram early?"

Aggrieved, as if it pained him: "Coming to help just this minute, Johnella," Ray Adams shouted toward the back room, standing before fixing upon his beloved a forlorn look. His hair had thinned. He was a man stretched like string shadows with a ball lump where his belly had spread while the rest of him hadn't. But he was weak—couldn't open the stored fig bottles, wouldn't even spar on account of Treble's fake hand, he said. Didn't want to hurt her, he'd opined oncet, but he'd seen her punch a block of wood in the yard with her club-fist a number of times, take down some neighborhood boys, too, so when he muttered that malarkey about not wanting to harm her, all tender, ready to burst with his own tremulous would-be goodness, she'd dressed him down right quick, whispering immediately under her breath, "You afraid I'm gonna tear your face off with this hand of mine, Ray Adams, aren't you? You and every other boy round here. Because I would—or I could. You negligent piece of shit."

He took a few weeks before applying his next flirtation. Brought her a few gifts that wouldn't be noticed. Lima beans? She had graduated high school the previous June. "Biggest nightmare, I'm going to get so bored here now," she told herself just then, listening to the shelf banter in the hall, picking up Ray's smoldering pipe and taking a toke, "that I might actually change my mind about him. Liking Ray Adams would be a terror. I'd rather punch his lazy face."

She practiced boxing regularly. Her father had been dead so long, thirteen years as it were, it seemed his long-ago pugilism lessons were fading, though ever-present, like the memory of his hands as he'd helped her up so many times, so she now extended these teachings with the help of his spirit's ghost inside her, for he was the only one she listened to, and she could hear him talking to her sometimes, when she paid attention quite close, encouraging her, like he had when she'd lost her hand at age ten—falling on the road, concussed after a few night rounds in his ring, laid on the roadside with her palm pointed toward the sky, alone and spread on the asphalt, as a '36 Plymouth full of liquored teens barreled down the country pass and ran it clean over, crushing every bone.

"Treble Ann, you gotta fight this," her daddy said then, "like you fight for everything. Don't let it take you down." Viewing the stump, lacking the digits that once wrote and picked up tools, no one thought she'd finish grade school, or high school, no matter her new prosthetic—but she had! Though her daddy'd passed soon thereafter, she learned to write with the other hand, fought more, fought harder, and kept his training paces. She used her prosthetic better than most gimps around, excepting she didn't want the tool hand so often. She wanted the blunt fist her daddy made her just before he died, the hitting hand that fit like a charm below her boxing glove and did some damage.

The real prosthetic she wore just for work at the Five and Dime. At home, she brandished the hardwood replacement, rounded, the one that bore no resemblance to the pronged metal creeper, and she lorded this about like an ever-held rock.

She grew. She learned. As her mama would say, she had blossomed. Through the years, she ran in the mornings, rain or shine, to keep up her stamina, breathing in the good country air, checking out the thorn vine growth from time to time, and climbing the hills steadily, insistently, breezing down them on her long, strong legs, darting behind and between houses in a pair of torn gray sweats getting shorter by the year, like a ghost of a girl who had always been a boy at heart. So powerful while running and hitting, she had no care for romance. Never had.

Probably why Ray Adams took a shine to her. He enjoyed no immediate competition, so often said when outside Johnella's earshot, "You shore do have a pretty face, Treble Ann," again and again, like the effect of an already poor compliment could increase by repetition alone. Treble Ann didn't want her pretty face. She wanted to fire her boss and reopen her daddy's store to sell hard liquor and playing cards out the backdoor, like he'd done when he'd been shot. She wanted to own every person in this town by knowing their secrets—the Cottons, the Hopewells, the Freemans, the Joneses, the Townsends—because you could know a family by what they bought: Who's an anorexic, false slut? Glynese Redhead Freeman! Who's sticking it to someone else's wife? Edgar J. Cant. Sure enough. Look at all that baby repellant he buys!

Treble Ann first wanted to re-own her daddy's store, and then maybe she wanted to beat every lousy boy at St. Mary's Christian Fellowship Academy who'd ever given her a moment's cruelty over her gone hand. That, or join a circus, though she had no marketable skills.

Still, the daily boredom wore her down. Mama's checks from the insurance were long gone, all casinos miles away. Most days, the house was still like a witness on the stand, this rotting house, and between Johnella's door-wreath fixings, selling hens' eggs, and working odd days at the post office, plus Treble Ann's small earnings from the Five and Dime, they had plenty of victuals, but no hope of expanding their horizons—unless there was a bank to be robbed or an inheritance to be swindled. So, the urge to hit something. Hitting things relieved her.

If Treble Ann had been born a boy, she woulda been a champ welterweight. Woulda been on television, knocking those fools out, even the black boys who thought they were something.

Truth was, even though female, or because of this, she didn't really miss her hand, often speculated that if she came upon some trouble, the wood her daddy had fashioned as a fist would work better than any fragile hand of skin and bone. Her wrist had not grown. The club-fist would fit forever, though was roughhewn with the beatings she gave it. The car that had rooked her fool hand could run over the club-fist five or six times, and it wouldn't be worse for the wear.

It was this longevity and durability she thought about while strolling to the wood porch as she saw a stranger sauntering up their drive, a young man—and what a sad sack of shit in an eye-popping blue suit he was, carrying some red-handled black valise like he was the Reaper's son, walking so full of himself, so inappropriately erect, like somebody had rammed a thick stick clear up his rear and into his spine. He was thin, coltish, none too clean, a half-smile perched on his face like a flatulent frog.

Initially, she had no hopes about his impending arrival, scrawny as he was, until realizing that, because he was a boy, because he was new around here, he might want to wrestle. Since attempted wrestles with Ray Adams had been more about restraining the hands of a deliberate tit-grazer than pure athletic sparring, she smiled at Mr. Thin-Whatever-His-Name-Was, hoping to appear engaging, or at the very least nonviolent. "Treble Ann, you must hide how aggressive you are," she'd heard her mama say so many times.

"Shut up your head, Mama," she'd wanted to say each time. "I studied boxing, not philosophy." But she viewed the new boy arriving with interest. His novelty sparked her fire.

"Why, hello, ma'am," the boy said, coming up to the porch, tipping his toast-colored hat from below.

"Hi, you," she replied, like she didn't care. "Fine day, no?" Tumescent clouds gathered on the hill's horizon, thick as clots. Where the day was blue and cold before, she could smell the impending rain.

"Your mama home?" the boy asked, hat in hand.

She rolled her eyes before answering, even waited to create some suspense. Then, "Yep. She's here," she finally agreed, tapping her club-fist lightly three times on the banister. "But she's enticing Ray Adams, so you'll have to come back." Treble smiled slyly. "Because she may not want your interruption."

"The Lord is never an interruption," the boy replied, sassy as a varmint. "Besides, I just walked clear across that field with all the pink flowers to get here. Up and down a buncha hills."

"No mean feat," Treble said, unimpressed.

"All right then," he replied. "Can you let me see her?"

"Ha." Treble Ann put her hands out in front of her, folding the whole one over the club-fist delicately at her waist. "Can I let you see her, salesman-boy?" she asked, raising the tail end of her inflected sentence. "Like I got a lease on yer dumb eyeballs? Or maybe you think I can just pull a curtain cord, and out Mama will come?"

He gave a disgruntled look.

She laughed, eying him scornfully, then asked, "How's about we whistle and see if that works?"

"I don't think you got a lease on my eyeballs," he replied, attempting cool and collected. "Any more than I got lease on yours." But his gaze had settled on her breasts, the large breasts she had never wanted but gained as God's gifting curse, those that filled out her blouses and dresses too fully ever since she could remember.

She felt a flush, asked, "What're you looking at now?" crossing her arms in front. "Bet you was just wishing you had tits like mine in your shirt," she went on. "Cause then you'd never leave home. Am I right?"

He considered her words like they merited his evaluation, touching his pointy nose with his left hand before saying, "Nome. I could just touch yours without having my own." He held out his palms like he would.

145

"But you won't," she said, stepping back and turning half away. "Can't touch mine. Won't ever."

"But I could," he replied. "Right now. As we speak, I'm even touching them with my mind." He didn't step close, just kept his dirty eyes glued to the front of her shirt.

"Could and will are two separate things, sales-boy," she said. "What you selling, anyway? Bibles I bet. Something not worth my trouble in this whole world of things not worth my trouble; just figures. Nobody sells nothing worth a shit 'round here."

He giggled in a way she deemed girlish. "Yeah, I got Bibles," he said. "But hey, don't tell your mama I said nothing 'bout your tits and maybe I'll kiss you behind that tree later," he replied. "I'll kiss you good and long and tell you I love you, maybe. After I get through with my business in there."

"Mama has a Bible," Treble Ann said, turning on her heel to enter the house, her head turned uncomfortably as she spoke, like to watch him from behind while walking forward. "You ain't got no business here. But come on up, if you're itching for it. You can try your wares on her."

The boy smiled with half his face, revealing a crooked tooth that Treble Ann liked. Her estimation of his attractiveness rose each time he went silent. "So what's your name, anyway?" she asked, sizing him up again, wetting her finger with spit and rolling another curl.

"Jeremiah Godman," the boy said.

"Bull. Shit," Treble Ann replied.

"Jason Strepper," he tried again.

"Hail Mary, Mother of God, what a lie," Treble Ann responded.

"Okay. Reginald Klepheart."

"Better," Treble Ann said, "but keep practicing that one." She hollered for her mama and then whispered to him, like this was some secret, "Well, Vesper C. Klitosis, make your home in our kingdom and come on in."

ELEGANTLY NAKED IN MY SEXY MENTAL ILLNESS

From the outset, Ray Adams did not like the boy. Treble Ann knew from the way the elder man stood stock-straight in his skin, like there'd be some cockfight or wager coming soon. Truth was, Treble liked the boy more and more all the time. If not for his own good traits, then for the distraction. Two men and two women here now—a good balance, even if you liked neither man. "This here boy is good country people, out selling Bibles today, Mama," she announced as they entered the parlor. "I told him how much you love the Lord's Word, how avidly you dote upon that Word, and though we ain't short of any Bibles here, we might think to show him some hospitality." She paused a second before saying, "He wants to sell you his favorite keepsake edition, gilt-edged Bible, from inside that there black luggage, don't you, James?"

Johnella smiled at the boy and then at Treble. Her perfume filled the room like a platoon's funeral bouquet. "What's his name again?" she asked.

"Henry P. James," Treble Ann replied.

"Henry?" Johnella said, astonished. "You don't say!" as Treble apishly smiled. "Why, that's my late father's name! You come on into the kitchen, now, boy, and take the weight off. Any child named after my father—"

"Yes. Show her your special fancy Bible then, Henry James," Treble Ann prodded. "You know, the one you shown me."

The boy opened his luggage, propped upright on the kitchen floor, but peeked in just a crack. Ray Adams stood as if to follow the boy's gaze into the darkened slit, staring him down, but the boy paid him no mind, groping in the hole of the aperture at what few books he must have assembled therein, rifling like submerging his hand in a narrow hole. He finally selected a blue Bible as he pandered to Johnella, talking all the while about how he had sold seventy-eight Bibles in the last five months, with four more on promise. He spoke up a storm, said he was born a middle child, always overlooked, until he'd decided to find his way by selling the Word of *God*, but that he was frail in the way of a lamb, with an ailing heart, mightn't live past thirty-five. "And heaven bless the Word of the Lord," he announced, near fervent enough to encourage a strong emotion in Johnella, assuming a red glow about him that passed for zeal and suffused his gaunt cheekbones and his neck with enough blood to lend an appearance of boyish optimism.

"Sit down and relax," Treble's mother said. "Supper's almost on."

Every so often, he leaned close to Johnella as she cooked or cleaned the table and clutched her hand, peddling his overwrought sincerity like a lemon on a car lot.

Johnella liked the attention and better liked his hand clutching hers. Before long, they sang a hymn or two and she invited this boy to stay for supper, which disgruntled Ray Adams but tickled Treble Ann, who kept humming, after the singing stopped, "Who's that yonder, dressed in black?"

"How we all going to eat?" Ray Adams asked. "I'm not splitting a chop with nobody."

"We'll make do," her mama said.

"Maybe you should split a chop," Treble Ann said, staring pointedly at his stomach. And, *Ray Adams can suck my dick*, Treble thought, bored of his proprietary erroneous righteousness. When she tired of the mixed banter betwixt he, her mother, and the kisser Bible-boy, after choking down some grits and green beans without the benefit of a chop, Treble Ann went back out to punch her boards. They couldn't see or hear her from inside and besides, if she had one hope it was that her mother would kick Ray Adams out for the evening and get it on wild-boar style with Bible-boy so Johnella'd have something salacious to talk about at church or in coming weeks. The desire for this indiscretion was so strong it welled within her, and Treble even began to imagine how the scenario might play out, the bony hips of the small boy ratcheting atop her plump mama on the parlor floor like a chicken's wishbone trying to pop back in, by force, to the plumper cooked meat.

Treble laughed. But because it was her mother in the fornication fantasy, she soon grew so repulsed that the urge to vomit rose steadily as she blasted at the splintered wood with her ragged club-fist, not to say she still wasn't hopeful.

"He who loses his life shall find it," was one thing she remembered the boy had said, and oh Lordy, did Treble Ann want something found, maybe just something nice for her mama, who was a good woman no matter what anybody said. It did rather trouble Treble that Ray Adams wouldn't give Johnella any sugar. Not like her mama didn't make him dinner, do his dishes. Not like he had a chance with Treble Ann.

Soon enough, though, Ray Adams left for the night, skulking, and the sun hung low in the sky. Not long after, Treble watched the boy exit, pressing his silly lips to her mama's round hand, kissing it again and again, like in queenly tribute. But they hadn't, Treble Ann speculated, done nothing.

Boy was still simpering, still too kind. Woulda had a taller gait. How boys were when they'd pounded something, and, "Fuck it all," Treble Ann said, sweaty from her exertion. She went into the field to run sprints. Again and always, while running, she pretended she was a boy. Maybe an Olympic contender. She was right in the middle of fantasizing she had won an enormous race, the crowds cheering madly, as Bible-boy came up on her. She would have let him walk right past. But he took to watching her through five sets of sprints.

At their conclusion, she huffed and puffed, ignoring him. Finally, she sat in the tall grass, crushing it beneath her. Then, "Why you still watching me?" she asked.

"Cause I want to," he replied.

She smiled before saying, "You sell any Bibles in there, Holy Man, weak-hearted boy?"

"No, but I think your mama mighta wanted me in her bed."

"So do it already," Treble Ann replied. "Would it kill ya? I'll give you a nickel."

The boy's eyes widened as he took an insuck of breath. "You say you want me to do your mama?"

She cocked her head, inspecting his lapel, his dirty pants with dust dragging on their hems. "You or somebody better."

"What's that on your wrist?" he asked, sat beside her, and said, "It's a wood-club, right? What? Can't afford a real hand? Not going to grab anything with that."

"I don't use it to grab," she said.

Giggling again, he then took her club-fist and brushed it over his cheek.

She pulled it back. "I got a real prosthetic," she said. "I just don't like it. But what else you got in that valise besides Bibles?"

"Oh, nothing," he replied. "Nothing you'd want."

"I bet something," she argued. "You don't know what I want."

"We should trade," he said. "You tell me just what you want out of this shitty asshole of a life—and I'll show you what's in my bag."

Treble Ann said, "Deal. I want to own my daddy's old store that he lost to the bank, I want to fire my boss, and I want to know everybody's business. Good enough? Now, open it."

"You're kinda pretty, Treble Ann," the boy replied. "Dirty hair and all. Think your mama can see you and me out here in this tall grass?"

"Why you ask?" Treble Ann inquired, interested. "You want to wrestle? Because I am happy to."

"Yeah. I want to wrestle against those tits," he said. "Be a good girl and give 'em to me."

"Oh, I'll give 'em to you, all right," she replied. "Stifle your face with them till you can't breathe. Like this." She made a couple of asphyxiated faces, clowning, then said, "But first show me what's in the bag."

The boy scooted his bony butt closer on the grass, weirdly whispering again, "I got a girl's leg in here. I got another girl's eyeball. Can I have your club-hand now, Treble Ann? To place in my hand. To put in my valise. I think I want it."

"No, you stupid piece of shit," she said. "You can't have nothing you want."

He laughed, another stream of high-pitched giggles, and then said, "Peep in the bag if you want to."

She grabbed his valise and threw it open. There they were. Just as he said. And a real Bible and a fake Bible too. "Shitfire," she said. "You weren't kidding."

"I may look like one, but I don't kid," he murmured, tracing his fingers across her breasts. She trembled. The sensations were confusing, sweet and menacing at once. Not like she'd had much romance, nor cared for it, but since she remained quietly under his touch in shocked deliberation, he put his other hand deep in her trousers just after unbuttoning them, watching her eyes blink rapidly as he started to massage her there with his dirty digits, saying, "Oh, yeah, sweet thing, let's get to know each other a lot better," before shoving one sharp finger deep inside her.

With his other hand, he pushed her down. On the ground was his open valise. *There's a girl's leg in there,* she thought. *Another girl's eye.* Using one wrist for two of hers, he trapped her arms above her head. She did not resist. "I could scream," she announced, like she was weighing it.

"Sure could, babycakes," was his reply, leaning over her with breath reeking of whiskey. "But you won't. Who is going to hear you, Miss Treble Ann? Your mama, drunk as a skunk, hymn-singing in the smoking parlor—the gone Ray Adams? Your neighbors are a mile away. So, come on, Treble Ann. Let's have us a good time. I'll get to know you real good inside. And then I'll take your hand. But first I'll be gentle, so let's see what Mother Nature gave you." He unbuttoned her shirt, leaning heavily on her and saying, "I want to see those big ole tits. Let 'em out."

Treble Ann viewed him like some kind of monster, one forged from both hope and desire. Maybe she wanted him, too, or just knew nobody new came around too often, but it took until he unbuttoned his pants, still thrusting his other hand's fingers, one to three, in and out of her while licking and kissing on her bare chest, that she realized she should put a stop to this.

"I don't want to get pregnant," she said.

"You won't," he replied. "I can't make a girl pregnant."

"I don't believe you," she said, staring at the tip of his erect member now pointed to her or at her, fully freed and flopping, as he yanked at her pants with a series of pulls to take them first down over her hips, then to her knees, and finally to her ankles, taking her undergarments with them.

"I'm gonna do it," he said. "I'm gonna do whatever I want, girl. Because I ain't like anybody else. I take what I want, and now I want you. You want some whiskey first? It'll make it hurt less. You're different and special. I can see that."

He pulled his immersed hand out and away from her body, and used it, wet and gross, to grab and then unscrew the flask in his nearby valise, leaning heavy to hold her down, swigging a gulp, and then pouring some liquor into her unready mouth such that she coughed and sputtered, whiskey flowing down her face.

"I could take you down, scrawny," she said. "You're not taking my club-fist with you, or anything else—even though I have another hand at home."

He smiled, said, "You're already down, girl. So now we gonna have us a real good time, but don't you cry—cause I don't like that none. If you don't cry, I'll be real sweet; I promise."

"You gonna need that Bible in a minute, sinner," Treble Ann replied, the sexual heat in her blood cooling faster than grease dropped in snow as she realized that he regarded her as a lamb, his dumb, waiting lamb, whom he would enjoy taking—and harming. He was, she saw, a harmer. He reached down, stroked himself, smiling, sipping more whiskey, and pressing what he could of his body tightly against her, rubbing against her. "Any minute now," he said. "I'll be ready."

"So, come on then," she replied. "Get down here, boy, and get to know me."

As he settled his skinny limbs on her, reaching to position himself, she pressed her legs together for a second, aware she could whip and hog-tie this boy any day of the week, but kissed him once, drawing his hands to her breasts, before she kneed him hard in his privates and pushed him off. She stood, pulled up her pants, zipped them, buttoned them, and said, "You want to fight me now, Bible-seller? Really fight? Let's have a go."

Wincing, in fury, he stood, eyes flaring with rage. "I'm going to take that fist of yours today," he taunted, wheeling around her. "I'll have it with me before I leave this hill." Him in her periphery, Treble Ann looked at the innocent hill, the pink flowers so delicate on the upslope, glowing faintly with the dropping sun. She crouched into her fighting stance.

"Gonna be night soon," she told him, tilting her head, and using her club-fist to gesture for him to approach.

He came, but feinting and jabbing, quick and easy on the ground, she took him down in three blows, ducking his attempts to hit her. She hadn't had a real tussle in a long time and couldn't quite explain the anger that swelled within her as she touched him, made her want to hit him more and more, even after he stopped fighting, but she kept swinging her club-fist, pummeling his face until it was as red and unrecognizable as a tainted valentine outside the month of February, and he rested still as the fake shutters adorning a distant house, his lips and cheeks a chop of bloody meat.

"That'll swell something awful," she said. "Iffen you should wake up. But I don't think you might."

She took the girl's club-leg out of his black valise, hefted its weight, and swung the stump like a bat in a wide open swing, cracking the air to the stars, then boxing his ears with the tapered end for good measure. From the valise, she took the other girl's eyeball and held it aloft, as if it could see all around her into the tall grass and beyond. The eye was blue. The hills rolled gently as always. Mama must be sleeping.

He'd do nothing for her, this fool. Couldn't even fight nomore. "You ain't got no real name, any which way, Bible-boy," she said. "No skills. And nobody could find you now, even if they wanted to. Nobody saw nothing round here but the hollow sky of evening turned to night."

She thought about being simple country folk, simple and complex, regarding again her thwarted seducer, monologuing with him for the sake of being an adult in his company, holding court, admiring his toast-colored hat with the wide red band which was now hers, which was fine and was laid beside him on the ground like a man-lily corsage gone wrong.

She then commenced to digging him a hole.

Horizontal
Scale   1:1

— Level 6 —

Vertical
Scale   1:1

P_V^a

LEDGE

Listen, I am telling you a story.

A young girl leans from a sixth-floor balcony, waving the elegant wave of a woman who knows the eyes of a lover are on her. He waits below, signals her descent. She nods. No, she will not come down. In the room beyond the window is her sister; together they stay in a two-star hotel overlooking the Seine and its narrow street scene, which is rife with aimless wanderers. *Listen, she does not come out. She does not come down.*

Her only sister bothers her, a girl of five with natural pin-curl ringlets and a three-day sunburn; her sister who tells and tells and tells. In this room they await the arrival of their father, who will bring his young business associate in their mother's absence—falsely blonde and brown-rubber tanned as their mother is fond of quipping—and the associate will, undoubtedly, treat the children with the polite civility of a supposed friend. She will not know them though she will try.

When she arrives they will smile and accept her gifts, recognizing them as attempts to buy the lasting favor of their father. They will call her by a stretched-out version of her name: Lila becoming Lighl*aaa*, or Maria being Mary-*i*-uh. But their voices will never sound friendly, and silently, cruelly, they will hate her, assessing her gold bracelets like thieves, feeling that they are round sickles near their father's back.

"Nevy, do you know when he will come?" the younger asks.

"Tomorrow."

"Will he bring Mother?"

"No. Another friend."

"I'm tired of waiting."

"You can't go out, silly. Look, you're as red as a pepper. If you'd worn sunblock we could go to the water again. But you insisted."

"You were supposed to put it on me," the younger will insist, but meeting the elder's glare, continue, "I'll wear it today. Promise."

"No. Today we wait."

"For what?"

"For tomorrow."

When tomorrow comes they will go to the airport, link arms through the crowded terminal and shake hands with the next speaking Barbie. They will seem to listen as she tells their father how adorable they are, how he should put them in commercials, how nice it is that he takes them on business trips, and the older girl will pry her lips apart in something resembling a smile.

She will sneer from her sixth-floor window as the couple leaves together in the morning, and consider taking the younger girl to a movie, perhaps two, because he gave her money, because she must stay out later than his prime business hours, because she remembers the last trip and what she viewed through a crack in his door. To punish him later, she will speak of how scrupulously he attended the real reason for his trip, precisely reentering each hotel through the night-use door in the early afternoons. For this reason, he will threaten to not bring her again, but also for this reason, she will make him change his mind.

On the next trip she will tell her younger sister what

happened. For once the young blab will have nothing to say. Then, late at night in their room she'll discuss each of the women they've seen and say aloud: "He only married Mother because he had to. She was pregnant. He was young. He didn't know what was out there. And she could have been anyone; you know why, Susan? Because there are no knights, only nights. There are no chargers, only charges. A maid is only perfect until she's been bled."

"I don't understand," the younger will reply.

"You will. I know you will," the elder will say. And she will be right.

~

Listen, I am telling you a story.

A young girl leans from a sixth-floor balcony imagining a rendezvous with a lover she has never met, one who does not exist. In the room beyond the window her sister squawks noisily about the boredom of remaining inside, and she, tired of listening, says again what she has already said: *Yes, they must wait. Yes, he will come. No, they cannot leave.* They are nineteen and twelve, pretty and plain. The eldest thinks of the blue stilettos her father gave her for her sixteenth birthday.

She has already taken the first steps to being like the last associate who opened as an exotic bloom in her father's arms: Pink skin, brown center, fuchsia core. She has already let the boys touch her in those places she saw spread wide and furred that afternoon, but has not surrendered fully because to each she asks: "Will you love me and only me for the rest of my life? Will you never touch another girl? Will you promise?"

To them, she is speaking a foreign language: The language of need. Word by word they translate, but always imperfectly. None has yet been smart enough to lie.

They know she is young. They know she is serious—but who

can make promises for the rest of their life? Whom, for what, and how? This is the dilemma.

On another day the elder will pretend to sleep as the younger makes a call. On the other end of the ringing line, their mother will pick up. "Mother, there's a problem," the younger girl will say. "Nevy's gone mad."

A sleepy, doped-up voice will answer, "She'll be okay. Tell her something to distract her."

"Mother, she's cut her throat. It's bleeding on the bed."

"Take her to the hospital then, or bother you father. If it's not too deep, ignore it."

The younger will watch her sister bleed, staunching the blood with her own cotton nightgown, wrapping it like a white scarf around her sister's hot, red skin.

~

Listen, I am telling you a story.

A young girl stares from a sixth-floor balcony, leaning over the ledge. As her sister snores, forgotten, she hopes for nothing but the night sky and the wind at her back, which beckons, soft and warm, like it may wrap and consume her. *The air is my guardian,* she thinks. An eventual fall is not the worry, only the impact. She will be an angel should she ever take a leap. For now, she retreats into the room.

The father has a new woman who annoys her. The mother is as absent as the catatonic grandmother she remembers from Detroit. As her sister sleeps, she invites a young waiter into their room. She acts the harlot and throws her arms around him, peeling off his white pants, white shirt, and black tie as soon as he clears the doorway. "Shhhh," she says. His flesh tears at hers. The pain is good. She does not ask his name.

This moment is the loss of her virginity: From when he enters the room, she does not speak at all. There is no need. She does not moan. There is a bright perfection to her silence, to her pain, to her stillness. Late in the act, her sister awakens to see the white, hairy moons of the waiter's buttocks, thrusting up and down in starlight. She sees his hairy back. Her sister wears a non-expression. Through heavy-lidded eyes, the younger watches them fuck. As he removes his shrunken penis and dresses quickly, the younger sees it: Nude like a short-stemmed portabella, shrubby. He has spilled his seed into her sister, which will only cause a stench in their shared room. Though he doesn't know it, her sister's blood will stain his uniform. He will have a pink, barely-there imprint near the front of his groin that others will see by the hallway lighting.

As he opens the door to exit, the youngest turns in her clean sheets as if she is sleeping, closes her eyes, opens them, and he is gone.

~

Listen, I am telling you a story.

The elder will plummet from a ledge on her twenty-seventh birthday—long after she has left that first encounter and found another. She will have invited up one of those once-imaginary swains from beneath her window, a man made real by time and circumstance, hours of endless flirtations, but somewhere in her awareness she will know he has never loved her and that even his perfect face holds a vestige of her father's duplicity.

In the interim, time will pass and pass and pass. The partners she has danced with will multiply like rabbits. Her last love will be her first love, but her fortieth lover.

She will have destroyed his love with questions. She will never have trusted and therefore never ceased her inquisitions. At first he will coddle her, telling her he loves her, or pretending to. And when her coquette's laugh fails to amuse him, her body fattens just beyond her liking, and, even for a moment, he stares too long at someone else, she will touch that scar on her neck with purpose, walk over that red carpet, fling aside the clear glass door, and from that balcony topple like a wax statue, freer than ever before in this final act.

And she will have no wings. And he will regret losing her, or simply being in the room, or having to make lame-sounding explanations to her younger sister who'll arrive first on the scene—the same younger sister who will then make her own lame-sounding excuses to the remains of the family, but secretly hate making them because somewhere, deep inside of her, as if a crystal ball had been thrust into her lap years ago—one that curiously resembled polished agate or a stone boulder or a red stain on a white nightgown—she will have always known this was coming, but never have known how to stop it. She will have planned her remarks for years, although, when she finally does make them, even to her, they will sound stale and dry.

~

Listen, I am telling you a story—this is the end.

It does not matter how often I say this. My sister is gone. My sister was beautiful. She dances in my sleep and woos handsome waiters in half-empty rooms. Her throat gushes blood as she spins in blue heels. I push the wound closed with my nightgown. She continues to bleed.

"Listen, Susan, listen," she says to me, before the jump

"I am telling you a story: Above the darkness of innumerable vacation cities at night, a young girl leans from a sixth-floor balcony, waving the elegant wave of a woman who knows the eyes of a lover are on her. He comes up. He comes up again and again. He looks like Daddy. He fails her.

"One day, she jumps. This is a short story. You knew she was going to die, didn't you? It's a ledge after all. And what are ledges for?

ELEGANTLY NAKED IN MY SEXY MENTAL ILLNESS

"Don't look so horrified, Susan. Let's play a new game. You're so silent. How about you tell me a story? No? You keep saying you are bored. How about we guess what hair color father's next associate will have? I say red. Do you say blonde? Listen. Talk to me! Stop turning away. What do you say? What do you say, already, Susan? I'm waiting. Give me my shoes. I'm preparing to walk outside."

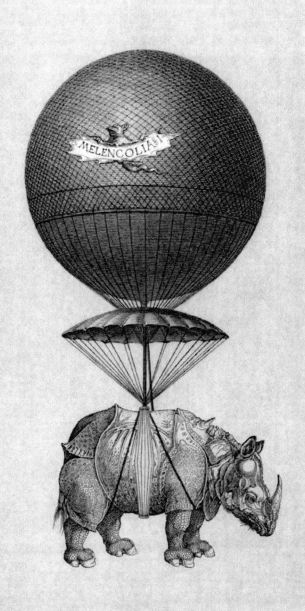

The banner reads: MELENCOLIA§

GIANT BALLOON ANIMAL TRAGEDIES

Since Brianne was small, hanging out at her father's apartment during the Macy's parade, eating halved pickles, pitted olives, jack cheese, and crackers on his small foldout card table in his living room, she kept hoping that if she watched long enough, she would see more than the twirlers and the marching bands, more than cheering kids and happy crowds. What she wanted to see most was one of those great balloon animal mishaps, but it seemed each time one occurred, she was only able to witness the after-carnage on the news.

Where were the cameras, she wondered, during the actual time when such a thing happened? Her father lived in Jersey, a far cry from Manhattan. He had a girlfriend named Lalaine with big brown eyes and slick black hair that fell to her waist. Perpetually, Lalaine smelled of pomade, mango, and sweet, sweet curry.

He would have another girlfriend after her, but while Lalaine was the one, a period that spanned from when Brianne was about six until Brianne was twelve, Lalaine walked around in loose emerald saris, exclaiming over one trivial thing or another, and she adored the big balloon parades. Lalaine's joy bothered Brianne. "What are you so happy about?" she often said.

"I'm just happy," Lalaine replied. "That's my nature. Unlike you, my darkling." Lalaine was a bird flitting from here to there. Tiny things pleased her and when she was adequately pleased, her soft lips fell open and she made a little squeak. This made Brianne feel violent, hateful. When Lalaine got too excited about the cuteness of the giant balloons, seated beside Brianne on the couch and finger-combing Briane's hair, Brianne liked to tell her about the horrible balloon-related accidents, those collected in her photo album memory book, but Lalaine would tilt down her half-Indian face, stop the dance of her fingers across the child's scalp, and make a sour face as if to say, "Don't do it. Don't ruin my happy."

This, of course, just inspired Brianne to continue, getting up to show Lalaine the newspaper clippings kept in her scrapbook from early balloon accidents, including the one from the 1995 glass-showering incident when Dudley the Dragon had bashed into a Columbus Circle lamppost. Many times, Brianne had imagined how that must have gone, how quickly the dragon must have deflated, what the people just below must have felt to see it fall upon them, all of these details. She told Lalaine how she'd read that in 1994, the Nestle Quik Bunny's ear and Snoopy's paw deflated as the result of a crash collision.

"Quik Bunny takes Snoopy out!" she shouted, cackling.

Lalaine grimaced. "Look!" Lalaine said. "There's a cute one coming!"

In response, Brianne told Lalaine that the 1994 collision would have been the best to see because Barney hit a lamppost, tearing a hole in his side, and the Cat in the Hat had injured a foot. Or wait! Or wait! In 1993, she went on, Sonic the Hedgehog, sixty-four feet high, smashed into yet another Columbus Circle lamppost, injuring a cop and a ten-year-old girl. A ten-year-old girl was injured! Also, Rex, an eighty-four-foot dinosaur, ripped his head section when he bashed into a light pole.

Lalaine tried to stop her from detailing anything further, muttering, "It's misery!" but Brianne was on a roll.

Did Lalaine recall, Brianne asked, that in 1989, as the first Thanksgiving snowstorm in fifty-some years brought wailing winds, Bugs Bunny's side was punctured, along with Snoopy's nose, so both balloons were grounded?

"I was in Delhi then," Lalaine said as she walked away from both Brianne and the set. This suited Brianne just fine. She wanted to focus, and while eating pickles and olives, she realized, there was an intensive sort of TV-watching that could be done if she didn't want to miss anything, one she had recently mastered, where beverages or food were brought to the mouth with no perceptible movement of her eyes from the set.

It was only the Thanksgiving parade she watched this way, but it was because this one weekend a year was the only time her father got her and her mother had no television for her earlier years, but even after she bought one Brianne could only watch it for one half-hour a week, for educational shows with learning games.

Granted, most children liked balloons. Brianne was no exception. Not that she'd had many. But Brianne, despite Lalaine's horror, felt there was something gory and fantastic about balloon accidents—the large, false gods stuffed with helium; those created in the shapes of monstrous felicitous atrocities, elevated and rolling in the breeze, their people-handlers off to the sides, holding them down with ropes—and who had conceived of this? Let's make a big balloon and resist taking it into the sky; instead hold it close for gawkers to watch and lampposts to gore? And what adult could say with pride, "I'm one of fifty handlers for the SpongeBob SquarePants? No, not one of the stooges, but an experienced member of the twelve-person leadership team"? Most parade balloons, in Brianne's experience, were mascots or cartoon animals meant to appeal to children.

As a child, Brianne found every one of them terrifying. Perhaps this is why, when they ripped, when they crashed, she found it so satisfactory. The feeling of joy at their collisions never quite went away, even when she lived in Manhattan and could watch the parade out her window at the age of thirty-five. *Down with corporate America*, she sometimes thought as she witnessed the event in her adult years. Two-point-five-million people gathered to watch a bit of nothing? A marketing extravaganza? *Down with greed! Down with stupidity!* That's what half of these balloons were—colorful ads for more colorful ads for action figures. And down with people wasting time and money on enormous balloons that would enjoy one brief spotlight per annum and likely be out of commission soon enough when something bigger and dumber was invented.

It was like these parades had become her target for what was wrong with the world. Frugal, Brianne could make two bags of groceries yield eight meals. She could, with a combination of coupon clipping and bargain shopping, make a Thanksgiving dinner on sixteen dollars. Lalaine left her father when she discovered his gambling addiction was not something she could solve. His next woman, Connie, liked Brianne's fetish for these animals, but Connie was cruel and reeked of marijuana. Brianne didn't quite know what motivated her.

All she knew was that her hatred for this annual festivity was also connected to an obsessive need to watch, and then an obsessive need to track the huge balloons in such close proximity to her flat that there were entire moments when, as a balloon passed, the color of the animal's ass or arm, like a big orange or yellow patch, was all she could see from the window.

She had become a tax accountant. She still visited her father in Jersey. She had married a man who was busy like her. By all accounts, she was well-liked and successful.

So, she didn't know what made her snap on the day she threw a kitchen knife out the window to burst the mammoth passing

Minnie, the one whose blackness blocked her window for a good two minutes, but she threw the knife and waited. Maybe it was the memory of her last trip with Lalaine through the park. They were walking and a man was selling balloons. Lalaine's eyes lit up to see the array in his hands; she grabbed Brianne's hand and her eyes seized upon Brianne's, conspiratorially, as she said, "Would you like one? This might be my last chance to give you something." Lalaine's eyes were red-rimmed and she wore a dark-violet sari. Her smile was a slim pinion of sun in all her recent rain.

The night before, Brianne remembered, Lalaine and her father had a blowout.

"Go ahead and fucking leave me, then," he said.

"I will," Lalaine said, her voice soft like a drizzle of butter in Brianne's awareness. "But you are leaving me. This is my lease. So, pack. Pack now while I am taking your daughter for a final walk in the park. She needs air. You need to go."

And the walk, this walk that she and Brianne took in the park, as to allow him to get his things into his car because Lalaine had said, "We will split up, but this is my apartment." So it was decided that Lalaine would be driving Brianne back to her mother's house after their walk.

Thanksgiving Day had been arguments, the thick sound of her father's wounded voice against the flapping of Lalaine's, and the television. No balloon accidents.

The parade had passed uneventfully; Lalaine hadn't even pretended to be a stepmom like she normally did. Brianne wanted to comfort Lalaine, but her loyalties were still with her father. Brianne was, she decided about herself, heartless, just like him. He too had scorned Lalaine's constant joy. But she was crying as she thought about this later and hated him more than anyone she had ever hated for making her this way, not soft enough to make Lalaine love her or keep her, because that day in the park, looking up at the balloons, when, "Whichever one you want,

173

honey," Lalaine offered, Brianne mimicked how she'd often seen her father shut the woman down, rolling her eyes and looking away. She thought instead about how her father had promised her a balloon on an earlier day but at the last minute had shaken his head, pulled his pockets out of his trousers, and said, "Babe, I've only got enough money for a pack of smokes, okay? Another day, right?" But that future day had never come.

Likewise, he had never taken her down to the streets lining the parade route as he'd promised. He'd never done a single thing he promised, but here was Lalaine, pretty, happy, soft-spoken Lalaine, with her little beaded pocketbook out, saying, "Whichever one you want, honey. Which one did you want?" And Brianne could have picked a butterfly, or a crane, or a big anaconda balloon with *Happy Birthday* up its length, though it was not her birthday, but this would be the last kindness Lalaine would extend to the sulky man she had given up on and his dark-dreaming child, so Brianne refused. "No. I don't want anything from you."

And it was the black glitter that was a tear in Lalaine's eye that long-ago day that Brianne saw when the Minnie balloon passed years later, that horrible gleam, with Brianne's fresh recollection of the man and his handful of balloons standing before them, *pick a balloon, honey, pick one*, then losing interest because she said she didn't want a balloon like a princess or a tiger, when she really, so desperately, did. Even at twelve.

And then Lalaine was leaving. Lalaine was waving goodbye. Lalaine was out of there, *hasta la vista*, never to be seen again. Not by Brianne. So there would be no one happy around anymore. Her mother was kind, but never happy. Her father was angry or flashy, but seldom just light. She hadn't known anyone like Lalaine before and feared she'd know no one like her again.

And it was in that moment, thinking about Lalaine and looking at Minnie, that the kitchen knife went out the window, aimed at the huge Minnie's ass. But it fell and clattered to the ground. The winds were strong, didn't help. There were no lampposts on her street, at least none near her building.

Brianne watched the next colors pass: Red, blue, white, green, yellow. She took another knife from the butcher block and another and another, flinging them out her window until there were no more knives to throw, but she had hit or ruptured nothing. How could she miss a target that big? The closer she got to the window, the farther away the balloon appeared from her fourth-floor view. There was no way she might have hit it. She looked down. No one was stabbed on the sidewalk.

It was not that she wanted to hurt anyone, not really, not like the woman in a coma from one of the accidents or the two sisters hurt in another, but Brianne wanted to pop one of those balloons because it was big and it was smiling from above; they were all smiling, the balloons. She walked downstairs to see if she could retrieve the knives, gather them up, and maybe, if the feeling had not yet passed, try to sail them out at distant targets once again. But her husband had not been home for days, and so wouldn't be there to help, and she found she couldn't recover them all. One had stuck into a dumpster in the alley that flanked her opposing window. Many had been chipped by the cement, blown into the wall of her own apartment building by the same gusts that brought the animals close enough that their colors filled her window, but some were simply missing altogether. The parade continued without cease, and though Brianne still most urgently wanted to see a giant balloon animal tragedy happen right then, right in front of her, there was nothing but a glimmering black eye in her recollection and these childish animals gliding by without a hitch, fifty or more people on the ground below them guiding them through low winds, happy people more than likely, pulling down on those happy animals' helium-lifted strings and coaxing them right on past her door and down her street, while her hands were full of banged-up knives.

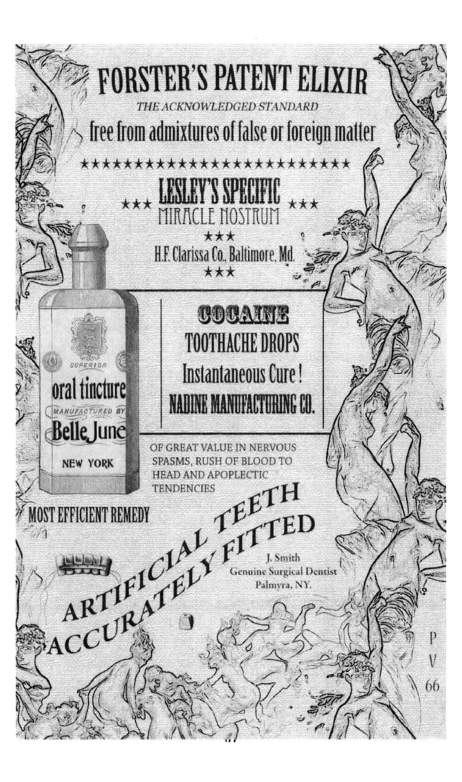

HIS OTHER WOMEN

The first thing you notice is that they're all so pretty. So pretty you could puke. They're all super thin, too, the kind of thin you dream about becoming when you are on a treadmill at the gym, wishing against reality that the few short sessions you've endured so far with a personal trainer named Phil will count for a lifetime of their better metabolism or good nutrition. Not only are they pretty, the ones you've targeted as threats, but they are smart. They are fantastic. The kind of girls you wish were your friends.

Most of them are married to someone else. Most of them laugh easily at his jokes and engineer reasons to touch him. If this goes on long enough, your watching of them, you imagine yourself attending a Pleasing the Cheating Asshole seminar with them one day, a seminar located in a room where someone other than him, maybe a woman he has cut loose but once loved, teaches. You imagine them taking thorough notes with black ballpoint pens, one in each of their writing hands, one to spare on their tabletops, with you sitting there, your pencil eraser chewed to bits, chewed down to a nub, where the paper in front of you reads only, 'Fuck that twelve-timing prick!' This has been written and erased thirteen times.

But you don't imagine you left the class when first angered. You imagine you stayed to watch the women, thinking: *This here is an ode to the beautiful blonde hair of Clarissa. The glowing smile of Nadine. The hot, sexy rumination of Belle June.*

It's not like you see these women often outside the office, not like any one of them has ever called you up on your cell and said, "Please. Please come over, single, ridiculous Lesley. Timmy is sick and I need your help." You barely know them well enough to borrow a purse pen at the market. You overhear them rather than "converse with." When you do converse with them, the act strikes you as somehow wrong—like talking to the birth mom of a child you are about to adopt about how hard it will be for her to lose her casual-sex baby, no matter what a hooker she is, so you can take it home—like you are the asshole because you are sweet to their pretty faces, but will be ax-grinding later, vehemently, in their backs.

Sometimes you watch them in public places, like parks, where you go to walk your dog Buster. Sometimes you watch their children, who always pet Buster, and think, staring down at the downy tops of young heads: "Your mommy is fucking up your idea of love as you pet my sweet dog! I am sorry, poor child! You will know this by and by."

Sometimes, you fantasize about viewing these women in their private moments, watching them doing disgusting things like belching or scratching their abdominal stretch marks, or lying to him when they are upset, about how small his dick is, or how little it pleases them. You imagine them leaving irate messages on his windshield, like you do, and you wonder if he has stock in the neighborhood Motel 6s.

He's a dentist and there's one located right across from his office. As he drills on someone this morning, he tells you about his conscious sedation training. "It's like a patient has had five or six glasses of wine," he says, looking at you through those sporty dentist glasses that have extra bug lenses built into the larger protective glass. The bug-eye rounds are set like bifocal peering lenses, blue and purple, iridescent. They are slightly mirrored. Convex. If you look deeply past their curved surfaces, you can watch his lashes flutter; you can see the magnified blue-green of his eyes. His huge pupils. You watch him touch the patient's shoulder, softly. "You okay?" he asks.

"Mmmhkemmm," she says. She's pretty, too; long slim legs he can look down on as he grabs his tools. This one's been here an awful lot the last month. But you do not question what he says or what he does (or whether anything is anything) because if you mention the other women, he's cold at the office and doesn't call for weeks. He conditions you to accept small satisfactions. Behavior modification training. When he wants to soothe you, he lies, says: *You are unique. You turn me on. I'll try to be more honest.*

But his eyes and hands rove. He seems always to be touching someone. His women keep multiplying, the ones you think he wants. You see him as a plotting mastermind. You wonder if he makes maps; one woman per city block, peddling his wares of faux sensitive and laying on thick his "I'm a just a regular man" bullshit game—his "I just want to see all the photos of you ever taken—your name is so pretty, my pretty girl" routine. Or, "Look at that million-dollar smile!" This he says as he grins brightly when he talks to little girls. Older girls, too.

You are his dental hygienist, so you've heard every line he uses, though you sometimes wonder about his private lines. About repeat customers who return for whitenings. Like Belle June.

Belle June. The Italian one. You ran into her at the deli the other day; she's one of them—you are absolutely, somewhat, mostly sure. He touched her thigh as she sat in the chair. But there is no definitive way of knowing this bears witness, except the other small gesture you watched happen between them at a weekend potluck he threw for patients when her hand slid over his and paused for half a second too long. She said something idiotic then, something like, "Don't burn my hotdog. I like mine barely warmed." You took that as a sexual pun, wondered if she had a pussy like a fridge. Was that an inside joke? An inside joke about his wife? It may well have meant nothing, but who likes a lukewarm hotdog? Her teeth are white like a baby's. Even her x-rays are good. Does she really need the dentist so often? Is there such a thing as blinding white? Come on.

And you see her at the deli, eying the ham. "I think I'll get Black Forest," she says to herself. "A pound. Oh, hello, Lesley!"

"Hello!" you say, grinning at her like she is a normal woman, one you could get close to, one you don't perceive to be on his screw-on-a-fast-track list. You make small talk, the kind you forget the second it leaves your mouth. You don't act petty or small-minded. You don't ask how her husband is doing, nothing barbed or ill-mannered. You don't say what you want to say, what you need to say, which is: "Are you taking a number for him, too?"

There are no numbers at his office. He calls everyone into the luxurious back suites by first names. Belle June has a real number in her hand now. Deli number 30. Your deli number is 23, and damn if that doesn't give you some small satisfaction later as you buy low-fat yogurt, as if you have won something. Hell, yeah! She'll wait longer, you speculate—for ham, him, and everything else.

You visited another of his patients, the blonde girl Clarissa, one day, at her home, upon her invitation. She has scoped you out before. You think she knows something. She is complicit. She is cute and she is wary. You swear she saw you duck into the office bathroom with him one day and the way your cheeks were flushed when you left, the taste of his semen on your tongue. "Oh, wary, wary Clarissa—I will not scalp your new babies," you want to say. "I will not steal your man. He isn't mine in the first place. In fact, we're kind of like Mormons. Will you be my special Mormon sister? We can be the dentist's lovers together. I will brush your hair. I will kiss your cheeks. There can be a schedule—I would like him on Tuesday evenings, if that's okay?" Of course, you mean, and say, none of this.

And maybe you should spend more time watching her, checking out her house as you enter, but as soon as you visit and clear her oak doorway, you find her spouse is more far interesting. What is his tragic lack, you wonder? How doesn't he please her? He seems innocent enough, watching a Mets game, his feet propped up. He seems virile, too, and like he looks at her with love's eyes. But your cheating bastard has his claws in Clarissa, you know, you think. He has his claws in all of you. Sometimes, you imagine yourself and these women as a herd of sick sheep, sheep that oddly want to comfort one another. Sometimes, you want to make love to his women, every single one of them, so that you can enjoy the pleasure of taking what he has enjoyed. You want to send out a support group email to the ones you think are closest to his sexual fan club—or a snail mail letter, privately, to every single one, that states: "Does Emma Forster's husband tell you he loves you, too? Does 'cleaning your teeth' ever have another meaning? Here is a picture of he and I in bed together, though he is sleeping, so you can know that I am not lying. If we ever arrange a meeting, I will bring my sheets as proof."

But what if they aren't his other women, these other women? What if they are just women he chanced to say a kind thing to in front of you, women he has been gentle and sweet to on occasion, women who know his every friend and acquaintance and wife— the sort of women he does not deserve to be villainized in front of? What if he is just a dentist who loves you? Or what if you told them what you thought you knew about him, but you were wrong? And they knew about you then, about you and him, which would ruin you and him—and then what if they stopped coming to the office? He makes a mint on female clients. He's not stupid. He would kill you. He would be so angry. Yes. This could happen.

Though what if, instead, when he comes to your place (a rare visit) and puts down his things, when he sits on the couch beside you and rubs your neck, when he whispers in your ear, "I'm so tired. I have been wanting to see you all day," you can be sure that he is telling the truth? Are they all nothing to him?

It's just you and him. So what if, as he says, "I would leave my wife for you if it weren't for the children; I would do anything for you—anything I could," you could at least partially believe? Relatedly, what if you could forget all the evenings he doesn't have free and the times he is unreachable by cell—and forget that you never bother him with your real troubles because he is not there for you that way and never will be? Well, that would all be fine.

But his hands smell like pussy when he walks through your door tonight, though he hasn't been home for the day. You haven't been to work. Is that canned tuna he had for lunch? Is your house just a quick stop on his many-drop routine before his wife? Will he leave within an hour? Are you his only girl this evening? Do you love him enough to let him move the wetness dried on his fingers into you, because you and that other woman are the same? Is it a montage as he fucks you of the gorgeous visual streams of his other women stripping nude, slowly seducing you with pole dances, upbraiding you, and then falling into your arms and crying with you, about you—and about him.

There should be an about-him weeping spot. An about-him burning place. An about-him lovers' grave. Who are these beautiful other women? Why does he need so many? You want to ask him this. You want to shout it out, beating on his chest, and let him tell you that you're wrong.

Because he could love you. He could have no other women. You could be imagining things. You are about to have your period. He did call twice today. He could just like the pretty people. Everyone loves the beautiful. He is not alone. You could be his only other lover.

ELEGANTLY NAKED IN MY SEXY MENTAL ILLNESS

Yes. And pigs could start flying any day. Keep your eyes peeled to the sky; some kind of odd pork product might wing by sweetly and repetitively oinking, "I Love You and Only You," (Parenthetical: As Well As My Wife), and you can't tell those other women a thing. Not till you're sure. Because you don't like to be wrong, so for now you keep smiling at them, those beautiful, suspect other women.

You tell them trifles about weather and vacations as patter, as small talk. You suck saliva from their mouths with a small vacuum. You squirt their tongues. You scrape plaque from their teeth. You probe their gums for gingivitis and bone loss. Nothing you say you can remember. Not while you work on them. Not ever. You shine a bright Pelton and Crane LF-I Post Mount Light on their faces, wondering if they note the scratches on the lens surface: "A little wider," you say. "Open. Turn toward me. Good." You nudge their cheeks with light, safe, and plastic-covered fingers. You want to finger-fuck their mouths.

But you cannot admit things to them, even as you watch their mouths bleed, their full lips opening, their eyes growing a little glazed and fearful, like most people's do in a dentist's chair. Not like they can talk with your hands all up in their bites anyway. His wife, however, could use a good long message. A good long talk. You don't work on her teeth. She's a mousy, brown-haired woman with a genuine face. She's his angel. His Madonna.

But you don't hate women. You've always loved women. More than he does. Evidently. So isn't it a higher moral ground, even after you stop sleeping with him, to let a man keep his family of four children, let his wife maintain her illusions?

You don't know about his other women, but you know about you. You know what you've done, what he has done to you. You know exactly the things that would hurt the wife most—how you already know about all the small troubles of each child, how he tells you she is cold to him and turns away, how there are times he's spent with you that she thought he was away at a conference somewhere, how you and your whole life are just like his new class on conscious sedation—a few glasses of wine later, lay back.

"Lesley, can you hand me the clamp?" you hear an imaginary him say. "Good. Hold that. Hold that. Steady that curing light. Suction. And very nice. I'm going to reach down now…" His hands slide over a woman's imaginary breasts. His body mounts another in the chair. "They don't," he says, pushing up a silk skirt with his palms, moving lace panties aside with his index finger, pulling himself clear from his garments to make entry as his hips move in wide, surrealistic thrusts. "Remember a thing."

But each of his other women, or the ones you think he gathers, are beautiful and kind. And you wouldn't want to hurt anyone, really, not even his wife— not even if she called you and asked you directly, though you would tell her your side then. You would tell her anything she wanted to hear.

It will have been bursting to come out. You will have email and text messages and hotel receipts and pictures and voicemail. You will spill to her, spill it all, bright canary singing, just because she asked and you could unburden yourself, like you have been longing to. After all, she is the only one who could hurt him and change his life for the long haul. She has his four children. His other possible women would have to be approached as nebulous possibilities, but to touch his wife with your knowledge, with your pain, would be real and powerful and immediate. But sure as shootin' sister, for now, you don't want to hurt her. You don't want to hurt anyone. You're a soft sell, a cream puff, a darling, somebody's only darling once. You could not even kill butterflies as a child, house flies, or dying birds.

Though, in your fantasy, in your real life, "Tell me what happened right now," Emma might say, standing in his office one day with a baby on her cocked hip and two more standing behind her, the fourth child seated in a chair. Or, she might call and say, "I need you to admit something to me. Please. Be honest, Lesley.

I've always been with you." Or, she could come knocking on your front door, screaming like a banshee, "Come out, you fucking cunt! You fucking whore! You home-wrecking bitch! How could you? How could you do this to me?"

But no matter her approach, you would let her touch you and hit you. You would tell her everything. You would cry for her, for you are sorry. You would tell the other women everything, too, if they asked, if they brought it up, just admit this was a sickness that you shared with them, that what was true for you was true for them, too, had been for a long time.

But you'd wait for that admission. And even after you got it, after Clarissa or Belle June or Nadine came to you and laid it on the line, you'd still have one question left, one question left for all of you, including his wife, because you would be happy to let loose the sordid, unhappy story, unload it and be rid of it—but you needed to ask, wanted to know:

Dear God, *where*, oh where, to start?

20/200

20/100

L

E T

R A V

20/70

A I L R

20/50

pv66

E N D L I

B R E L E T

R A V A I L R

E N D L I B R E

20/30

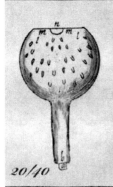

L E T R A V A I

L R E N D L I B R E

ARBEIT MACHT FREI

20/40

20/25

20/20

SUMMER ROSE

Tamar sat before her vanity, cinching her wet hair with a tortoise clip. Arms up, head straight like a dancer, she found her appearance romantic, nostalgic, like a painting she'd seen once at L'Orangerie in Paris. Tangerine light, filtering through her windows from late-autumn leaves, cast golden shadows on her empty walls. Mystical with this orange quality, her apartment could have been anywhere, anytime—until the New York street noise cut through her fifth-floor window, bringing with it the shuffling stop and groan of a city bus. She drew herself to attention. Soon, she'd have to go. She'd wear the de-feminizing slacks and shirts that had become her trademark—but at present, water trickled from her shining limbs, and she ignored the staining mess on the carpet, rubbing her feet back and forth on its soft fibers. It was an oddly sentient day. Her face and figure seemed at once old and new, her reflection revealing a person who may have been disappointed yet still hoped for unspeakable tenderness.

At thirty, with her hourglass hips, full breasts, and flat belly, she wondered when her body would show her age and go to ruin. When was her last lover? Eight months ago? Six? She thought of the last slew of casual sex partners, particularly the ones who lasted beyond a single night. More relationships ruined by her need to control?

For a moment, the mirror-stranger chided her, put a finger to her lips, and she felt that the way she chose to define herself could shift at any time, any moment, simply by her saying: "I won't be harsh anymore. I won't be demanding. I won't do things that mean nothing. I won't be me."

Then a thought of her flyaway father destroyed this musing. Her natural scowl returned, her reticent identity restored in the mirror's unblinking eye. "You fit into me," she said, thinking of him, recalling an Atwood poem she'd read: "'Like a hook in an eye. A fish hook. An open eye.'" She didn't know if she quoted perfectly. When her phone rang, she answered it, then she hung up. The thoughts evaporated now, but just before her shower, during her shower, she'd felt softer, pretended an imaginary lover waited behind her bedroom door, or in her kitchen making breakfast. one who would call her Tammie like her father had when she was young—before he disdained her.

This lover would never be cruel, would never leave voluntarily, and he would never disappoint. He would be handsome, too, she decided, perhaps with tiny square specs. He would not demur to her like the cowards at work, and she would not want him to. She would be his moon and wrap herself around him as if she held the last remaining child to her breast after an accident with few survivors, and she would be complete, they would complete each other—but the fantasy between sleeping, waking, bathing, and preparing for her day left as she donned liquid eyeliner in harsh, black strokes. A bit of it burned in her eye. *My day fits into me*, she thought. *A fish hook. An open eye.*

And how ridiculous to even imagine a lover, she thought. Was she daft? She had no lover, no children. The kitchen was filthy from last night's dinner, and there would be no one there to greet her except a tiny betta fish in his small bowl with a mirror behind him so he might mesmerize himself, entice and later be hostile. She yanked on her bra and panties as an industrial rhythm filled her head, life awaiting.

Pitching her towel into a hamper, she readied herself for work, humming a battle tune. Only later did she realize it was a rapid, military-style march. This made sense. She had already engaged in acerbic communication with her assistant before ever getting dressed. Standing naked, angry, it had been strange to pontificate in moist and shaking flesh, but her office was full of hard voices and difficult manners, the kind her father hated: "I want those papers on my desk, now, Julia," she barked, chest and ass bouncing with her vehemence. "Get someone up here today. Yesterday! I don't have all year!"

She did not think this day would be different after a second latte from the convenience cart convinced her that the ulcer she'd begun to imagine lodged in her stomach might actually be real.

"My stomach burns, and I can't be a warrior and a flower at the same time," she said to no one. "But we all know what happens to flowers. Crushed underfoot."

~

Charles lifted Karin's envelope to his lips and inhaled. Tapping his toe on the curb and yanking the onion-thin missive from its folds, he examined Karin's script, wondering if today would finally be the day. Hesitating before the street, he read her letter again, until her voice seemed to float above the words, fusing audibly with her small, sweeping scrawl: Voice and ink, ink and pen, throat and word.

> *Since you'll get there before I do, Charles,* her letter read, *wait for me at the station with a red carnation. I'll be there as soon as the Liebermans' daughter has her baby—as soon as Mother no longer needs me, maybe in one more year. There are many*

things I can't now relate. Dear Bumblebee, I wish you were here almost relentlessly, but at the same time, am glad you're not. Paris is irreparable. We're poor. The streets are full of strangers. Who would have thought? We've moved to Loiret where Mother makes miracles of single chickens and Lisette has grown three inches since you last saw her.

She's still blonde, but the blue of her eyes has deepened. In case you've wondered, my hair is as dark as before! Lisette is precocious. You always loved her so much. If she hadn't been four, I might have been jealous, but jealousy seems foolish to me now. It's Tuesday morning, and I lie in bed, remembering that afternoon at Normandy and the sandwiches you made with the crusts hacked; I remember how the gulls swooped down and ate them—and how we laughed. You kissed me then with the lightest pressure, and I remember your face was stained with my lipstick as you left. I must say, I liked you in pink!

But I do have a question for you, Charles: Why can we not suspend time in a package and unwrap it at will? Your mouth felt soft as peaches that day, and if I run my palm across my mouth, I can pretend you kiss me now, in this ugly room, which is a small comfort with so many dear ones packed together like boxed sweaters. There was a crack in the left lens of your spectacles. Have you repaired it?

Over and over, I think how you draped your jacket over my shoulders that day and sang, "I love you, Karin," then turned as if I would reject you. Then, I thought to say something witty or pithy, maybe something bold, but instead I said, "That's nice," and your face fell. I should have said I loved you. I would have meant it. I should have gone away with you, but do you believe I thought Paris was the city I'd die in? Here in Loiret, Mother wheezes and cries. Lisette whines. A dull look remains in her eyes. If there is regret, this is the tree it pins its aching dross upon…

ELEGANTLY NAKED IN MY SEXY MENTAL ILLNESS

And to think I thought you thin, and that it would cause a rift between us at the worst of times! Think of it as a girl's foolishness, though it's hard to imagine a girlish bone in my body now. Again, a black note. I'll start again (I put this letter down hours ago, and have just resumed):

It's noon. The overcast sky smells of sulfur, mold, and grit. Out my window, a girl hops in the street with her friend. She's four, maybe five, with scarlet ribbons. Her friend is a new little boy with blue suspenders who follows her every step—if I hadn't been so foolish, she might have been our child… Do you forgive me? I'll pretend you've said yes and that I'm in America with you so Europe can vanish.

The lure of its cobbled walks has faded. If you'd asked me to leave this week instead of before, I'd surely agree, but I'm glad we were able to resolve things that day in Mother's darkroom—though I know I was cruel. Please tell me you forgive me. Tell me I'm still dear to you. My mind plays tricks on me here; I forget flowers, words, names, but never you. I wish I could hold your hands under the stars at the Trevvechio's like we did that June when your sister got the mumps, stealing kisses under the moon, but it's hard to imagine anyone doing such things now, and yellow does not go well with my dresses, of which I have two: One to get married in, and one for other days. The second is in tatters, as you might expect. Think of me fondly. I'll write when I can.

I love you.

Your daisy,

Karin

Charles stepped away from the curb. As always, the closings of her letters burned him since they forever worried he would forget her, he would not think of her, he needed a reminder. He paused in the street, imagining her, creating a melody from her name. Would she look different now, less like a girl? It had been years, he knew—so many things were possible. He smiled, tucking the letter into his pocket and thinking they'd speak French like when they met, the Parisian French that warmed his ears. He hoped she'd notice his manlier build and sharp brown suit, muttering, "I'm no longer thin, Karin," then looking at the concrete sidewalk.

As he scanned the ground, a black Omni zipped past, almost knocking him back. A dull wind swept past his ears. He thanked his stars he'd not been hit. Broken bones were not a good way to spend the winter—bones, bones. What had she said? Not a girlish bone? He doubted it.

Even as he touched her, when he touched her, he'd always feared she'd break. His stomach rumbled. His wool scarf felt too thin to block the wind, even wrapped twice, so he tugged it tighter and crossed the boulevard, regarding the shoddily maintained facades across the way. One had fallen to strike a pedestrian last May. And how typical of New York, he thought—the city was crumbling slowly, like a rock in a milk jar, the old buildings languishing. One after another, historic landmarks dropping like kicked women.

It was sad to visit the once-immaculate churches, rain seeping through their foundations, remaining inside the sacred walls till they swelled and cracked. Structures built for grace and grandeur were lost due to neglect, due to the elements—and he knew how that worked. Nothing lasted forever, not even Rome.

Truthfully, he'd cared little for this notion when he worked for Aberson and Crowl, neck-deep in blueprints for repairs, struggling on shoestring budgets to keep old structures whole—but if only for an ounce of prevention, as his mother often said, they may have been saved. Either way, long-since tired of convincing spendthrift landlords to pay to avert invisible disasters, his new bakery job was a relief. Twisting dough each morning, he felt infinitely lighter.

It was easier to create than to fix. Yes, the bakery job was pleasant, and then each day at noon, because she abhorred anything but midday trains, he went home, put on his dress clothes, and went to the station. But Karin had not yet come. It had been three months, and there had been no more letters, but no matter: He knew where to go.

And his brown suit looked fine with his burgundy dress shoes, which he'd retrieved last fall from a box mistakenly thrown in with older boxes during his move. He considered the callus on his instep, breathing deep to avoid wincing, as he paused beneath an awning to regret his lack of gloves. Thrusting his fingers beneath his scarf, he shivered.

His hands were cold, but reeked of onions and flour and the stray odor of crushed blueberries. His stomach grumbled again. He would eat anything but bread; the bakery had dimmed his taste for it.

Stopping at a hotdog stand, he said, "One dog, please, no bun," and the vendor dropped the steaming morsel into crinkly white paper. He took a bite and closed his eyes, at sway, then looked up to see a black woman in a bright jade dress swaggering toward him on the walk. Huge and boisterous, her hair in a half-blonde, half-ebony weave, she flared like a splash of color swung through the gathering crowd, taking more than her side of the road.

He stepped aside as she smiled, saying, "Well, aren't you handsome, sir! With that flower in your lapel!"

He tipped his hat, noting her red earrings, thinking of several other good omens this morning: An embryo in his breakfast egg; two women walking past in nearly identical red dresses; a hospice worker stopping by with crimson poinsettias; and best of all, a girl playing hopscotch on the street outside the bakery, wearing three scarlet ribbons. He'd watched her while cutting the dough, kneading it with his fingers and thinking: This is the girl Karin told me about. She will come today.

The black woman's earrings were not just red, but glowing

with flashing lights, the kind that held tiny holiday bulbs. This was a good day, a grand one. Still, as he got closer to the station entrance, striding forward, he worried that he'd missed Karin at the station last week. His fever had been 103, and he couldn't leave his building, but, *She didn't come then,* he consoled himself. *You saw no omens that day, Charles. You'll find her.*

He stepped forward from the curb into a chorus of horns.

~

Tamar phoned the doctor at eleven, professing an interest in talking about her father's therapy, but the nurse had left her on hold so as soon as someone got on the line, she was prepared to give her complaints about his case. He'd wandered around lately, she'd say, and he talked to himself while running bizarre errands—but when the doctor finally picked up, "I don't have much of a window to chat, young lady," he announced, spouting some random "we care" message she was sure they'd made him memorize in Putting-Off-Patients School, one that truly translated to "kindly fuck off, and goodbye," because he was, as she well knew, always in a rush.

She tapped her red-enameled nails on her desk. "Listen, I've got a problem. I can't control him from here. Tell me, what should I do, doctor?" she asked, furious at having to waste more work time dealing with her father's lunacy, especially after she'd begged him to stop doing crazy things, to just stay where he should. Inevitably, his only response was to ask who she was and what she was doing there. "Leave me alone!" he'd screamed on more than one occasion.

In some irrational way, as the children of his patients must often do, she'd managed to decide it was the doctor's fault, her father's acting out, his worsening memory. "You see," Tamar told the doctor slowly, "he doesn't know me as his daughter anymore, but my mom is dead, and the other kids won't—" She paused from a clutch of emotion in her throat, trying to think of happy things until finally the constriction loosened. "Not a stitch of help from Eitan. Talia either," she stated. "I just thought you could—"

"What do you want me to do, Tamar?" the doctor asked dryly. "I've heard all this before. Should I drug him until he can't move? Would that suit your lifestyle?"

She played with her paperclip holder, dumping then tossing the clips—only barely repressing the urge to say, "Thanks very much. Yes, that would be good—at least until the Jamison account is finished." Instead, she listened to him wait for her reply and stared out her window.

On the sidewalk, a large black woman hustled down the street in a wild, green dress. *She looks happy*, Tamar thought, but felt listless as the woman peeped through office windows, glancing in to where workers toiled—and Tamar hated the woman then with all her might. Happy woman, easygoing woman. She wanted to hurl something heavy through the plate glass, a brick or a rock perhaps, anything to deter such joy and progress—but "Tamar?" the doctor asked, dragging her attention back to the phone. "Tamar? Are you there? I asked what you want me to do..."

Yes, I'm here, but I'd like to be outside, she thought, *despite the weather, my arms swinging free, wearing an open coat, happy and fat as I please. I'd like to find a—*

"Tamar! Can you hear me?" the doctor asked. "Have we lost connection? You know, I have another appointment in three minutes."

"I hear you just fine, but I don't know what to do, doctor," she finally replied. "Can you at least tell him again that he has to remain in the building? Repeat it a few times. At least do that?"

"That's the problem," the doctor said. "He doesn't have to remain anywhere until he's a danger to himself or others."

"He is!"

"He's a danger to your schedule, but to himself? And Tamar,

you really…because it's in the best interest… If you could hear yourself…have to…busy…father."

Tuning the doctor out, Tamar glared at the black woman, who then fell in a lump to the pavement—as if she'd twisted her ankle or caught her heel in a grate. "Oh no," Tamar said then, returning her eyes to her papers. Guilty.

"Tamar? You could at least —" The doctor yammered on, but she ignored him, watching the woman gingerly rise.

"A big help, as always, doc," she said then, hanging up. "Goddamn HMO vampires." She maintained a brief, acidic pause where she cocked an imaginary rifle, aimed it at the receiver, and fired. "They should all be shot."

~

The black woman—beautiful, blossoming, and bold—Eugenia to distant relations and telemarketers, Genie to friends, was on her way to meet her nephew Truman at the station, but she first had to pick up some dark chocolate. It had been eight years since Truman's last visit, so she wanted to have his candy ready.

Still, the morning had not gone well since she'd fallen, so she hoped the accident would be the worst of her day. Truman, her favorite of her sister's six children, would have loved the chocolate treat, but with an aching back, she sadly reconsidered her options. She'd been having an amazing day, had woken up without a sore back for the first morning in many weeks, then put on the green velvet dress that reminded her of blues festivals in Tennessee, cinching its large, gold-buckled belt as she'd donned the thin, emerald heels, three inches high, and last, her coat. Several scarves had followed, hanging free from her lapel. She'd walked out the door with her jacket unbuttoned, but after the fall, had to close its folds, feeling colder as her vertebrae absorbed the compression from that jarring bump, and the muscles in her back flared.

She pulled a compact from her purse, frowning; her hair, four hours in the salon, had been wrecked, and she looked disheveled, not the perfect Auntie she'd wanted Truman to see. Luckily, a taxi pulled behind her just then, so she got in, regrettably abandoning the chocolate, saying, "Grand Central Station, please," then asking, "Hey driver, do you know if there are chocolates there for sale? My nephew loves chocolates."

"Lady, it's a super-mall these days. You can buy anything there," he said, never glancing up. *He looks Pakistani*, she thought, pondering his tiny, dark eyes; then she noticed how the picture on his license did not resemble him—in fact, was not him—and so she stared out the window, just wanting to get there.

The car had already swung into traffic and wove at breakneck speed through more cautious vehicles. Other New Yorkers could be seen, still waving for taxis—so at least she was in one. "Lord have mercy on my soul," she breathed. "Just get me to the station today."

~

Charles waited on a bench, clicking his heels. It was 1:30, but he hadn't lost hope. It was not that she'd told him specifically when she'd be there, but he cherished the notion of surprising her, an unspoken way of relaying that he remembered her little habits and preferences. He spent enough time at home and at work thinking of her, removed—but the nature of waiting for someone felt more charged when one was seated in the area of their possible arrival, and she could come breezing through those doors, wearing the scent of lavender and freesia, ready to kiss him hello. He adjusted his carnation and glanced at it. The flower was not a bit wilted; it was jubilant even, like a floral maraschino cherry, but still, he could not remove the bud from his buttonhole just yet.

If she walked by and saw him without it, they might never find each other, so he forced his hands down, folded them onto his lap, and listened to a scantily clad woman on a cell phone ranting beside him. Her breasts leached from the sides of a stringy latex top, and she spoke in an exaggerated voice, swinging her nail-bitten hands, and declaring through swollen, plum lips, "Fuck that shit," and, "Fuck him," as a plastic-tipped barbell scraped over her teeth while she listened, and, "Yeah. Yeah," she said. "But a blowjob is definitely out of the question. He can fuck himself if he thinks—"

Charles stopped listening. *Vulgar*, he thought, *but pretty*. She stopped mid-sentence and glared, so he glared back. Then he stood to locate another bench, but, standing, was bumped by a swinging hip in a shade of green so bright it shocked his eyes. The woman he'd seen earlier! Yes, there she was, but now she frowned something fierce. The young woman walked off still hollering into her phone, so he sat back down, nursing his cheek where the hip had ploughed into it.

"Hey you!" the green woman suddenly said. "Sorry I bumped you. Can I sit here?"

~

"I know you don't want to move to New York, Eitan," Tamar said, "but Dad needs you."

"He does not. You're such a baby, Tamar—always whining. He does have a human relation in the city, after all—and that's you. Besides, we'll be down during the holidays."

"December is too far away," she said. "If your wife didn't have you on such a leash—"

"Just call the home. Talk to Papa," Eitan said. "He always remembers you after a while."

"You call the home," she said then, ready to swallow her tongue. "You could at least do that."

ELEGANTLY NAKED IN MY SEXY MENTAL ILLNESS

"Tamar, I'm busy," Eitan said. "I do call the home. Call up Talia if you want to complain. Did I mention my wife is pregnant? And the children are screaming? I've got to go."

She hung up, rapped her knuckles on her desk, then dropped her head. Damn Eitan for always making her feel worse. She dialed again. "Hello? Is Talia there? You busy?"

~

"Hey, I remember you!" the black woman said, grinning and shaking her finger. "All dressed up! You have a hot date? Oh, it's so good to sit! My feet are hurting, and my back, too. I had a bad fall. Almost broke my leg."

"I'm sorry," Charles said. "It's very cold today."

"Sure is," she replied. "Freezing." She dug in her purse for a sack of dried apples and ate them as the crowds rolled by. "Who you waiting for?" she asked. "You know if they sell dark chocolate?"

"Don't know," Charles said. "I'm waiting for my fiancée."

"How nice! Well, I'm Eugenie, and my nephew's coming today, so I wanted to go to that chocolate place up the road from where we met, but my heel got stuck in a gutter, so bad luck, black as a Halloween cat—and I fell, but, oh! The pain is killing me!" She shrugged. "And I'm dyin' to get home and take these shoes off, but not until I find Truman, cause I have to pick him up."

"What time does he come?"

"Least another hour. What did you say your name was?"

"I'm Charles," he said, showing her Karin's photo, "and this is who I'm waiting for."

"She's pretty," the woman said, looking close at the photo. "You sure she'll be on this train?"

"I hope so," he said. "I've been waiting a long time."

"What'll she wear?"

"Oh, I don't know," he said, worried again. "I didn't ask."

"Well," the woman said, letting her warm, apple-scented breath linger close to his face. "Don't fret. And don't worry yourself about it none, Charles. I'll help you look."

He was about to reply, but just then she saw the chocolate store, so darted off, shouting, "I'll be right back," scuffling away in her high, high heels.

~

"You say he was here earlier, but he left around noon?" Tamar asked, her nerves stretched as tightly as the fabric strips on the potholder looms she saw in the craft workshop.

"Yes, ma'am," the old lady said. "But he's gone now."

"And you don't know where he is?" Tamar's gaze flitted past the entry hall where a few ladies sat, bent over, making decorative things—but when she looked too close, a lady in a mauve polka-dot dress spotted her and shouted, "Emmaline!" gesturing frantically. Though Tamar did not know the woman, she smiled sardonically, thinking: *At least someone recognizes me*, and cursed her father again.

The lady at the desk had still not replied. "Listen, lady," she said, "I just want to visit my father and leave. You sure you don't know where he is?" The smell of cooked cabbage drenched the halls, but the woman at the desk was impervious, her hair done immaculately, her eyes vacant. She just smiled and said, "I remember he mumbled something about the station, earlier. You might try him there."

"What station?" Tamar asked, wishing the woman had a speed dial like a record player. The other woman who'd called out to her was determinedly grabbing her walker, ready to approach.

"Grand Central, of course," Ms. Desk said.

"And how," Tamar asked concisely, "will I know where to look?"

"Can't help you with that, missy," Ms. Desk said, tonguing a fissure between her dentures and gums, then sucking her teeth tight to murmur, "Don't know. I suppose you could wait here if you want, being that it just started to snow—going out'll get mighty cold. Just look out the window."

Tamar glanced to see the flurries drifting with unnatural quiet. Already the roads were salted, and it would be bad walking weather, but the crazy old bird still waved and called out. "Thanks," Tamar told the secretary. "I'll find my way out."

She hurried to the street, shivering as the snow fell in flakes at her feet, twisting and dancing in the wind. She felt like a tiny person in a life-sized snow dome then, and, "Papa," she said with a rare burst of exuberance, one of the few expressions he'd taught her as a girl, "*Voila! La neige!*"—Look, the snow!

To her left was a French bakery and a French boutique, and *how à propos*, she thought, but in the resale boutique window she saw a dress that stopped her, a retro number with three-quarter-length sleeves and a modest sweeping neckline. It was beautiful. The color was brighter than her dull slacks and pale yellow blouse but would look fine under her black trench.

Eying the mannequin's matching jewelry, she craved the entire outfit, and thought: *This will please him when I see him.* After all, her father had always said, "You look better in jewel tones, Tammie. More radiant with that dark hair." She walked into the boutique as if lured, pushing down the ugly thought that he still might not recognize her.

Inside the store, she peeked at the outfit when a salesgirl sashayed up in a short summer dress. *What an odd outfit for the season*, Tamar thought, but simultaneously found herself longing for the energy displayed by the pure light color and also by the black woman's ensemble on the boulevard earlier. Still, thank God, the boutique dress wasn't green or white! "Would you like to try it on?" the salesgirl asked.

"I'd love to," Tamar said, surprising herself.

The dress did fit, as if made for her, the sleeves and hem perfect, but after a quick tour in the fitting room, she realized she had only pale pink lipstick to wear. Luckily the boutique had a burgundy one under glass, so she put it on her bill. She applied the scented wax to her lips, which smelled of flowers. *So romantic*, she thought, looking at herself. *So different*. Like her time spent before the mirror that morning.

There seemed a softer crook to her stubborn chin. Even the dress had come from a different era, a different time. Tamar handed the girl her credit card and applied mascara, muttering softly, almost as if in prayer, "I'd like to be seen today. I'd like to be known."

"*Et pourquoi pas?*" the salesgirl said with fabricated mirth. "You look *magnifique!* There are shoes that match the dress, too! Do you want them? Size seven and a half, narrow... Oh, and a purse."

Tamar's feet were at least an eight, but staring at the carmine shoes with fluted leather, she bought them anyway, shoving her toes into their narrow berth. She did not buy the purse though, because its clasp was broken. According to her mother, now gone ten years, a broken clasp always augured lost things.

She'd lost too much already.

~

Charles saw the black woman's nephew a mile away, waving and whooping. *How happy they look*, he thought, and Eugenie was shouting and jumping, too, but awkwardly, because under her right arm was the sack of chocolates, which she held tenderly and offered as the young man arrived.

"Auntie Genie!" he called, sweeping her up in his ropy arms. "I hope you haven't waited long?"

"Not long, Truman," she said. "Gorgeous boy! You ready for New York?"

"Sure am." Truman said, tearing at the bag of chocolates, "I love New York!" He was humming and saying, "Thank you, Auntie!" through his full mouth as Charles watched. When he swallowed, the young man said fondly, "You look young as my sister, Auntie. Even thinner than before!"

"Don't lie to this old bag, chile," she said, "and don't eat yourself sick." Then she noted Charles' eyes watching them, and so introduced him. "Truman, this here's Charles. He helped me look for you, so say hello."

"'Lo, Charles," Truman said through chocolatey teeth.

"Hello," Charles said and waved but looked away as Eugenie asked, "How's your mother, boy? Mind if we sit a minute?" He pulled out Karin's letter, scouring it again and wondering when she would arrive. Time was ticking.

He began to doubt himself, churlish in his disappointment, but when he glanced up again, he saw a fantastic sight coming toward him. As she neared, his eyes widened. It was her, same as before, walking closer with that slow, clumsy gate, stumbling in her shoes.

"Karin," he said, standing with open arms. "I do love you. I miss you. I truly do."

~

Tamar had walked the terminal for the better part of twenty minutes; the crowds had saddened and amused her. As always at train stations, she felt a sense of nostalgia, such passionate comings and goings.

For a moment, she feared finding her father, watching with envy as a little girl in a blue coat rushed out to greet her waiting mother. Tamar had no such sweet reunion to anticipate, only her father's lack of recognition, the stale companionship she received at her stilted office job, or the clutching frenzy of old, desperate people in the home. She needed a young man in her life—even a brief, passionate affair. She looked down and blushed. These were not normal thoughts.

Though her shoes were too small, causing her pain as she walked, she felt unusually beautiful on this day, like a hothouse flower, and noticed the eyes of men upon her, especially those of a dark-complected man in a beige suit. She smiled and winked; he grinned and waved. In this renovated station, wearing her vintage dress, she felt out of time. Hundreds of children roamed free on the platforms, warming her with their bustle. The crowds seemed friendly and familiar, not hostile. She started to realize that, in many ways, she did not want to find her father at all, not until she got back her chilled demeanor.

Nonetheless, she roamed aimlessly across the crowds, stopping her hesitant, swivel-walk only when she saw a familiar emerald dress and its larger-than-life wearer. Curiously, she neared. Was it that woman? It was! And she stood not thirty yards away, a mocha-colored man beside her.

Beside him was an older man in a brown suit, holding out his arms. Her eyes throbbed as they recognized the familiar face. *Papa*, she thought, *I've found you*, but she said nothing, afraid her voice would break the tenuous spell.

~

Charles called to her even before she arrived, but as she neared, he fell quiet. What might he say, he wondered, that her beautiful dress reminded him of one she'd worn in Normandy? That she looked exactly as she had then, a free spirit on the sand, as if the sea breeze had ripped her tension away, leaving her hair to float on her shoulders, uneven and marvelous, as it had years ago? No trace of ripped seams lingered on her dress, and this relieved him.

She's here, he thought, *finally here—with me.* He remembered her question: "Why can we not suspend time and unwrap it at will?" *We can, Karin*, he thought. *You're here, and I'm here*, but just then, Eugenie shouted, "Hey, Charles. There's Karin. Look at her!" patting his back with quick, heavy thumps, and he grinned at her vigilance.

"Yes, there she is," he said, still reluctant to speak. But when Karin drew close, he wrapped his arms around her, inhaling her flowery scent. The aroma was not freesia and lavender, but sweat mixed with musk. She'd changed her perfume, and he was glad. Out with the old. In with the new. He'd always known change was inevitable.

~

When Tamar saw him not ten feet away, her heart heaved. His arms were akimbo. He looked so happy that her eyes teared up immediately, and it had been so long since he'd looked at her with any kind of pleasure that a blast of guilt stabbed her like a knife for her absences over the past five years. How petulant she'd been. How unforgiving. "Remember me?" she asked, rubbing her nose in the decaying fabric of his suit's lapel as she leaned in. She almost called him Papa in the old affectionate way, but paused, still afraid to speak. This was a moment to think of the future, to start again, to be silent.

With kinder eyes, she noticed how silver his hair looked around his aged face—how wonderful he looked. He loved her. He knew her. She would be fine.

In that moment, she smiled so widely that everything seemed to glow in her sight and she was glad she'd worn the dress, glad she'd left work early—even glad that she, of all her siblings, had stayed in New York. His aloof French regret at his children's Hebrew names no longer bothered her. His apathetic love. His hard, merciless character.

Tamar tucked her head into his shoulder, reminded of days in that dusty paper factory where he met her mother before receiving his degree, when he'd taught her to waltz on the factory floor during his thirty-minute lunches. She had stood on his shoes.

He held something in his hand, an ancient paper, as he hugged her tight, but her elation started and lasted long after he let it slip from his shaking fingers, long after she flung her arms around his midsection again and squeezed with all her might, right up until he pressed his dry lips to hers, like a lover, declaring sentimentally, "Like peaches, Karin. Your lips are peaches." She did not move, not even when he stepped back and said, "Am I too thin? Do you find me thin now?"

Tamar could not respond, only partially glad that the black woman and the young man had not seen this exchange. She was mortified: *Her father's lips on hers—passionately.* There was nothing to be said. To her right, a bag lady approached with a basket of kittens. There was one blind kitten in the basket. Tamar fixed her eyes on its mewling face, knowing it could not see her, then stood very still as if her feet were weighted, crossing and uncrossing her arms. "Karin," he'd said. *Who was he talking about, and who was he talking to?*

"Ah, you've found each other," the black woman said. "Your Karin." and Tamar wanted to punch her so hard those little green pumps would fly off her feet, but the young man dipped between the two of them just then and handed Tamar the paper her father had dropped. "Excuse me, miss," he said. "I think your father dropped this."

"Thank you," she said, but her father shouted, "She is not my daughter, sir. She is not my daughter!" so the young man looked away.

Tamar lifted the letter. At the top-right corner was a date, one year before he'd married her mother. *Like peaches, Karin,* she thought, *your lips*—and she realized she did know that name, remembered hushed whispers heard just once or twice in her lifetime: Karin. The one her mother hated. The one her mother never quite measured up to.

In the here, in the now, her father beamed. "I am so happy to see you, Karin!" he said. "Did you have a good trip?"

"Papa," she told him, unable to restrain herself. "I'm Tamar, your daughter."

"I don't have a daughter," he said. "Don't joke, Karin. You know I'm not fond of jokes. Aren't you glad to see me? *Alors! Tu m'as manqué! Est-ce—*"

But when he switched to French, Tamar stopped listening. Still, in his eyes was such a misty look that she found it hard to shift her gaze away. Then anger welled in her, pressing like a vise, and his happy face caused her to shout, "I'm your daughter. Tammie, old man. Tamar. Remember? Not Karin!"

His posture drooped, and he squinted through an old pair of glasses marred by a crack in the lens. He asked softly, "Must you be so mean, my love? I don't tease you."

"No, Papa," Tamar insisted. "Karin is gone. She's gone. I'm Tammie!"

He did not speak.

"I know what happened to Karin, and so do you," Tamar said, willing herself to stop, but at the same time, unable to. "Remember JoJo Klein's letter, Papa?" She closed her eyes as she pictured the places she'd visited six years ago on that long, sad vacation across Europe. She remembered regarding the piles of shoes, the unfinished mattresses stuffed with human hair, and the photographs of watches and jewels. She remembered, too, looking in terror at showerheads where gas leaked out near high windows. "I am not Karin," she shouted hysterically. "I am not!"

"Then I don't know you," he insisted with a trembling voice, and she said, "After Loiret, Karin went to Drancy, Papa, then from Drancy to Auschwitz. Remember? You never heard from her again."

"Auschwitz," her father replied, staggering with a black look. His face dipped between his hands, his proud head drooped, and he sat on the bench as tears leaked through his closed fingers, covering his eyes. It was the first time she'd ever seen him cry, and it was painful to watch.

She wanted to throw herself somewhere closed and dark for saying what she had, but, "Please, Papa," she begged, "forgive me. I won't say it again."

He had no comfort for her. She stared at the quivering shadow of a face beneath his hands, and gingerly caressed his silver-white hair.

The black woman and the young man were now watching them intently, but her father did not move. His shoulders remained bent until he looked up again at the clock before searching the crowd. He no longer registered Tamar, and she felt five again, exactly how she remembered after the first time she'd lied to him when he'd turned his back, refusing to speak to her for weeks. The shame had grown in her heart then, like a briar thorn, and how angry he'd been. "My daughter should not lie to me!" he'd bellowed. "I want nothing to do with you. Talk to your mother if you must tell lies—but do not talk to me!"

She wanted to feel angry at him for how much he'd hurt her over such tiny things, but his tears had stolen her rage. He was so broken, and then he was nothing, floating off as if she'd never spoken. She knew she was nothing to him then—and this frightened her, realizing as she did that he would not try to speak to her again. This, if nothing else, prodded her action. "I'm Karin, Charles," she said, forcing herself to speak. "And I can visit you often, but you can't kiss me again because I've married. Just last year."

Her heart broke to say these things, but her father looked up brightly like a lit Menorah. "Of course you've married!" he said. "I didn't expect you to wait for me, Karin. I always thought you'd fall for someone else."

"Then, let's go," Tamar said. "I'll tell you everything in the cab. How I've missed you, P—Charles. Have you missed me?"

"Yes," he said, "I have. Desperately." His fingers traced a

serpentine pattern in her palm before he said, "You're the only woman I ever loved."

Tamar tripped on a tile and nearly fell, wanting to shout, *How could you? How dare you do that to Mama?* but she said nothing, letting her tears blur her sight until they cleared the rims of her eyes.

"Don't cry, my dear," he said. "It's not your fault. If you loved someone more it's only natural, but please stop crying. It pains me to see you this way."

"I've changed my name to Tammie," she said. "So you must stop calling me Karin."

"Tammie," he said. "A vulgar, American name. I liked Karin better." He spoke conversationally, dismissively, and her heart burned.

"Well, that's my name," she said harshly. "So I want you to use it." She softened as she noticed that he watched her in a way that made her feel young again and proud, like a beautiful, different Jewish girl, able to turn him away with a flick of her wrist.

Still, she felt battered by the wind and cold, as if naked in the crowd, while pretending to be someone else—Karin, not Tamar; not Tammie, Karin. She lost her identity in that instant, but it didn't matter. She had the rest of her life to be someone he'd never loved, and the rest of his life to be someone he did.

And it was no small consolation, she realized suddenly, that she could finally know his true self, the one who longed for a lover she'd never met, the lover he'd turn to while dying or losing his mind—the lover who stayed fresh in the vaulted halls of his memory like a summer rose in a New York winter. And, she thought then, shivering with cold: *Throw it up in the air like a coin. Toss it. Which would you choose?* She'd already made her choice in the instant she sat across from him on the bench, after speaking the name of that horrible city, pleading for his gaze, hungry for it, but invisible.

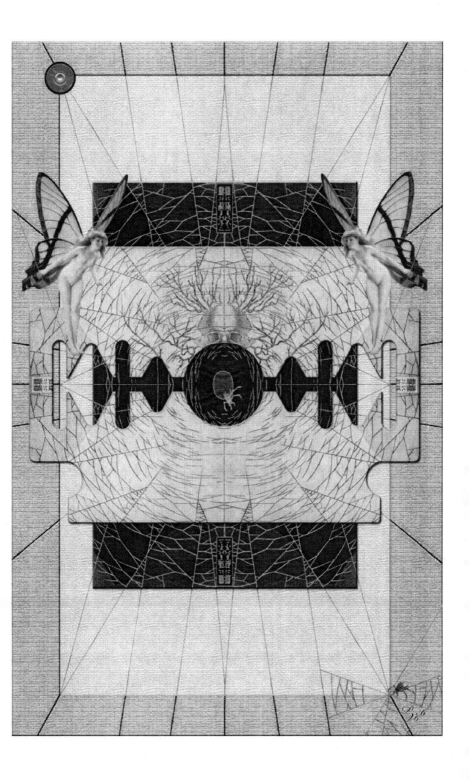

THE GRAY FAIRY

Hesther says there's a gray fairy she hears when she's alone. But she hears this fairy other times, too, like when she's with me. Hesther is seventeen, though you wouldn't know it. She looks twelve. Wearing her long Goth dresses, her light brown hair hanging to her waist, no makeup, it's easy to mistake her for a child who found a trunk in the attic and played dress-up with her grandmother's clothes, but Hesther is far more grown up at other times. Her wrists are scarred from the three times the Gray Fairy outsmarted her caretakers.

With me, or people like me, Hesther can walk and bike, but she cannot drive, or be driven, unless absolutely necessary. This is because she will sometimes try to throw herself out of cars. She cannot be alone in public restrooms, either—because this is where she tried to slit her wrists. Thus, if one of us has to go to the bathroom, we use the handicap stall that is large enough for us to look at each other. A suicide watch breeds a special sort of intimacy. She has no personal privacy. She has small blue eyes rimmed with short, blonde lashes. At five-foot-one, she is a skeleton of a girl, indentations where her bones create their imprints without padding. Like ballerinas who dance too hard or live on air, she has no breasts to speak of. Her face is delicate, as if someone importuned to press upon her cheeks would cause a crumble of dust—a ready pink debris of sugar shard.

Everywhere Hesther goes, she is accompanied. When I take vacation days, someone replaces me. If her family wasn't so well-off, Hesther might have killed herself ages ago. Or the Gray Fairy would have killed her. She tells me everything the Gray Fairy communicates. The Gray Fairy tells her to take the blade from her father's razor and score her wrists. The Gray Fairy tells her to drink a large glass of water and down it with a bottle of her mother's pills. The Gray Fairy tells her, too, to take a coat hanger and jam it inside her until she cleans out all the dirty matter the Gray Fairy is certain rests up there. "There are webs, spider webs," the Gray Fairy says. "You have to clean them out."

She was not born into this family; an orphan, she left Romania at the age of five, but you do not hear the foreign strains in her voice now. I have worked for the family for seven months, and though this employ is low on actual hard labor, it is daunting, every day, to keep such a close eye on this slip of a girl. My job is both to watch Hesther, every moment, exhausted or not, and to convince Hesther not to listen to this Gray Fairy. It's a strange job, but the psychology of the fairy is quite interesting.

Sometimes Hesther's face takes on a conniving look and she lets the Gray Fairy speak to me. Most days, we plan picnics and go through her home-school materials, but it is a strangely sterilized space in which Hesther lives. There are no knives and no glass. Since the pills incident, there are no pills; since the hanger incident, only felt-wrapped hangers or rounded plastic hangers, not that Hesther couldn't break apart and use one of those, but clothes can't be left on the floor because her mother considers it gross, so some kind of hanger must be available.

All the packaging for items bought is cardboard. And soft plastic. Sometimes cling wrap. In the fridge and freezer, foods are those that do not need to be cut, easy-use items like sliced lunchmeat, bread, strawberries, apples, sliced deli cheese, sauces, carrots, and microwavable food. Hesther insists the Gray Fairy says her parents are out to poison her.

All day, I argue with the Gray Fairy. Example:

Her: The Gray Fairy says she has no idea why they take away all things they think I'll use to hurt myself. Don't they know those sauces in the fridge could be used for broken glass and I could simply poke my jugular? Don't look away, Sarah. I could do that in less than a minute.

Me: But you won't do that. Remember that the Gray Fairy is bad. She doesn't want you to live. She doesn't love you. What can we do to kick her out of our games today?

Her: The Gray Fairy doesn't want to be kicked out of our games.

Me: Can you tell her to go away now so that we can spread out the picnic blanket together?

Her: The Gray Fairy says that it would only take one roll of cling wrap, wrapped around my head to do me in. She says you could help if you wanted.

Me: Hesther? Hesther! Please come back to me today. The Gray Fairy is not welcome.

But Hesther thinks the Gray Fairy is beautiful. She wishes she could fly like her. Even on good days, when the Gray Fairy is nowhere to be found, she dreams of soaring on glimmering wings. The Gray Fairy might be beautiful, but she has an ugly voice. When Hesther lets the fairy speak through her mouth, the Gray Fairy's voice gives me chills.

It is springtime. I have been contracted by the family through the summer; Hesther and I are to go out and purchase swimsuits today. The Gray Fairy has been gone for a week. I appreciate this because when Hesther and I are on outings, I seem a few cards short of a full deck when I start arguing with the Gray Fairy and consoling Hesther.

I'm not a psychologist. Sometimes, we talk so clearly and

avidly about the Gray Fairy, though I know she's not real, I do start to feel distinctly like there are two people sharing Hesther's body—Hesther, who is naturally sweet and retiring, and the Gray Fairy, who is morbid and constantly dreams up new ways for Hesther to off herself. Today, I get Hesther dressed and I tell her we need to go for an outing, so she wears a pair of tomato-red shorts and a white-and-black-striped tank top.

When we get in the car, she says, "The Gray Fairy doesn't want us to get a swimsuit."

"Yes, she wants you to have a swimsuit," I say.

"The Gray Fairy says I'm too small for swimsuits," Hesther says.

I can't help it. I'm tired of the fairy and wondering how terribly this trip to the store will go, so I say, clicking the blinker to switch lanes, "Doesn't the Gray Fairy love death by water? How easy would that be?"

But Hesther starts to cry. Clearly, she's here today. "I'm sorry, Hesther," I say. "I didn't mean to hurt you."

Hesther pulls at the belt loops on her shorts. "You'll be sorry for saying that," she says.

"I probably will," I agree, but we buy her a lovely lime-green swimsuit for the family's trip to Cancun. The outing goes off without a hitch. When we get home, Hesther wants to go to her room.

"Don't look at me," she says, knowing I cannot stop.

"Tell me about the Gray Fairy," I suddenly say. "Tell me where the Gray Fairy came from. Is she Romanian?"

"No," Hesther says. "My mother knows who she is. She comes from a blackness. She lives in a blackness."

I haven't spent much time talking to Hesther's mother. As a family, this one is strange in that they move around one another in this big house, and when I am here, I am here for the daughter.

"I'm taking a nap," Hesther says. Within an hour, I have watched her twist and turn and finally fall asleep.

I know I shouldn't, but I take a stroll into the main rooms. In one room, her father has motorcycle manuals, sports magazines, and a computer and a desk. Her father interests me. He is a tall man I cannot remember ever hearing say a word. I lean into his piles of things, staring at the hobby items he buys that clearly go unused. And then I see something. There is a clutch of children's books beside some baseball gloves and a hockey stick.

On one of them is a terrible fairy. A gray fairy. This fairy is stick and bones. She wears a horrific grimace. *Tales from Dark Fairy Land*, the book says.

I take it and enter Hesther's room. I am reading about the gray fairy as she sleeps, her breath light and measured. When Hesther wakes, I ask her about the book: "Hesther, does the Gray Fairy come from here?"

Her face is furious. She pulls her mouth into a pinch and turns away. I am given my notice the next day. Two-day notice, but to be paid for two weeks. "I'm so sorry," her mother says. "We know how hard it is to find good care. But, I have to let you go."

Her mother is a small blonde woman. They hire all their helpers in the local help-wanted mag. I can only imagine who next will be watching Hesther's light face, talking to her about this fairy she hears clearly.

"Does her therapist talk to her about the Gray Fairy?" I ask.

Hesther's mother looks at me in surprise. "Yes, he does," she answers.

"What does he suggest?"

"He suggests the fairy is a figment from her time in the orphanage," her mother says. I go get the book. I press it into her mother's hands. I tell the mother the only useful thing I might have learned. "Hesther says the fairy does not come from Romania. I don't know what this means."

Hesther's mother wears a white blouse with long silk sleeves and a prim neckline, fully buttoned. She wears a slim blue skirt, beige nylons, and cream pumps. Despite the air conditioning, her fingers play at the buttons on her neck and she releases a few. "It's a condition," her mother says. "A depression, of sorts."

As I'm leaving I can't help but wonder if Hesther will wear that green suit in Cancun and find a way to dart under the waves, quickly, silently, like how she once slit her wrists in that Nieman Marcus. How will her caretaker keep her close, unless with a leash? I did enjoy the easy check, but must admit it a great relief to never speak of the Gray Fairy again, to never watch that thin girl, to leave those unhappy lives back where I found them.

Next, I will watch a happy old lady who needs only board games and cooked meals. This will require me to sit in a hot apartment and listen to her heyday stories about touring as a musician, but I will think about Hesther. Does she still wander through that house in strange, ill-fitting dresses? Does she still not eat and listen to the voice that tells her all manner of strange things? Is she on medication? Who is her therapist? Why did I never take her to an appointment? Is he, too, an illusion?

I will think about the dark, silent father, and the strange, Victorian mother. I will think about that day when the mother fiddled with the buttons at her neck and the long, slim scar I glimpsed there as she shifted in her seat.

And the Gray Fairy—is it her mother? Is it her father? Is it the virtual neglect she has lived with for so long, in the care of strangers? Hesther was an orphan once. Maybe each of these entities has for her the same index for reality. But the little blonde girl in her big airy house will continue to be watched.

It is not my job to keep her safe. Not anymore. And I couldn't do it now, even if I'd do it for free. It is a foolish thing I do next, but I buy chiffon and tulle remnants in pink, orange, green, and yellow. I buy pieces of every whispering, sheer fabric I can find at the store and I have the basketful delivered to Hesther's door.

I am watching from my car as it arrives. Inside the basket is my note: "There are more than gray fairies, Hesther. Look, they come in many colors. Sarah."

Hesther looks around for me when she reads this. She doesn't find my car in the patch of woods where I'm parked, watching from binoculars. Her face tilts up as if she perceives a new register of sound. *The Gray Fairy*, I think. *Talking to her.*

Hesther rips up my note and shoves the basket outside until she can close the door. I keep watching. A minute later, she opens the door in tears and grabs an armful of the fabric to her wet face, touching each piece softly and bringing the basket in—but no sooner has she done this than she again pushes the whole thing beyond the doorstep, angrily, and kicks at the basket's wooden weave.

Watching with great confusion is a caretaker, a young girl like me in close proximity, talking in silent clips, for I can see her mouth moving and her confounded posture, along with Hesther's furious reactions. Hesther's face screws up and snarls. Hesther's face cries and smiles. Hesther's face goes through all of its contortions.

Hesther picks up the colored fabric again, a lime-green piece, touching it gingerly, appreciatively with her bony fingers. She looks out toward the trees where my car is parked, still not seeing me. She presses it to her face. She sinks to her knees.

I watch her. I watch it all. Then I drive away.

TIGER MAN

The Greatest
WONDER
of the Age

TIGER MAN

"You know what your problem is, Terry?" Jane asked, crooking her finger in that annoying way. "You're too nice! I don't want to break up. I just want to fight. Fight! You hear me?" He rubbed mentholated cream on his chest and stared at the gap between her teeth as she said, unwilling to give up, "I mean, get a little riled."

She was seated on the bed and sanded her foot with a pumice stone, craning her face to stare at him. He watched her breasts shake back and forth inside a small, flimsy bra. Below her chest, her beige slacks pinched a sliver of flesh. He was more interested in the view down her white poet's shirt where through her ripped brassiere and beneath the aqua lace, a round dot of nipple made a pulsing period of pink.

"And Terry, you…" He was not really listening. He noticed, beneath the shadows of her shirt, that her body had that odd, patterned look that sunbathing gave women, especially women with bikinis, patches of white and darker tan appearing like opposite coordinates. Two daubs of sunburn appeared on her upper shoulders. She smelled of Noxzema. As he watched the stipple of nipple bounce, foot dust flying, she went on, "Another thing, Terry. I am tired of your limited attention. I should be your main interest. Are you listening?"

He was not. As beguiling as her nipple was, it was a spot of gold on a bland and empty road. In fact, he had more interest in whether it would rain tomorrow, and why he didn't have a wife like Salvatore's down the road; Salvatore's, who served dinners piping hot each night, wearing that soft look, and maintaining that delicious sense of closeness she always exuded when she went out with her man. Comparably, Jane was wretched.

He had one question: Had Jane always bored him? Had he always bored her? In honesty, she had not, but thinking of that time was like thinking of a kingdom twice removed, in a land far away. Through the window, he saw foxgloves and dianthus but inhaled only the pungent mint of his mentholated skin.

Jane's fingers twitched. She waited, gripping the pumice loosely before beginning another bout of exfoliation. "Well, what do you think of all this?" she asked. "Fight. Let's fight."

"Let's not," he said.

"Listen, Terry," she said. "We will fight. Now."

He wanted to roam to the avenue and drink a latte, maybe stop at the hotel bar on Genser for a rum and Coke, but "Fight?" he asked finally. "You want to fight?"

"Yes," she said. "Exactly."

We never communicate, he thought. *We always fight! You avoid me each time I try to touch you, and we fight without speaking as often as we breathe—and if you don't know that, we're in bigger trouble than I thought!* In his mental vehemence, his lip quivered, but to her, much calmer, he said, "About what? Fight about what?" as if he too had suffered a lapse in integral memory. He focused on her pumice-battered feet to ask his second question, "And then what? After we fight?" On her heels, the whorls of skin prints were all but hidden by the dusty opaque of dead cells.

"What? Anything. Fight. Make-up. And then fuck. Fight, make-up, fuck. Understand?"

"I have to do the ledgers," he announced, "so I'm sorry." *Stodgy ass*, he thought to himself, of himself. He'd spoken to her just like he would a client. He walked to his closet, and she followed him just long enough to yank a beige sweater over her head, blonde curls springing up, and say, "Then find another wife." And she left.

If she can walk out, he thought, *so can I*. He would not give in. Instead, he pulled on his green winter parka. Mint ointment stuck to the fleece, and he peeled the fuzz from his chest hair as he walked away from the apartment and down to the business district. Heart pounding, adrenaline driving, *I am leaving*, he thought as he strutted, but soon forgot what made him so angry. It was possible, he realized, to feel so distant from a relationship for so long that negative conversations were simply redundant.

If, for example, she had said, "Terry, I love you. You look so handsome," he'd still be reeling, thinking about it again and again, maybe blushing in the old way and out to get her flowers. But her discontent was so pervasive, it warranted no further thought.

He ducked into the local bookstore. Passing the window, he saw a book entitled *City Men, Emasculated*. On the cover were a man's granite balls, separated from an iron phallic sculpture. He winced. The separation looked painful. One hundred thousand copies sold, the jacket advertised. *Balls and penis separated*, was all he thought.

He walked in, and picked up the book. "The problem in today's society," the author Dr. H.P. Ballis announced, "is that men have hunter-gatherer genes, and nowhere to hunt or gather. Forced into monogamy, they—"

Terry had just begun to dip his head for a deeper read when a wholesome clerk pointed a sensor gun at him like a small, denuded orchid, saying, "Sir, you can't take that book from the display."

"Just a second," Terry said.

"There are plenty of copies on the shelf," the clerk said. "Please leave the display copy where it is."

"I will not," he said and read aloud: "In the cement infrastructures of downtown, in the land of the suburb, men are resigned to planting herb gardens and mowing lawns. Unmanned by society, they cannot be their true selves. Whereas, women—"

"Sir, I must insist," she said.

"Are distinctly more demanding in the modern context," Terry pointedly concluded. He shut the book, dog-earing the page, and wandered into the coffee bar to stare at his indistinct reflection in the espresso machines. What would the clerk do? Call the cops? He hadn't left the store and by God, he would buy the display model. He should get a discount, but he wouldn't haggle.

"Good," he said, and shouted, "I'll buy this book and a double cappuccino, low-fat." He considered having a Bacardi at the hotel afterwards, two or three Bacardis, but didn't want to walk. He continued reading the book as he left, sipping his coffee, almost stumbling over an uneven curb.

The wind was pleasant on his face, but he coughed, fighting a slight cold. At the park up the street, the swaying trees and shouts of children playing in the sandbox were calming—until he saw a girl in a purple headband pour a bucket of sand over a smaller boy's head. He wondered if Jane's, like the little girl's, main purpose in life was to give men difficulty.

What made it worse was that he'd always been the kind of boy girls trusted with their purses. It seemed incredibly unfair that he was meant for an easy life with women, yet didn't have one, and lately, bit by bit, had begun to hate them. They smiled, yes? They made things comfortable. They seemed to answer too many questions at once and pose them back with flourish—but it was only once they owned you, once they sunk their talons into to-do lists and home repair that they became the bane of man's existence. And why argue over details like socks askew from the hamper or counter crumbs?

ELEGANTLY NAKED IN MY SEXY MENTAL ILLNESS

With the chest cream aiding his breathing, he swung his arms and kept moving forward, then looked at his watch. Jane would be in the shower, washing her hair. By the time he returned, she may not have even realized he was gone, so, "This is silly," he told himself. "I have work to do. I have to get home," but, reluctant to leave, he sat on a park bench and read more of the book.

When he got home, Jane sat in front of the TV, her hair turbaned in a towel. "Hi," she said. "Did you have a nice walk?"

"The problem with men," he announced, "is that they cannot be their primal selves in today's society."

"Did you get condoms while you were out?" she asked. "Not that I want sex, but there aren't any."

He craned his neck to see *Casablanca* flash across the screen and notice Jane's eyes. There they were, wet with longing for Bogart, not even noticing him. Upstairs, he opened a computer spreadsheet. The boxes were lovely and plain, so plain his eyes could follow their grids forever back and forth across the page. He loved how gently the arrow keys swayed the little black box across dividers. Swaying, bouncing—he then got an erection, remembering Jane's bouncing breasts, but did not picture her face: Lately, she was safer to conceptualize in parts.

"Jane," he called, "Jane, are we done fighting?" He received no reply. "Jane?"

He walked downstairs. "See," he said, pointing to the bulge. "The fight worked. I am now my true self."

"You have a hard-on," she said. "That's all."

"We fought, and I forgive you," he said, magnanimous.

She flipped the channel to an infomercial on implants that seized her attention. "You call that a fight? That was barely a disagreement. Go away, Terry," she said, but the next morning when he woke, her hands were glued to his face.

Hair mussed, eyes half-open, she scrutinized his face like a bad fortune, a fortune that says nothing specific, like, "If you make the right choice, you will be rich." She checked him for fever, running her fingers through his hair. He suddenly intrigued her.

"You were pushing me away last night," she said. "All night. Are you all right?"

He felt like a primate-grooming partner, an ape she would tend to and pick morsels from, so he did not open his eyes again and pretended to lapse back into sleep, waiting, waiting patiently—and then, shouting at the top of his lungs, "AAAAAAAAAAHHHHH!"

She fell off the bed. When she got up, she smacked him in the face, screaming, "What did you do that for? What did you do that for?"

"I don't know," he lied. "To surprise you?"

She glared and froze him with her eyes. At work, he asked Frank, "Do you think I'm boring? Jane wants to fight because she says I'm boring."

"Women," Frank said. "They want you to be Mr. Sensitive, then Tarzan. Tarzan, Mr. Sensitive, Tarzan, Mr. Sensitive. No matter which way you go, you're screwed. Go caveman, and you get: A sexist pig, outmoded, and an overt representation of 'the man.' Go sensitive flower, and you're emasculated for not being a bodice-ripping Fabio. Women inspire personality disorders." Frank was right, but Terry noticed he had a disturbingly long hair poking from his earlobe.

"Women!" Terry said, wanting his grooming kit. "I hate them." He paused, took a sip of his coffee. "Frank, did you know you've got a hair sticking out of your ear?"

"I know. Flame likes it. Says it's natural."

Flame! Frank's annoying girlfriend. All day Terry had been picturing those granite balls disembodied from that iron penis, and suddenly her name was a connection to that picture. He hadn't met her and didn't want to. Even so, at least she wanted Frank to be natural. "You are right!" Terry affirmed. "Don't ever cut it off. Never cut it off, man!"

Frank was surprised. "Okay, man. I won't."

And the balls need the penis, Terry thought. *The penis needs the balls.* But he found himself staring at Frank's abhorrent ear hair and picturing a jungle of vaginas instead.

Jane was cooking when Terry came home. *Bodice-ripping Fabio,* he thought, saying, "Honey, I'm home," kissing her and ripping open her blouse. The tear of silk was liberating.

But Jane said, "Terry! What the fuck are you doing? This is a two-hundred-dollar blouse! My God! It's ruined." Backing away, he tried to remember why he'd done it. Then he decided to do it some more.

She held up a spatula to ward him off.

"Ooohooo," he said. "A spatula. Hit me!" He lifted her onto the island and kissed her again, which she seemed to enjoy, at least partially, until the scent of burnt garlic filled the air. "Great!" she said. "Dinner's ruined, and you sat me on the cutting board where I chopped onions."

Suddenly, he wanted to toss her down. "Maybe I can't be who you want me to be, Jane," he said.

She said, "Yes, you can, baby. Go into the living room."

I am not her baby, he told himself, wandering to the bedroom to change into the bleach-stained sweats she hated.

His phone rang. It was Frank. "Hey man, want to go to a sweat lodge?" he asked.

"Jane's cooking."

"So?"

"She'll be mad," Terry said.

"She wanted to fight, didn't she?"

Terry wavered.

"Come on! She wanted you to fight," Frank said. "So, start a fight! Let's go."

"All right. Meet me out front."

Terry looked back toward the kitchen as he ran out; Jane, wearing a "Kiss the Cook" apron, squinted at bell-shaped pasta through her reading glasses. He slammed the door behind him, and there was Frank. "Let's go!" Terry said and ducked into Frank's backseat. Then he noticed an Indian woman beside Frank and said, "Who's the Indian girl?

"Native American woman," she corrected. "But if you really want to be correct, womyn. W. o. m. y. n."

"Terry," Frank said. "This is Flaming Flower. Flame." She smiled in a nasty way. "She teaches Women's Studies at Bell U," Frank continued. "Flame, this is Terry. He's the accountant whose wife abuses him."

"I'm sorry," she said. Her smile widened and he gave a hostile glare.

She wore a leather beaded dress like that on a museum display, so he almost said, out of spite, "How now, brown cow," but held back. Her breath reeked of hummus. She and Frank looked happy. "This is going to be fun," she said. "We'll sit in the steam and tell stories."

"I'm shy," Terry said.

"You don't have to speak," Frank said. "Relax. We'll mingle. You'll get out for a while."

Flame had a soft voice, and spent the trip singing Indian chants, her voice increasing as they neared the reservation. "Frank," Terry asked. "What does it mean to be a man?"

"Ahhhh—llloooooo," Flame sang. "Saaaaaahhh."

Frank, debonair with the top down on his convertible, said, "Being a man is becoming and belonging to yourself." The words sounded so familiar, Terry paused for reflection—and then he looked under Frank's seat and saw *the book*.

"Ahhhh—llloooo," sang Flame. "Sah!"

"Do you have infantile regression disorder," Terry asked and Flame glared.

He glared back, but the clay dust kicked up by Frank's car had already begun to bother his eyes, and he wondered if Jane was at the dinner table, tapping her double-jointed finger, cursing him. Maybe she had already called her friends to complain about his behavior.

"That's the brakes, Terry," Frank said. "What did you expect from married life? I've had five wives—didn't like any of them. It's my girlfriends I've loved."

"Frank and I agree," Flame said. "Wedding rings are signs of ownership. The man wants to feel he owns his woman, and so he marries her."

"That's right," Frank told her, parking in the dirt, "so we'll never get married!" He looked at Flame with a meaningful glance, but he smacked Terry behind the seat.

When they arrived, a few Native Americans stood by a steaming structure that resembled a locker room, and a bitter scent tickled Terry's nose. "It's sage," Flame said. "To ward off evil spirits." Then she kissed Frank.

"Will we be here long?"

"A while," Flame said, already looking so happy she actually smiled as Frank introduced him around.

"Can I have something to drink?" Terry asked.

Frank said, "Sure. The cooler's over there."

Terry walked to the cooler, which looked like a mirage in so much dirt, and exhaled. Flame bugged him more than Jane did, but he couldn't put his finger on why. Considering her, Terry leaned toward the chest and noticed a man behind it, crouched. The man's face had been tattooed with orange and black streaks.

His fingernails, like gnarled talons, grew inches past his fingertips. His body was completely nude, also tattooed. They stared, man to man, until the hair rose on the back of Terry's neck. The Tiger Man looked fierce.

"Hey man," Terry ventured, and the Tiger Man growled. "I'm Terry Goodwin," he said, extending his hand, but the Tiger Man stood tall, snarled, hissed, and fled. Terry admitted the exchange bothered him mainly because he had barely been acknowledged and the Tiger Man had looked bored. He returned to Flame's side, pointing and asking, "Who was that guy? With the tattoos."

"Oh," she said. "The Tiger Man. His tribe did that. A punishment." She yanked Terry into the steaming structure. On a clay plate, more sage burned but he ceased to smell it. "Think about something else," she said.

She and Frank necked like teenagers. Terry watched. When he got home, Jane snored into her pillow and he wondered about the Tiger Man. He thought of living with those tattoos. What had the man done? He went to work the next day, stewing it over. "Frank, hey Frank!" he said. "Did you see that guy?"

Frank gave him a blank look.

"The Tiger Man," Terry said.

"Flame doesn't like him, so we can't talk about him."

"And?" Terry asked. "What do you care what she thinks? She makes me ill: W. o. m. y. n! What's so great about the Y?" This pissed Frank off, and then Terry noticed that Frank had clipped the long hair, so he said, "Hey Frank, what happened to the hair?"

"Flame cut it while I slept."

"She's awful," Terry said. "Just awful." Infuriated, he sped through the day, slicing through spreadsheets until his boss called him in. "Terry," Reginald Allen said. "Terry Goodwin. You've been with us a while, haven't you?" When Terry was seated, Reginald asked, "Do you know why I wanted to see you?"

"No."

"Accounting. Each day we prepare our clients. Each day we make sense of the numbers—and do you know what I found today?"

"What?" Frank asked.

"You lost this company a million dollars."

Terry held his pen. "I what?"

"You deleted a loss denoted by Orion Angels, which falsely boosted their profit margin—they believed your spreadsheet and bought new machinery. Then, they wrote a bad check. Suffice to say, they are no longer our clients and could sue. Need I say what I'm going to say next?" Reginald was smug.

Terry felt tears in his eyes. "No, sir." He drove home, practicing what he would tell Jane. Opening the door, he was about to say, "I've been fired," when she interrupted.

"Terry? Did you tell the Lippinskys that we couldn't meet them for dinner?"

He walked upstairs to their bedroom. "No, I forgot." He could picture contempt on her face and didn't care. He imagined the Tiger Man walking into Barkers Restaurant to growl at the Lippinskys.

Jane threw on a loose red dress and red Birkenstocks. "Damn it," she said. "I can't depend on you for anything. I reminded you to call them today. You know I can't call from work, and, now, when I wanted to put my feet up and relax in front of the television, I have to get dressed. You should get ready too. Right now." She threw him a look. "I'll wait for you in the living room."

"Rann, wann, rann," he said, imitating her. "By the way, Jane, I got fired today."

"So you need to put on a nice outfit," she called up from the stairs, not hearing him.

"I deleted you today," he said, thinking simultaneously: *The Tiger Man wouldn't get lectured. He would growl. He would rip open her back and tear out her spine. Then she would beg for mercy. Or, maybe she'd be dead. Spine-tearing probably meant dead.*

"Did you hear me, Terry?" Jane yelled.

"I heard you," he said, but he didn't get dressed. He got naked.

He stood before the mirror. "Primitive man," he ranted, swinging his penis from side to side like a wagging finger, "would not lose his job over the tap of a key. His job was to hunt and gather. If he lost a rabbit, he wasn't afraid! There were more rabbits!" He had almost worked himself into believing his rant when he looked in the mirror again. There he was: Just a dumb yuppie trapped between the shower and the bed, naked and pitiful, with strange tan lines from his socks. "Arrggggh! Arrrrrrrrrrrgh!" Impotently he growled at himself.

"Hurry up," Jane shouted. "I'm ready!"

"I'm not going anywhere," he whispered, opening her cosmetics drawer. He took out an eyeliner and painted one stripe on his face, then another. He opened her eye shadows and found a putrid shade of melon, put it on the counter, and then ripped off his wedding ring, saying, "Primitive man did not wear a slave band of feminine ownership." He tossed the ring into the toilet and flushed. He flushed again.

The ring did not go down; he painted another stripe of black on his nose, then dipped his free hand into the toilet to retrieve the ring, wrapped it in toilet paper, and depressed the lever. This time, it went down beautifully and, "Jane," he shouted. "We're going to have a fight."

He picked up a second tube of eyeliner. By the time he was done, he had completed his entire face and arms. He walked out of the room wearing only this makeup and a black speedo. Then the Tiger Man, like a voice from a loudspeaker, spoke to him, telling him what to do: "Don't let her intimidate you!"

"Ter—" Jane started, then stared at him. Her strident voice paused mid-word as he crouched beside her.

"Be a man," the Tiger Man said, like a ghost in his periphery, "but also, be an animal."

"Terry," she ranted. "What in God's name is wrong? Is this some kind of joke? What kind of sick—" He snarled and whirled, knocking magazines off the mahogany rack. "Terry? What are you doing?" There was concern in her voice, and fear. He moved closer.

"The only thing you need," the Tiger Man said, "is to know you are feared."

"What is your name?" Terry asked, spinning around. "Your real name." He could see the Tiger Man in front of him now, like a mirror image. It was his mirror image.

"Jane, your wife," Jane said.

"Not you," Terry said. "You."

"Ballis," the Tiger Man said. "H.G. Ballis. Like the book. Listen to me closely, Terry; hear my words." Though Ballis stood directly in front of Jane, she did not see him.

"Who in the world are you talking to, Terry? It's me, Jane!"

"You are the man, Terry," Ballis said. "I am invisible. Pay attention. Don't let yourself be castrated. Don't let her cut us off. Leave. Leave now."

"I'm leaving now," he announced. Terry walked out the front door and headed for the boulevard. He snarled, traipsed, and pranced. He growled at everyone. Everywhere he turned, people feared him. He leaned toward them, and they retreated. Women began to cross the road as he approached; those who didn't were sniffed and pawed before he progressed.

With every step, his power grew and he believed more in Ballis. Even when the policeman cornered him on 3rd and Main, he did not speak, but instead growled and roared. His eyes were a Burmese tiger's, surveying a jungle. He felt alive and on fire, alive and on fire even as he bit the policeman's wrist, sinking his teeth into the tender pink flesh and gnashing it to the bone.

He realized he smeared his wife's makeup all over the officer's sleeve as he did so, but he thought of her nipples, pale pink periods in a restraining aqua mesh, bouncing, tempting, blocking his sight of the officer until he could not think, until he could not imagine a thing but: Women and how they'd destroyed him. W. o. m. y. n. "The problem in today's society," Terry said, "is that men have hunter-gatherer genes, and—"

"Do you hear what that loon's saying?" one cop asked another. "He's mumbling. Gibberish. Somebody tell Sally to get a sedative, please. Hurry."

The woman Sally came in and knocked him out. "Jane," Terry said as he began to feel less steady. "We're going to have a fight." But his eyes already burned from the makeup and he saw in the stainless paper towel dispenser that the stripes on his face had smeared to a reluctant orange and gray. Suddenly, he felt ashamed his costume was ruined and he had no real clothes. "Jane," he called out when she walked in, but there was nothing to hide him from her hideously dissecting eyes.

I am a Tiger Man, he thought, as he stood in the wide concrete cell. *And the only difference between today and yesterday is that I can see the bars of my cage clearer than ever. Somebody's going to put clothes on me, domesticate me. Primitive man did not have to put up with this shit.* He crumpled to the ground in the powerful fist of the tranquilizers, seeing more than one of his wife, albeit unable to see himself at all.

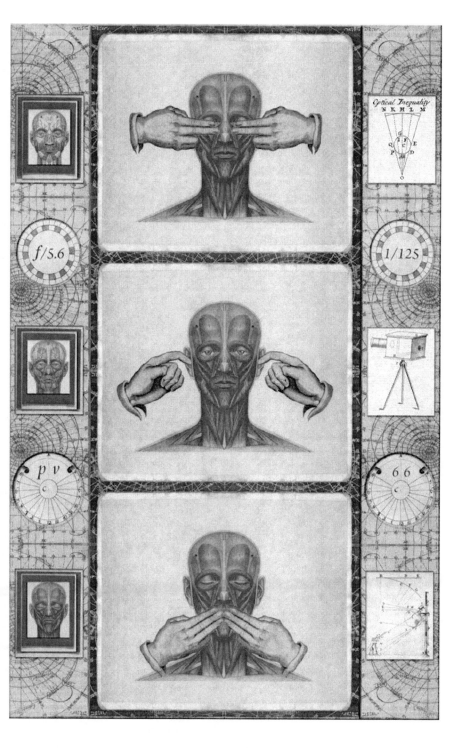

.

THREE PHOTOS

Photo 1: Family Portrait, Sunday

. . . .
?":,,,,,,,,,,,,,,,,
,,,,,,· · · · · · · · · ·,,,,,.
@@@ !!! ...
*() ? !!!

The first photo above plainly shows five children outfitted in suits and dresses. There are three girls. Each girl wears a yellow sundress with chiffon ribbons. The boys have been terrorizing them—the girls, not the dresses. Then again... Then again... It is agony.

Can you tell this by the finger of the largest boy poking into the side of the girl on his left? The shorter boy, the pudgy one whose shirttails overhang his slacks, is my brother Jebediah. In the terrorizing, aside from instigating in his own sly way, he did not participate much.

There are no parents in this photo because my mother lingers behind the lens and my father is out in the shed. The shed, comparably, would be about five inches to the right of what the photo frames. The house would be six inches to the left. This is all imagined perspective. All is ash.

But the shed is where he stores his liquor that works as "hair of the dog." It is actually Jack Daniels. There is no hair involved.

If there were a photograph an hour, or perhaps a photograph of each significant instant that transpires, this day would document as such:

Mother dresses and prepares children, who squirm and snarl.

While she curls her coffee hair, she tells the children to go play in the yard, but, "Don't get dirty or I will tan your asses!" she exclaims. "Church is in an hour—Jebediah! Come!" She wipes the snot from Jebediah's nose with a kitchen rag. Kitchen rags are the preferred rags.

Then two little girls pick wishing wands from the lawn weeds and blow. The eldest tells them how to be fairies.

The eldest boy says they are just stupid little girls. He pulls the ribbon from the eldest girl's self-done braid and pinches her right arm. They fight, ripping the hem of her dress as he steps on it, but she hides this by finding a piece of tape in the study, working hard to repair the damage by positioning and pressing the frayed fabric to the tape, then rushing to the bathroom to cry, without sound, staring in the bathroom mirror and rinsing her freckled, reddened face before re-emerging to the impending afternoon's radiant light.

In the yard, the two littlest girls play at kissing each other's hands and mouths. There is a discussion of Prince Charming. The pudgy, short boy wants to play, but only if he can be the court lion. The girls disagree about his role. "We don't need a lion. We need a prince."

"Yuck, I'm not kissing my sisters."

"You could just pretend."

ELEGANTLY NAKED IN MY SEXY MENTAL ILLNESS

"No, I would rather be a lion. RAAAAAAAAWWR! You need to run."

The girls do not run. They laugh. A car arrives.

The [our] father [who art not in...] returns to the yard, stinking of booze and "loose women" we might conclude, were we so inclined, as Mother often does, though we do not, at this moment, know what that means. Do we picture these women as sliding, slippery things? So loose they could slip through our fingers? "Motherfucker!" he says, kicking the car's tire. We do not address him for fear of his rage.

The oldest boy whispers to the oldest girl, "Shhhh. Don't tell him about the dress." The mother appears.

"Where have you been?" Her finger is up, wagging.

"Wherever the fuck I wanted," the man replies.

The adults retreat inside. There is yelling. Mysterious things clang and bang. Maybe a piece of furniture brushes close to a wall. As this happens, the eldest boy says to the eldest girl, "I'm going to punch you in the arm, and you better not cry."

Before this, the girl steps away and Mother emerges, immaculate, hair curled, makeup heavily done. She winces as she walks, a large black camera in her hand. We line up like bowling pins. "A photo!" she says. "We need a picture before these clothes get ruined."

Father goes to the shed. A picture is taken without her and without him. The younger version of him, her eye, through the lens, captures.

We load into the station wagon and leave, crinolines rubbing together. Mother gives advice to those outside the church, artificially smiling. "Good thing to plant the hyacinth about this time. Nice day, yes?" Do they pity her? Some [or all] of them know.

Mother cries through the entire service as though she is enchanted by God or the Good Word. The eldest boy thinks, "Motherfucker" is the good word. "Praise be! Praise be!" the mother intones. She sings loudly in her mezzo-soprano, an angel in chains. In song, her voice attempts to escape the roof. Only I hear, "Hussy," hissed through her teeth as she glances three rows up and two parishioners to the left.

She comes home. Lets us out of the car. Yanks off her shoes and sprawls on the couch then checks on Father and brings him a glass of water and an aspirin. She cuts up chicken for dinner with particular vehemence. She cuts up his shirt, abandoned in the living room, with particular calm. There was a red spot. At first, she cuts out only the spot, but the red bled to pink and then the hole is so big, right on the collar, that her shears dance to en-ribbon the rest. When she points, Jebediah gathers and carries the pieces out to the garage to be added to the rag pile.

We are on our best behavior, as we always are when she cries. All day. This day, fear creates goodness. Fear induces acquiescence. It is always this way. Imagine the photograph repeating (though it never does) with the garments getting more and more worn and the children getting more and more ill-behaved. One of my sisters will die at nineteen, of rebellion. For now, my mother adores the word "hussy." It remains under her breath like a forbidden sigh.

~

Photo 2: Mother and the Vacuum

```
/> ~   _
  ~   :::
  >>>>
```

See her here, above, how she holds the handle of the upright so high as if she is holding a prize fish? The vacuum does not touch the ground, except its trailing cord. She stands outside the house. Her lip curls.

Something is changed about her. The handle is like a staff. She is mighty. She is also, for the first time [in a long time], relatively happy. The change comes with the fall wind. With that change, my father stays home more and goes to the shed more. It is nothing as drastic as an announcement, may even possibly be the air with which she carries herself. Her every word is heard. Quiet, soft, strong—perhaps God-breathed. Father obeys her then. We do not know why.

And only she is in the above picture, this one where she stars as Queen of the Vacuum. She wears a housedress in a lime green color, if you cannot tell. She wears pale pink lipstick and had just finished cutting flowers before the shot. Tulips. For her vases.

Weeks before this day, on the day the appliance is purchased, I remember she walks into the house, addresses my father like she's speaking to a pulled weed left drying on the sofa, and takes his wallet from the table. She pulls bills free then gives the man several hundred dollars. "Work harder," she tells my father afterwards. "I need more than just a vacuum." He does. And, for a while, there are no more red spots or nights gone.

There is only the way a man looks down at his shoes when he has done something so unspeakably wrong that he defends himself from nothing. He works harder, lording over us at nightfall with a swinging, fisted bottle, issuing sharp commands. We linger like leaves from his tree. But there are days when he is gone, when she is gone, or when they are there but not there, if only because we are out of view. On these days, we four, after school, roam free. We move, unphotographed, in the yard.

The vacuum salesman comes back. The mother no longer needs a vacuum, but she invites him in. The father works hard. The eldest girl is told to stay outside, as is the boy.

Standing in the grass, watching windows of nearby houses, the two littlest girls play at biting each other's hands and mouths as the pudgy child watches. Then a neighbor child comes to play. Jebediah dislikes him.

This other boy will be Charming, no lion. They couldn't care less about lions, they say. The girls are in love.

When he has to go to the bathroom, they enchant him to stay, but he can't go into our house and doesn't want to go home, so the littlest persuades him to shit behind a tree. She will let him, she says, use her dress to wipe.

The pudgy boy wants to watch, but the girls wave him away. "I'm your brother," Jebediah says. "Come on."

The girls disagree about his role. "No, brother. We don't need a brother. We have our Prince."

The eldest girl and eldest boy stand behind the house, out of view, under the shade of a tree, listening at their mother's window. There is moaning. "I would like to see in," the girl says.

"I would, too," the boy agrees.

"You lift me first," the girl says.

There is a gasp and a low growl. These sounds echo in their ears like sin and pain. The girl puts her tan shoe into her brother's waiting hand and he shoves upwards, straining to support her as she leans against the house.

Her mother is below the man on the bed, head thrown back, hair spilling over a pillow in a circle around her face. The man is kissing her mother's neck. His hands roam her mother's breasts. There is a sheet pulled up to cover their waists, but the shape of the man's ass, even under fabric, is clear. He undulates and thrusts. The boy lets his sister down just as her cheeks start to redden.

The girl tries to lift the boy, but he is steady for only an instant, "Be careful," he hisses down, and they both fall, almost soundlessly, to the grass. They roll upon each other. "Did you see anything?" the girl says.

"Yes," the boy says, lying on top of her, where she feels a hardness grow on her leg, "but only for a second." He thrusts his hand up under his sister's shirt and pulls down her bra with dirty fingers, letting his rough touch move over her nipple, circling and pinching until she gasps. "These have gotten bigger," he says, meaning her breasts. He lifts her shirt and puts his mouth on one. He suckles her until she moves against him.

The [our] father [who art not in...] then returns. In the yard, he finds the neighbor's kid defecating and begins to shout. "Motherfucker! Motherfucker! What are you doing shitting in my yard?"

In the back, the eldest two, flushed, disheveled, stand.

In the bedroom, the mother pushes the man off her and dresses.

The man dresses, too, for nothing is left in the house when we check later for clues of him. Somehow—we won't know how—she will get him out and away.

It is a fact that only one set of events can be viewed with any interest at any one time. Everything out of view becomes a story. The eldest girl hears the mother's explanation as the neighbor child's parents are called.

They are effuse in their apology.

"He is Charming! He is Charming!" the girls protest.

The eldest are called to task for not watching closely enough.

The neighbor child's father picks up the boy's feces and his parents carry it between them to their house, hung in the pocket of a rag, as they berate him. A garage rag to be sure; it stank of oil before it found the pile. They are so mortified, they say. This will be a story for later. "Remember when B_____ was small and he shit in the neighbors' yard?" they will whisper to each other, though not at cocktail parties, for it is not the sort of story one issues in public. I can never again look at them the same way, not after what happened with my brother that day and afterwards.

"What the fuck were you doing?" my father asks my mother, later, when it occurs to him that she had a role of some sort.

Vacuuming," she says, and this is all.

~

Photo 3: A Funeral

```
{...    /??
:.":.":.":."
    <<<   ///
  ///  //
........  !!!
!!!!!!!!!!!!!!!!!!!!!!!!!!!!!!!!!!!!!!!!!!!!!!!!!!!!!!!!!!!!!!!
```

This third photo, if you must know, is the last I really remember. It's not like we took many pictures. When we did take them, the mother would develop them and we would view them, and then she would store them in a box in the shed. This was taken at my Uncle Tom's funeral. Do you see my mother again, in a black suit? And that's my father! They are standing by the hearse.

His hands, in his pockets, tell more of the story than anything. They can hardly look at each other, so each stares straight ahead, daring death or anything else to come and take them. This is taken a week before the shed incident, right before my father begins, again, to stay out late and come home stinking.

After the vacuum salesman leaves, Mother invites in others closer to the house. All married. All men. I'll do what I want as long as he leaves me alone, she can be heard among the children to say—but when the fighting recommences, she takes to finding God again, possibly as the plea of the faithless. And perhaps that's the way of the wicked. Forgive me Father, for I have... Oh, again. Yes, again.

Fallen angels retain their beauty.

The children are weeds. The children are leather. Toughening. Shoes do not fit. Pants go high-water.

One night, under the full moon, the eldest boy and the eldest girl experiment beyond what is right. Jebediah, from his bedroom, observes them in the chill and shadows. And then, there is an awakening. The mother had hers days before the funeral, but we don't hear about it until the day the father comes home from work, tired, ready to slink anywhere, discovers his woman with a man, a man he knows well, and, "Motherfucker!" he shouts, paling. "Get the fuck out of my house."

The man leaves, but Mother is angry. "Why did you stop me?" we hear her shout. Anymore, she doesn't care what we hear.

Two little girls play doctor with the neighbor boy, who is splayed on the lawn like a small white animal under a sheet. They are poking him with a sharp stick and listening to his heart. "You should have been a lion," Jebediah is saying. "Now look at you, Charming."

The eldest boy and the eldest girl sway under the sycamore tree. Close. Finishing.

"I am your husband!" the father shouts.

"But am I your wife?" the mother asks. "I keep your secret," she goes on, "But I can't live this way. Eduardo and his lipstick on the roughhewn floor of that place... You do what you want."

"I can't be the laughing stock," the father says.

"Why not? You made me one," the mother replies. "Does it matter if they don't know with whom or how?"

The father walks out to the shed, past the eldest children, and around the front. He looks at no one. In the shed, he shuts the door. There is smoke and then a boom. No one is called.

Look at that photo above. See him. This is how he looked, the last time I saw him, before he was ash. I understand that there is only ash before you as I speak of these pictures, but that is because on that day, I remember, he lights that shed on fire and locks himself inside. Photos curl and burn.

He takes his Smith and Wesson before the smoke gets too thick and snugs the barrel up to his chin as if it were a fist. One shot takes off the back of his head. So charming. Charming. Prince, what?

And there is fire: Crackling, snapping. And the mother is screaming and crying and praying for forgiveness. Does she finally hear back from God? We do not know.

Sure, the eldest girl survives. She and the eldest boy give each other up—eventually. The young girls, for the moment, also survive. Jebediah becomes an ineffectual cleric. The mother, our mother, survives by hair of the dog, pickling her liver.

We do not move. We are poorer than before. Our dresses and clothes grow bedraggled faster than we can blink. It is like time-lapse photography. Regarding photography, that day in the shed, the camera burns as well, hardens and stiffens wherever there was softness or padding.

It records no more. And, later, does it really matter that there are no photos left as I paint their relief in ash? Isn't it enough that I describe the three I remember as if they exist, as if you could see into my memories to pluck out or embolden those images that remain hardwired in the spaces behind my eyes?

Remember: Energy is neither created nor destroyed. Put this ash on your finger and dab your forehead. Is it Wednesday? If you look close enough, ash can be anything. A mark of Cain. A question mark. A colon. A dash.

Remainders of a burn.

In Pompeii, as the volcano rained soot, fire, and hot air, people turned to fossil, pressed cloths to their mouths as they ran, or cried out to the sky that it was the end of the world, that God had abandoned them, yet one hundred miles away all was tranquil and green. My childhood was tranquil and green. Do you believe me? Do you see your childhood, too, in all this ash?

I can, perhaps, and I tell you: It is beautiful—no matter how it was. Look again: Look left. Look right. Look into the whitest, hot spot of the flame. Green, green, green: With the right amount of denial and forbearance, about anything, you can feel the same.

ELEGANTLY NAKED IN MY SEXY MENTAL ILLNESS

Première année — N° 29   Un numéro : 10 centimes   9 Août 1868

RÉDACTEUR EN CHEF
ELIOT HARPER

ABONNEMENTS
PARIS

Un an.............. 9 fr.
Six mois........... 5 90
Trois mois......... 9 »

Bureaux : Rue de la Tristesse, 36

L'ECLIPSE

DIRECTRICE
PAOLA BAIRD

ABONNEMENTS
DÉPARTEMENTS

Un an.............. 9 fr.
Six mois........... 5 90
Trois mois......... 9 »

Bureaux : Rue de la Tristesse, 36

Mlle BARET (Ophélie)

 LA TERRE

L'AIR

aliénation mentale

démence

manie

folie

f.

aliénation mentale

démence

manie

folie

f.

L'EAU

LE FEU

Dessins de PV66

THE SCENE THAT YOU COME UPON IS MADNESS

The nurse briefed Eliot Harper before he entered the therapy room. He stared at the girl. Michelle Baret, age thirty-six. She was nothing to look at, dowdy with stringy brown hair, small eyes, slightly plump and wearing the sort of clothes he thought appropriate for an old backwards woman in a nursing home. "And she did what they said?" he asked, incredulous.

"Certainly," replied the nurse. "But what they haven't yet determined is why. That's your job. Wipe the shit off the wall and go to work."

"Thanks, Lucy," he said.

"Welcome, doc. Have at her. She used to be a nurse, they say. So don't be leaving any syringes nearby."

"Gotcha. Ten-four."

Eliot Harper entered the room. The girl, name Michelle, looked up at him, unperturbed; she regarded him as if he were an Ivac entering, or a new chair. "Hello," he said.

"Hello," she replied.

He took out his notes. "Do you mind if I ask a few questions?"

"Mind," she said absently. "Why would I mind?"

"We're here today to talk about your interaction with Paola Baird. Can we talk about that, Michelle?"

"I go by Mickey," she said, staring down at her tan loafers, which were stained with rainwater and falling off her feet. "Yes. We can talk about that."

After a few preliminaries regarding the courts and signatures, she agreed that she knew what she had done. She agreed that it was necessary, at the time, and that she was likely suffering from some sort of mental illness. "So what I'm giving you here, Doctor Harper, is not a confession, which I already gave the police—it's a statement of my understanding of the events. But you're a psychiatrist, so maybe you can tell me what to do. Prescribe me some drugs?"

He asked her the necessary questions about background and upbringing, cursory though these were. To them, she said, "I had a fine childhood. My mother was rather cold, I suppose, and my father emotionally unavailable, but what child does not feel this way? Unless you are one of those strange people who is, to this day, strapped to your mother's side, I think people always think this about their childhoods. And besides, this thing that I have done—it happened well into my thirties. I should remind you, Dr. Harper, that I stabbed her after she was already dead, so I am no accessory to murder. I neither caused the murder nor wanted the death. What I am charged with is arson. But I didn't burn down the house to incinerate the body. I burned down the house because it was evil. An enclosure, if you will, for the most terrible sort of pain any person can endure. And it housed Paola, who was a menace. But I was crazy in that moment. In the moment, that is, that I burned down her dwelling—because I honestly thought that if I didn't light that match. If I didn't soak that curtain in kerosene. If I didn't take that kerosene curtain and liberally apply the flames to every possible room, she would return. She would come back and torture someone else."

"You started in her employ via the Mangrene Agency, correct?"

"Correct."

"And you had no knowledge of Ms. Baird before your three-month engagement in her service?"

"Correct."

"Why were you hired?"

"At first, I was told she had heart problems, and I was simply to attend to her and call for medical help in the event that she needed it. I was to assist with her small details, such as handling her mail, helping her with bills, cooking or lifting if such things were required. She lived alone in that house, Dr. Harper. And let me tell you, the house itself was a disaster. Imagine, if you will, driving down a long country driveway after entering through an enormous bronzed gate. The driveway was full of wildflowers, oak trees, bends and curves, around which you would see the great lake in front of the house—the one with the water lilies, much like Monet's famous paintings. And once you drove past that driveway, you would find yourself in a rocky area, graveled, where you might park your car in the roundabout in front of the estate. Nothing was kept up. The paint cracked on the outer walls. The giant pillars were coated with bird shit. There was a junkyard out front and off to the side where appliances and old bits of rubbish had been flung willy-nilly. The doorbell didn't ring. And when you went to work, you were let in by Paola, who kept herself fastidiously if nothing else, by a curt nod of her head. Some days she said, in a tone beyond contempt, 'Oh, there you are.' She was a monster. Ice cold."

"Were there altercations?"

"It has already been established that I did not kill her, doctor," the girl remarked, and though she had appeared drudge-like and sparrowed when Eliot first viewed her, a strange fire burned in her eyes before she looked up at his clock, staring at the timepiece as if to pointedly say: "You bore me. Continue."

The first frisson of nervous energy then traveled up his spine. He wanted to exit the building and return for a different patient. Her brown eyes were so cold. He took it back to the casual level. "So your average day would consist of what, Mickey?"

"Oh, cut the bullshit. Let me tell you something, Dr. Harper. The reason I wanted out of there, and I asked my employer repeatedly to reassign me, is because Paola never said or did anything that you could label as hostile, which is to say, every slap she offered was behind the scenes, was easy to rationalize as something else, had a certain level of plausible deniability. So I give you this example, but only so that you may understand the type of tasks she set me to. One day she placed her address book on the table and said, 'I need these letters hand-addressed for all my Christmas cards. I need one for every person in this address book. Can you handle that, Ms. Michelle?' I said yes. This was when I still tried to smile at her, when I thought it would be possible—difficult yes, but possible—to gain her good graces. So I spent three hours addressing envelopes. And then, when I was done, she walked by again. She squinted at the address book she had presented to me and sighed. 'Ah,' she said. 'You did a fine job, but I fear I gave you the wrong address book. These people are all dead.' And then she sat at her table and set me to polishing silver. But I do not wish to talk about that. About the details of the accidental horrors she subjected me to. I wish to talk about the house."

"What would you like to say about the house?"

"I would like to say that sometimes, when a dwelling feels like a place of death and decay, it seems the very soul or representation of its master. The stairwells were dusty. The rooms were dusty. Every one of them was full of accessorized, expensive furnishings. There were fourteen bedrooms in all, many bathrooms, and Paola endlessly sent me through the house looking for things she needed. 'Go, Michelle, and get me the tortoise brush from the Red-and-Gray Suite,' she'd say. 'It is on the mahogany dresser.' And I would. But this was all I did, every day. Get things. Do things that she would comment were either not done right, or not needed. To stand with her in that house was like standing with a mother who had never wanted you. I was lonely. I was bored. Paola was poor company. She stared at herself endlessly, solipsistically. She spent hours doing her hair, fine gray hair, with bobby pins, into a severe style. Her makeup was immaculate. If there was one living thing in the whole place, it was her bathroom—her trash there, the debris of her self-maintenance. Sometimes I got down sweaters from back closets. I took out furs and on rare occasions I had outings. But I told my employer that to remain in that house, with that woman, was like death to my soul. It depressed me."

"And their response?"

"'Use your cell phone. Bring along books. Entertain yourself. It can't be that bad. She pays a lot of money for your company and the economy is bad. This job is full-time. Didn't you want that, Michelle?' At first I said I did, because my brother was about to get out of jail and I would need to help out until he could find work. But when I started to feel myself falling into the dark corners of Paola's house, I had an instinct for survival, you might say. I called my employer again. 'Please fire me,' I said. 'Or reassign me. This particular employment is troublesome. I'd rather wipe the shit off some guy's ass or help the bedridden than stay here with her. Give Donnie the job.' They said they would look into it. The next day they called me back and said that Paola was willing to pay me double to keep me there, that she had apologized for her lack of attention to my feelings, and that it was no problem for me to go back. She'd be kinder. So cheerful! It's no problem! They further expressed that they had no other opportunities that would pay as well. So, of course I stayed.

"At this point, Paola became more inquisitive. She asked me countless questions about my home life. She asked about my parents. She asked about my romances—not many, I confessed—

and the more detail she had, the more interested she seemed. As I walked through the house after this, it was like my voice and my past were comingled. I saw myself in every mirror, just after I had told her some particularly personal detail. And I was ashamed my stories were so small. Why would a woman who lived in an enormous mansion and travelled the world want to know about my mouse of a life? She didn't want to know. Or she did. But her reasons were not standard. I thought she would never die, that fucking bitch."

Eliot opened his file and looked at pictures of the house. "Her uncle gave her that house," he said.

"Yes," Mickey said. "The uncle who molested her."

"Her grandmother was the collector of all the furniture."

"Yes, her grandmother who beat her when she was seven for not putting away the china."

"She was married four times."

"Each time to someone colder and more ruthless."

"You know a lot about her."

"Of course I do. We were each other's only companions. Or, I was her mouse."

"I would like to talk to you about the day she died."

Mickey slouched in her chair. A series of expressions traveled her face, one of which was fear. "All right. Let's talk about that."

"She had a heart attack," Eliot said.

"Somebody give you a medal for observational skill," she replied. She glared at him. "I know she had a heart attack, Dr. Harper, because I sat across from her as it happened. I held her hand through it. We had just been talking about me. About me. And then it began."

"Would you care to let me know how you experienced these moments—the ones just before her heart attack and those leading up to the one when you began to torch her house?"

"I'd had enough." The girl reached into her bag and brought out a faded brown wallet. From that wallet, she took several scraps of colored paper from the billfold, folded them again, and placed them in her pocket.

"Which means?"

"Which means there's a breaking point for everyone, Dr. Harper. What do *you* fear?"

"Snakes. Big men in alleys. Staircases. Dark places that lock, where people are trapped."

"Right. So what if I told you that Paola's most special skill was to ferret out every single thing you feared, and then repeatedly go in for the kill, when you least expected it—stabbing you with your own fears and inadequacies—whereas moments before you thought her your closest friend and best mentor? What if I told you that she liked to hurt people, but was psychotic enough to make you need her or lean on her before she dealt the most stunning blow? Paola knew well that the worst injuries could not be inflicted by those distant, had to be by someone up close. A Judas kiss. And just before her heart attack, smiling with glee, she inflicted upon me such a kiss, said the most terrible thing she could utter. As I watched her, she backed away. She was consumed by emotion and said she was planning to leave the whole place to me, her house and property, but she needed to contact her lawyers. And then she needled me with cruelty, before I could be shocked or grateful for the previous announcement. And you know what caused her heart attack, doctor? It was not fear. It was not age, not anything negative. No, it was an excess of delight as she continued to accost me with my own painful personal details! She grinned and wove her web of pain before me. She laughed most terribly, just before she clutched her heart. And I had asked her for nothing. Well, I had asked to get to know her. But the very last thing she said, just before she passed, still smiling in the most serene way, was, 'I suppose I will not have time to talk to the lawyers. Be good now though, girl. Everything we said is nothing in the end.' And this is why I stabbed her with that letter opener from her table. She was dead and had just shared with me the worst horrors about myself that my smaller brain had never been able to articulate or understand—understand me?—and then she promised me the world, her world, while grinning, and then acknowledged, just before her death, that I couldn't have it after all, none of it—and then she passed, a chill smile on her face as she lay immobile. It was a cruelty itself, her smile! A horrible injustice. The job was over. She was over. I was over. So I stabbed her in the heart for what she did to mine. And then, because I was certain she would come back and entrap somebody else as she had done me, I lit up her house like a fucking Roman candle. I couldn't believe she was gone for good. She was that powerful to me. The woman was everything. And I cried as I watched the whole thing burn. That's where they found me. In the lake. With all the Monet lilies. Watching her house and crying. Shivering and crying and moaning her name through my blue lips as if she were some kind of mother or grandmother I'd never had, whom I both hated and adored with a furious passion. For me, her loss was that complex, that stunning and that painful. I loved her and I hated her more than life."

She looked at Eliot Harper as if he were no longer there, as if she could see through him, and she coughed once. He lifted his eyes to meet hers, but found himself staring at the wall behind her, as if he could not—or did not want to—meet her eyes.

Mickey waited. After a moment of shared silence, she laughed, leaned forward, and took Eliot's chin in her hands, murmuring to him as if he were someone she'd hated her entire life, or as if she'd hated everyone in her entire life, and he was just one in a long line of idiots to stand in her way. "So, doctor, tell me—do you have, could you possibly have, after all of this, any further questions? I feel I've been extremely clear."

Elegantly Eloquent: A Cabinet of Curiosities
By Pablo Vision

Avoiding tautology is an important guiding principle behind all of the artwork created for *Elegantly Naked In My Sexy Mental Illness*; not betraying any of the delightful secrets of the stories in an untimely manner is another. These notes are intended as an appendix, and should only be read after *all* of the stories in the collection. The visual narratives and cross-references are embedded in complex spirals throughout the illustrations, and these notes inevitably contain information that should not be received before the stories have been allowed to impart their original messages. The first experience of anything is, by definition, unique. The almost infinite number of subtle associations each reader automatically attaches to the smallest detail of any written work also makes reading a uniquely personal experience. I found the *Elegantly Naked In My Sexy Mental Illness* experience to be so extraordinary that I was inspired to create this cabinet of curiosities.

I have aimed to reflect the remarkable diversity of the stories by striving for distinctive variety in the sequence of illustrations.

Similarly, the images are intended to be immediately exciting and engaging, but also to actively reward deeper contemplation. The stories demand repeated reading, and their power extends far beyond the real-time experience of the page; the images endeavor to accomplish parallel objectives.

The illustrations are all abstractions of a number of extrapolated ideas that inspired me personally. Each illustration could have taken entirely different elements as conceptual catalysts and developed in radically different directions. The nature of these notes is similarly selective in what I have chosen to reveal; however, the pleasure of future surprise and discovery is a worthy consequence. We may never be able to experience that *first time* ever again, but we might actually find ourselves privileged to stand on the cusp of an infinite number of other unique and amazing journeys.

The Hand-Licker
Palmistry chart and occult diagram chimera

The seven planetary mounts introduce astrological symbolism and tangential trajectories to other illustrations, "Speak to Me With Tenderness, Howard Sun" also sharing Mars and Venus gender implications. This anachronistic chart suggests that diagnosis and treatment—rather than divination—can be read from the hand. Three types of personality disorder are listed under Jupiter, and three antipsychotics appear under the influence of Mercury. The male and female symbols are repeated on the plinth of the hand. Various visual suggestions—including the combination of mouth, tongue, yoni, and cunnilingus symbols—are stylistically influenced by sex magic 'hand' diagrams in occult books. The Richel-Eldermans Collection (archived at The Museum of Witchcraft, Cornwall) exerts a particularly strong aesthetic influence on this design. The partially hidden eyes are included to reinforce the visual concept of the arcane occult, and also as an abstracted story reference to the morphing visual delusions. What might initially appear to be crudely drawn symbols are revealed as two tablets placed on the tongue. The title is from a palmistry book by Adrien Adolphe Desbarolles, published in 1859. The rectangular matrices at the bottom of the chart are Braille for 'h' and 'and'—acceptable shorthand for 'hand.'

Losing Married Women
Designed to be suggestive of the major arcana tarot card

Modern decks often depict the pouring of liquid from a jug, and older packs sometimes portray a figure pointing at a star—both elements are present in this design. The Star may also be known as The Astronomer in alternate decks, and this illustration also points to both the preceding and succeeding—*astrological and astronomical*—images in the sequence. The star is introduced as a reoccurring icon that appears in "Good Country. People." and "Con Yola." There is an obvious reference to the protagonist's name and to lesbian love; oblique implication of water represented by swimming; and abstracted inference of 'crossing the line' insinuated by the image continuing beyond the natural border of the card. ('Crossing the line' is a phrase often used when referring to someone who has the audacity to not conform to traditional patriarchal stereotypes: a sexually assertive *female* marriage-wrecker, for instance.)

Speak to Me With Tenderness, Howard Sun
A complex flowchart

Starting with the simple line of arrows from Venus to Mars, and progressing to the obsessive, elaborate, detailed, correlated schematics, the trajectories abstract the two main characters and their motives and modes. Planets (or cryptic shadows) revolve around Howard Sun. There are cyphers and decryption mechanisms. And even beyond the multiple layers, and the pseudonyms, and coded clues, Howard sits behind the labyrinthine fortifications. As the complexity increases, identifying the organized from the disorganized becomes as difficult as discerning genius from madness. Howard's positioning in the center of the circular maze is echoed in the illustration for "The Gray Fairy." Mutations of the background image are used in "Ever" and "Three Photos." The sun rises in "Con Yola" and descends in "The Scene that You Come Upon is Madness."

Taking Celine
A visual exploration of some of the possibilities suggested by the idea of 'gargoyle tree' nightmares

This illustration is constructed entirely from mutated elements (arteries, veins, muscles, bones, and labeling) from an anatomical drawing in Ephraim Chambers' *Cyclopaedia*. The use of symmetry is intended to imply a complex Rorschach inkblot. The labelling includes interior muscles and 'Fore-part of Genitals of a Woman'— the latter suggestive (given the proximity to the skeleton-branch phallus) of the cold, clinical approach of Celine's nemesis. As well as setting the tone for the desolate mood, the bleak, winter-bare, needle-sharp deciduous branches are also of distinct relevance to elements within the story. (See "Tiger Man" for further information regarding the background concepts.)

Blood, Hunger, Child
Abstraction and mutation of several visual elements to alter inference

Text from Jean-Jacques-François Le Barbier's *Déclaration des Droits de l'Homme et du Citoyen* is positioned over the 'card cut-out' guillotine. Le Barbier's original painting includes a winged allegorical figure pointing to the Eye of Providence. The Eye of Providence has been recreated from parts of constantly morphing icons used throughout the sequence of illustrations, and, in turn, reappears with modified significance in "Con Yola." The winged figure (and much of the background) is recreated from various elements from Gérard de Lairesse's allegorical title page from Govard Bidloo's *Ontleding des Menschelyken Lichaams*. (Incidentally, this is the same title page that William Cowper used thirteen years later in *Anatomy of the Humane Bodies* [1698] without any acknowledgement of Lairesse or Bidloo.) An unborn child is placed in the circular card cut-out (and— *simultaneously*, therefore—the guillotine's lunette); there are also depictions of young children and skeletons, collectively inferring birth and death, and also imparting retrospective historical reality to the original idealism of the Revolution. (Le Barbier's figure—deposed here—returns triumphantly from exile in "Mother's Angels.")

Ever
Old-fashioned record label design

Revelation Records is intended to cross-reference the illustration
for "Good Country. People..," as well as being an integral part of the
Bible-belt insinuation. 'Ever' and 'Light'—as in the title and the
protagonist's last name—are evident in the title of the disc; less
obviously, the central character's house and telephone number are
embedded in the catalogue and order numbers. Conceptually, the
theme of the illustration is tangential to the daunting religious
undertones of the obsessive, fanatical stalker and his equally creepy
mother. The recording artist is a many-headed monster obviously
satirizing the naming conventions of *certain* religious factions: a
variety of splinter sects referenced are deviations of the Church of
God (relating to the stalker's Tennessee accent); the inclusion of
speaking in tongues, snake-bothering, treasure-finding cults—
'Tabernacle Choir' providing an additional link to "His Other
Women" (and furthermore to the obvious correlation between the
manner of promotion, and authenticity, of snake oil products and
snake oil faiths); and, with further reference to "Good Country.
People."—O'Connor's wonderful literary invention of Hazel Motes'
Church Without Christ competing against his rival's Holy Church
Without Christ. The background echoes a subtle shift of "Speak to
Me With Tenderness, Howard Sun." The circular windows, this time,
only reveal the absence of things.

Con Yola
*An advertisement for an exported brand of mezcal with logo and name
similar to a popular beverage*

The burlap label is intended to imply the authentic, indigenous,
rustic pedigree of the product—as well as relate to the burlap doll of
the story. The sales of mezcal con gusano (with worm) is actually a

marketing gimmick dating back to the '40s, so here *con gusano* is both part of the mezcal *mystique* and integral to the written work. In much the same way that advertisements for absinthe might visually imply that one might be transported to Nineteenth-Century Paris by the green fairy, this poster *infers* that our worm (lovingly fed peyote by Aztec gods) imparts a *particularly* spiritual and hallucinogenic ambience to this *particular* brand of mezcal. Better than Orange Sunshine Acid, this is the *real thing*! One might have difficulty advertising a drink or a perfume by *verbally* stating that the product is exclusively used by the beautiful, the successful, and the cultured, yet a glance at historical and modern advertising reveals how psychologically suggestive images can easily circumvent this inconvenient problem to great effect. This story also revolves around a number of *mostly* wordless transactions (cash and *other*) between Myles and Yola, and the dollar signs and the return of the Eye of Providence, in the overall context, make further allusion to this. (The Eye of Providence—as seen previously in "Blood, Hunger, Child"—is also used on the back of the dollar bill.) There are also visual flashbacks (and flash *forwards*) to "Speak to Me With Tenderness, Howard Sun," "Good Country. People.," and "Losing Married Women." The mechanical hands that form the pattern at the bottom of the image can also be seen to lift the edges of the paper on which the poster is printed—a small inclusion of *impossible reality* that visually paraphrases, *anachronistically*, the work of M.C. Esher. The influence of LSD blotter art informs part of the design.

Mother's Angels

Having previously created the 'womb to tomb' skulls as an icon used in a series of illustrations for *Antique Children's Kingdom Freaks & Other Divine Wonders*, they are now further developed—*or evolved*—as these ominous, descending angels of death. Consistent with the liberal use of foreign language and/or archaic linguistics in other illustrations, the apparent title of this illustration is named after the white kitten of the story; but, given the dark allegorical nature of the image, 'hope' becomes disturbingly incongruous and distinctly wayward. However, the driving forces behind the insistent nature of life—and the will to survive, and to *evolve* ever-greater resistance—may be considered partly fuelled by something akin to *hope*. The other winged figures relate, by substitution, to "Blood, Hunger, Child," and, when viewed in conjunction with the apparent date of the illustration and representation of the deathbed, serve to increase the visual allegorical reference to the story. The unusual perspective gives an intensified sense of depth to the image, as well as continuing the Escheresque theme of optical deception (as in "Con Yola" and "Good Country. People."). Lines extended beyond their natural parameters is a visual phenomenon also present in "The Gray Fairy," and prominently exposed geometry recurs frequently throughout the sequence.

Good Country. People.

This image is intended to work simultaneously on multiple levels. Just as the door-to-door Bible salesman might use his cover for ulterior motives, this fake Bible reveals a concealed compartment. Many of the illustrations use cut-outs to reveal underlying images or meanings and to provide an antiquated three-dimensional look, but here uncertainty is introduced: it can be viewed as both a direct representation of an object with such a cut-out as inherent, or as the entire image with windows cut out to reveal the different layers underneath. This duality is further exploration of the continuing optical theme of *impossible reality*. The hands holding the quill pens— seen to be partway through drawing a smaller version of the entire illustration and just completing the final flourish to the artist's signature—reference Escher's *Drawing Hands* (two hands drawing each other on a sheet of paper, in a circular visual enigma); the disembodied hands seen to be holding the book and turning the pages are also angled (and positioned relative to each other in the sequence) to suggest a partial view of an outward-moving spiral. The paradox of creating new images *after* Escher by use of the substantially *before* enhances the visual mystification. The border of the illustration is reminiscent of "Losing Married Women" but with abrupt disturbance to the left-hand edge; the intentional focal imbalance and 'crossing the line' also extend the related visual and metaphorical concepts; and, portentously, the stars have shifted position.

The object in the hidden compartment is a prosthetic, a fist, a religious icon, a political symbol, and (in turn, *simultaneously*) an astronomical, alchemical, biological symbol. The artificial hand and fist are both of obvious significance to the story; the cross can be also be perceived as an *inverted* crucifix; the clenched fist is associated with political protest and struggle; Venus and the female gender; and, in conjunction, as a whole: an anachronistic feminist symbol. Treble Ann (and by extension, Joy, of the related O'Connor story) get their vengeance: the symbol of their struggle is dominant over the sham religiosity. 'Revelations' relates to the *dénouements* of the stories, and the 'revealing' of the inner workings of the image and its construction.

Ledge
Architect's impression and technical drawing of partial, front elevation of unspecified building

The image presents a suggestively incomplete, understated, and enigmatic blueprint for an inferred event: horizontal and vertical arrows, dimensions and relativity, curves and angles, columns and arches, physical support and load transference, and repeated occurrences of balconies. The exposed geometry continues a theme present in "Speak to Me With Tenderness, Howard Sun," "Ever," "Mother's Angels," "The Gray Fairy," and "Three Photos." The implication being that the mathematics behind the science not only accurately defines what is, but, through cause and effect, describe what is likely to happen. It is not just the long *physical* trajectories travelled by the Voyager probes, but the very precise *plotted* journeys that have taken them to the edge of the solar system; the author of this story very astutely observes that certain events have very likely consequences. Some things, once put into motion, cannot be stopped.

Giant Balloon Animal Tragedies
Aeronautically inclined natural history plate

I wanted to capture—somewhat perversely, given the *palette range* of this sequence of illustrations—something of the wonderful tonal quality and expansive backgrounds of the *chromo*lithographs in Henry Louis Stephens' *The Comic Natural History of the Human Race*. Essentially, the influence was more of an ideal to aspire to: a clean, simplified, luxuriously *soft* tone; something that could actually seem gently *tactile* to the eye. The border and the background *colour* of this illustration are very closely related to those of "Ledge," and when viewed in order, "Ledge" performs the auxiliary function of visually slowing things down in order to set the mood. (The art for "Ledge" was concluded afterwards in order to facilitate this.) I additionally wanted it to be visually suggestive of old collectable trade cards. This illustration is also twinned *conceptually* with "Tiger Man": the image, in conjunction with the title, intended as misdirection.

The archaically spelled *Melencolia* comes from Albrecht Dürer's engraving and is positioned in the same location relative to the curve of the balloon as it is to the curve of the rainbow in the original image. Consistent with the mood and tone of the illustration, the reference to the reoccurring themes of the story derive their power from precise understatement.

The first idea I worked on for this illustration involved the unfortunate creature heading for a menacing machine inspired by the implausible eccentricity of Heath Robinson, and the aesthetics of steampunk. The frame and lettering were of Art Deco influence. But once the obsession with achieving a particular tone held me in its grip, it was only ever going to be this celebration of *timbre*, and of Dürer. *Melencolia I*, now approaching its half-millennium milestone, exerts a strong influence on the conceptual approach to the entire sequence of illustrations.

Mutated detail of the balloon reappears in the masthead of the journal depicted in "The Scene that You Come Upon is Madness."

His Other Women

A montage of words and images

A swirling orgy of women intended to parallel the escalating and circuitous nature of runaway conjecture regarding the 'other women'; speculation without absolute confirmation progressively twisting the perception of *conceivably* innocent action into the *plausible* smoking gun; the impossible calibration of suspicion and paranoia, given the circumstances and previous precedents. There is much ambiguity intentionally woven into the tornados of tempestuous (and tempting) flesh on show; what might seem like the depiction of several brazen acts of depravity could also be viewed as part of the choreography of the swirl: perception of the image depends upon *perception of the perspective*; it is the *presumed* proximity of the bodies that insinuate; it is the nebulous silhouettes on the peripheries that whisper accusation. The narrator is aware of her own excruciatingly difficult position, and of the many conflicts that render any single consistent, permanent placement untenable. Therefore, the frenetic, constant movement evades the jurisdiction which the more traditionally anchored must endure—but at the price of greater uncertainty and vulnerability: the voluntary surrender of rights that the self-exiled know so well.

There are visual echoes of "Losing Married Women," and

figurative foretelling of "The Scene that You Come Upon is Madness."

The archaic syntax of the advertisements suggests a bygone age contemporary to that implied in the illustrations for "Tiger Man" and "Ever": medicine shows, pharmaceutical almanacs, freak shows, snake oil, unscrupulous preachers—and the convergence of their similar cause and related effect. I've attempted to show the *essence* of what we commonly understand by the term *quackery*: fake, fraudulent, knowingly or *ignorantly* bogus; but also wanted to convey the loud, aggressive, competitive marketplace shouting of soapbox vendors flogging their questionable cures and dubious faiths. (All of the illustrations are designed to not only make reference to the stories to which they are attached, but also to expand upon references made in other illustrations, and, therefore, to threads of common themes found in these diverse stories. So, for instance, just *one* theme from "Good Country. People." has its *doppelgänger* parallel vision spread explicitly over the canvases for "The Hand-Licker," "Ever," "Tiger Man," "The Scene that You Come Upon is Madness," "His Other Women," *and* "Good Country. People.")

There are references to a variety of characters embedded within the illustration, a small cameo appearance for the author, and wayward allusion to a particular *mor*mountebank operating from Palmyra—a direct reference to a specific part of this story, as well as a part of the visual narrative arc described above.

Summer Rose
Oculist chart

Visually and thematically linked to the illustration for "The Hand-Licker." There are anachronistic elements embedded within a distinctly vintage design, and there is *slight* visual disturbance to both illustrations: the moiré pattern of "The Hand-Licker" causes the apparent oscillation despite the static nature of the image; and deviation and deception regarding the vertical, horizontal, and parallel lines, *and their theoretical continuations,* also occur in "Summer Rose." This subplot of optical aberration and eventual convergence of lines is revisited explicitly in "Three Photos" and "Ledge," and implicitly throughout the sequence of illustrations.

The central panel replicates the dimensions and spacing of a typical Snellen chart, and the numerical fractions distributed around the edges of the poster are the matching visual acuity scales for the first eight lines of this particular chart. Anatomical drawings of the eye surround the central panel, with the repeating eye icon (as used in "The Hand-Licker," "Blood, Hunger, Child," and "Con Yola") appearing at the top; the hooks perform the function of alluding to the Margaret Atwood poem referred to in the story, and as an understated link to the shocking opening scene in Buñuel and Dalí's *Un Chien Andalou.* Whether it is a passing thought, a nightmare, a poem, a film, or an infamous still, the juxtaposition of the delicate, vulnerable eye and unforgiving, sharp metal makes most people flinch as instinctively as any involuntary reflex action.

Throughout the illustrations I've made frequent use of foreign language (French, Spanish, and Italian) and also of archaic words and syntax. Reading the chart slowly will eventually, as one works out the language and where to insert the gaps, reveal three repetitions of 'le travail rend libre' before the phrase switches languages to become 'arbeit macht frei'—as chillingly displayed on the gates of Auschwitz. Likewise, as one moves in order through the outer segments towards near-perfect and perfect vision (20/25; 20/20) two small swastikas can be seen in the centers of the eyes. The ominous clues in the story are skilfully presented from the beginning, but only at the heart-breaking dénouement are the terribly sad truths made painfully clear. So, once again, there is the palpable *flinching* at memories, *flinching* at causing pain, *flinching* at suffering pain, and *recoiling* at the enormity of suffering for so many people. There is also the raw acceptance of the inevitable pain inflicted through the generations. It is almost as if the parallel lines of the dreadful transport railways extend their influence into a theoretical infinity too far away and too unreal and too large to quantify: lines forever unable to converge in order to enable full and clear focus. Instead, we are *haunted* by the abstracted, symbolic, peripheral visions of so many eyeglasses and so very many shoes; phrases and geographic places become synonymous with the undefinable horror we *feel* more than we can articulate.

The art is influenced by the sparse design of Holocaust memorial monuments, and the devastating *Games for Gustav* appendix to Yann Martel's *Beatrice and Virgil*: dreadful horror too immense to comprehend; atrocity too great to depict.

The Gray Fairy

"There are webs, spider webs," the Gray Fairy says. *"You have to clean them out."*

Multiple modifications of Katsushika Hokusai's depiction of a spider's web were used to create several layers. The first layer is intended to be suggestive of Peter Saville's cover for Joy Division's *Unknown Pleasures* (the desolate lyrics, music like slabs of mausoleum marble, and the suicide of Ian Curtis all delivering a multi-layered patina of reference, mood, and relevance; Saville's specific design for New Order's *Movement* and general strong typographic aesthetic also influence the design for "Summer Rose"). The second layer is cut to resemble a razor blade. Additional layers form the 'frame' and 'canvas,' with the radials extending outward; a similar motif is used in "Mother's Angels," with the underlying concept used extensively throughout the sequence. The central spider *lurks at the threshold*, and the 'gargoyle tree' figure (from "Taking Celine") is also skulking malignantly in the web. The sinister combination—partly camouflaged and somewhat disguised through abstraction—of the gargoyle tree figure, the razor blade, the spider, and the symbolic hole, is intended to represent the *malevolence* of the titular fairy. The mesmerizing vortex pattern, leading to the void, exerts a powerful and compelling force. The bullet, shot through the top left-hand corner, intersects two of the radials, and is, therefore, suggestive of forensic investigation mapping—with the two lines placing both the gargoyle tree figure and the 'good' fairy under potential suspicion.

The apparent *benevolence* of the depicted good fairy is intended as misdirection when viewed in the context of the title, a technique manifestly used in "Giant Balloon Animal Tragedies" and "Tiger Man," but she also conveys the poise and figure of a ballerina (tangentially referencing part of the text) and equally suggestive of a tightrope walker (paralleling the surefooted agility of the spider that traverses its web by avoiding the many adhesive strands).

Tiger Man

As with "Giant Balloon Animal Tragedies," this is a deliberately misleading illustration ostensibly reminiscent of a freak show poster for the named attraction. An essential component of the 'cabinet of curiosities' [*Assembled here for your Delight and Edification…*], it also performs a *major* function in a visual narrative—as detailed in the notes for "His Other Women"—spread over several images. Thoughts of P.T. Barnum are conjured up—indeed, the strapline derives from a contemporaneous parody of Barnum's promotion of Jenny Lind—to siphon off, by association, additional refinements to our flamboyant [*Step right this way…*] carnival of quackery. One can easily note the equivalents of freak shows and guided asylum tours in many types of current television programs; also, the plethora of self-help 'empowerment' books eager to divulge their *secrets* to a gullible readership is analogous to preachers' pamphlets and snake oils overflowing their dubious benefits on to the ill-informed, but ever-voracious, consumers of the past.

Charlotte Perkins Gilman's "The Yellow Wallpaper" simply *had* to be referenced in this collection: the title; the themes explored; and, particularly, the resonance of the evocative mood and situation in "Taking Celine." At one point, Gilman writes about how the pattern of the wallpaper, in certain light, becomes like bars, with women trapped behind them. This story—"Tiger Man"—concludes: "And the only difference between today and yesterday is I can see the bars of my cage, see them clearer than ever." There are various manifestations of the camouflaged, or hidden, *becoming* apparent in this illustration: the tiger stripes on the human face; the opacity of the central panel that momentarily postpones recognition; and the *suggested* three-dimensionality of the alternate dark and light bars that form the background wallpaper. The wallpaper was created using a repeated pattern generated from processing a detail of the anatomical drawings of female reproductive organs that were referred by the labelling present on the illustration for "Taking Celine"— it is also a small, wayward cameo for the 'jungle of vaginas' referred to in *this* story.

Located in the bottom left-hand corner is a dial: a rotation of 180 degrees clockwise will release the cage door, liberating our prize exhibit. Be quick, for he must have time to change his costume in readiness for his appearance in [*Ladies and Gentlemen, Direct from the Celebrated and Venerated House of Mystery and Mischief, We Proudly Present...*] "Three Photos."

Three Photos

A highly stylized progression of 'see no evil, hear no evil, speak no evil' developed through the sequence of the three photographs in the central strip. The sagacious triumvirate are intended to communicate the 'turning a blind eye' associations of the pictorial proverb. The story is a wonderful examination of the ominous no man's land and disputed territories that exist between the characters: an environment created through dark familial secrets and unspoken treaties of complicity; a fragile and volatile détente only sustainable by a conspiracy of wilful ignorance regarding events uncomfortable and threatening. The three main heads (and three smaller heads on the left of the illustration) are examples of the continually mutating icon that can be observed in "Tiger Man," but also used on the front covers of D.M. Mitchell's *Parasite Lost* and *Parasite Regained*, and on the RetroKoblitz poster for Jürgen Fauth's *Kino* remix project. The concept of re-contextualizing old images runs strongly throughout the cabinet of curiosities, and continuing the *development* of images by sampling some elements of my previous work seemed a logical evolutionary step. The hands are of the same genus used in "The Hand-Licker" and "The Scene that You Come Upon is Madness." Hand gestures are a common thread in this sequence. *The Ambassadors* and *Melencolia I* immediately alert the viewer that codes are likely to be embedded within these images, but subtle hand gestures—ranging from the symbolic (as in the *Mona Lisa*) to fingerspelling used as ciphers—have long been an important tool of obscured communication in art. From *Caesarean* shift to Vigenère and beyond, the complexity and transparency of any cryptic message can be pitched relative to those intended to be privy to the conversation. The background is an *astronomical* shift of that seen on the cover, and in "Speak to Me With Tenderness, Howard Sun" and "Ever."

The middle strip is designed to simultaneously look like three photographs with well-worn edges and three stills on a roll of film. The three smaller images (on the left-hand side) show a progression of transformation and are also intended to be suggestive of the accordion bellows (as seen front-facing) of old cameras, and *concurrently* to depict the layered framing of these portraits: *furthermore*, this also enables the optical illusion of alternate *décollage* and *collage*: reductive *excavation* and additive *construction*. This multi-dimensional portrayal of the simultaneous, and of the buried and hidden, parallels the external surfaces presented by the characters (in certain instances—and dependent on the relationship—and the prevailing dynamic of the nature of that relationship) to each other, *coexisting* with the hidden, labyrinthine, and more intrinsic subterranean internal *essence*.

There are numerous references to photography that are clearly conspicuous, but many of these also serve to intensify the geometric, optical, and optical illusion themes inherent to the cabinet of curiosities.

The Scene that You Come Upon is Madness

A pastiche of Francis Polo and André Gill's Nineteenth-Century newspapers—*L'Eclipse* not only succeeded the censored *La Lune*, but continued the splendid tradition of transgression against the authorities. This illustration offers particular reference to the issue featuring a caricature of a bottled Christina Nilsson as Ophelia. (Christina Nilsson was a Swedish soprano, as was Jenny Lind, and both are therefore represented by their absence here and, in "Tiger Man.") How Ophelia might have been perceived by Shakespeare and audiences of the time, and how too the portrayals have synchronized with the prevailing attitudes since then, is in itself almost a complete case study regarding predominant cultural perceptions of female madness, emotional instability, maniacal tendencies (including those of sexual origin), spiritual and ethical weakness, and so on. The first glance of Ophelia on stage would have instantly transmitted an entire psychiatric evaluation to the audience; likewise, her image in many famous paintings reinforces a prejudicial manner of presumption. All of this is perfectly understandable given the extremely patriarchal nature of culture and religion (each informing and shaping the other using strong motives to expediently make as few concessions to women as possible) throughout history. A cursory look at the types of historic crimes women could be punished for, or committed into asylums or conveniently deposited in convents over might lead one to conclude that simply being female *was* the crime, the mental aberration, and the sin. If one examines the reasons why the vote was—and in some cases, still is—denied to women, one might conclude that mental inferiority of women was *effectively* enshrined in law. One innate general societal understanding of madness is significant *deviation* from a broad range of *common* behavior: a person who *genuinely* believing they can fly would be perceived as mad, but not generally would a person believing in the miraculous transformation of wafer and wine on the tongue. One has to place the depictions and descriptions of women supposedly suffering from mental illness in the context of patriarchal definitions of how a woman *should* behave: any feminine deviation from these definitions would automatically be perceived as self-evident madness, rather than fair protest or reasonable non-compliance.

"The Yellow Wallpaper" is previously referenced in "Tiger Man" as an important contextual document; Ophelia, and the perception of self-evident madness, is equally significant; together they weave an essential pattern through the entire sequence of illustrations.

Various characters and story elements are embedded in the illustration, and there is some pertinent play in attributing gender to nouns. The four ancient elements are consistent with the ongoing allusions to alchemy, archaic science, and pseudoscience. This also allows for Fire and Water reference as integral to the story in abstracted and clandestine fashion. The arrangement of the hands, and other factors, create a smooth transition back to the first illustration of the sequence. Considered in traditional linear terms, this is the last illustration of the sequence, but, hating the end of anything good and always preferring the endless suggested trajectories that a spinning planet can imply in place of the prosaic one-dimensional clunk of *bad* tradition, this illustration actually sits at just one of countless beginnings of many fantastic spiraling journeys one could take…

There are echoes of images used in "The Hand-Licker," "Speak to Me With Tenderness, Howard Sun," "Giant Balloon Animal Tragedies," and "His Other Women."

The Cabinet Maker's List of Curious Components

A list of specific images sampled and re-contextualized in the creation of the illustrations

Anatomical Chart; Table of Astronomy; Table of Conics; Table of Dialling; Table of Geography and Hydrography; Table of Geometry; Table of Miscellany; Table of Opticks; Table of Surveying; and Warship Diagram from Ephraim Chambers' *Cyclopaedia or, An Universal Dictionary of Arts and Sciences* (1728)

Dental diagram from Pierre Fauchard's *Le Chirurgien Dentiste* (1728)

Albrecht Dürer's *Melencolia I* engraving (1514) & *Rhinoceros* woodcut (1515)

William Smellie's *A Sett of Anatomical Tables, with Explanations, and an Abridgment, of the Practice of Midwifery* (1754)

Maze detail from Georg Andreas Böckler's *Architectura Curiosa Nova* (1664)

Johannes van Loon's zodiac chart from Andreas Cellarius' *Harmonia Macrocosmica* (1660)

Anatomical illustrations from Julien Bouglé's *Le Corpus Humain et Grandeur Naturelle: Planches Coloriées et Superposées, avec Texte Explicatif* (1899)

Anatomical illustration from Richard Quain's *The Anatomy of the Arteries of the Human Body, with its Applications to Pathology and Operative Surgery* (1844)

Jean Auguste Dominique Ingres' *La Source* (1856)

Ambrose William Warren's *Aeronautics* engraving (1818)

Katsushika Hokusai's "View of Mount Fuji from Behind a Spider's Web" from *One-Hundred Views of Mount Fuji* (1834)

Anatomical illustration from Claude Nicolas *Le Cat's Traité des Sens* (1744)

John William Waterhouse's *Hylas and the Nymphs* (1896)

Diego de Astor's engravings from Juan Pablo Bonet's *Reducción de las Letras y Arte Para Enseñar a Hablar a los Mudos* (1620)

Peter Troschel's astronomical illustrations from *Astrolabium* (1660)

Advertisement for Eau de Cologne from the almanac of *La Nouvelle Chronique de Jersey (* 1891)

Luis Ricardo Falero's *The Butterfly* (1893), *Moonlit Beauties* (c. 1881), *Vision of Faust* (1878) and *Faust's Dream* (1880)

Gérard de Lairesse's allegorical title page from Govard Bidloo's *Ontleding des Menschelyken Lichaams* (1685)

Jean-Jacques-François Le Barbier's *Déclaration des Droits de l'Homme et du Citoyen* (1789)

Anatomical illustration from Johannes Kepler's *Ad Vitellionem Paralipomena, quibus Astronomiae Pars Optica* (1604)

Prosthetics from Ambroise Paré's *Les oeuvres d'Ambroise Paré* (1585)

Anatomical schematic from Magnus Hundt's *Antropologium de Hominis Dignitate* (1501)

G. Wingendorp's engraving for the Frontispiece of Regnerus De Graaf's *De Succo Pancreatico* (1671)

Emblem 45 from Michael Maier's *Atalanta Fugiens* (1617)

André Gill's illustrations—particularly Mlle. Nilsson as Ophélie—for Francis Polo's *L'Éclipse* (1868)

The stories below were first published in the following venues:

"Losing Married Women." *Literary Potpourri*. March 2002, April 2002, May 2002: Three Issue Anthology #2. Ed. Beverly Jackson. 195–206. (2002).

"Taking Celine." *Portland Review: International Journal of Arts and Literature Est. 1956*. Issue 56. Volume 3. Winter/Spring 2010: 120–125.

"Mother's Angels." *Penumbra. Literary Journal at California State University, Stanislaus*. 68–74. (2001).

"Good Country. People." *Necessary Fiction*. Jan. 2011. First Footing Project.

"Ledge." *Connotation Press: An Online Artifact*. 2011.

"Three Photos." *Sub-Lit*. Vol. 2, No. 1. Aug. 2008.

"The Scene that You Come Upon is Madness." *Kill Author*. Issue Twelve: The Janet Frame Issue. April 2011.

"Summer Rose." *Prick of the Spindle*. Vol. 6.3. Fall 2012.

Author's Acknowledgements

Thanks to fate for allowing me to live in good health, one day after another, creating art as legacy.

Thanks to my tears, which have been the glistening lens via which the world and its factual nature have come undone.

Thanks to colleagues and publishers who have selected my work and supported my strange vision for what words can do.

Thanks to the women writing and publishing both today and yesterday, who have come before and have continued to show me the way to be seen.

Thanks to those who have loved me and cared beyond casual greetings.

Thanks to the readers of this book who spend moments of their precious lives in commune with my thoughts.

Thanks to Stephanie Jed as the consultant on the Italian and Milos Kokotovic for reviewing the Spanish language use.

Thanks to Pablo Vision for wanting to make a collaborative work and for sharing his talent in this joint [ad]venture.

Most especial thanks to the following people, in no particular order, for believing in my right to make literature and for creating the permissive "we" space in my emotional landscape, so many times. As an aside, I love you all: Cynthia Reeser, Siolo Thompson, Rose Mambert, Erin McKnight, Josie Brown, Noni Romero, Odessa Smith, Reagan Myles, Laura Alonso, Cicily Janus, Heather Snyder, and Jennifer Geran.

About the Author

Heather Fowler is the author of the story collections *Suspended Heart* (Aqueous Books, Dec. 2010), *People with Holes* (Pink Narcissus Press, July 2012), *This Time, While We're Awake* (Aqueous Books, May 2013) and *Elegantly Naked In My Sexy Mental Illness* (Queen's Ferry Press, May 2014). Fowler's *People with Holes* was named a 2012 finalist for Foreword Reviews Book of the Year Award in Short Fiction. *This Time, While We're Awake* was selected by artist Kate Protage for representation in the Ex Libris 100 Artists 100 Books exhibition in conjunction with the 2014 AWP Conference. Fowler's stories and poems have been published online and in print in the US, England, Australia, and India, and appeared in such venues as *PANK*, *Night Train*, *storyglossia*, *Surreal South*, *JMWW*, *Prick of the Spindle*, *Short Story America*, *Feminist Studies* and others, as well as having been nominated for the storySouth Million Writers Award, Sundress Publications Best of the Net, and the Pushcart Prize. She is Poetry Editor at *Corium Magazine* and a Fiction Editor for the international refereed journal, *Journal of Post-Colonial Cultures & Societies* (USA).

Please visit her website: www.heatherfowlerwrites.com

Artist's Acknowledgements

First and foremost: the art is forever indebted to the collection of stories from which it was born.

Thanks to Heather Fowler for her inspiring and energetic enthusiasm for this unique [ad]venture.

Thanks to Erin McKnight for assembling *the cabinet* into a more refined piece of furniture.

I would also like to thank both Heather and Erin for making the entire project so pleasurable.

Finally, thanks to my *other accomplice* for continuing to share this most amazing journey.

CPSIA information can be obtained
at www.ICGtesting.com
Printed in the USA
FFOW03n1157210414
4916FF

9 781938 466281